THE THINGS ·YOU· KISS GOODBYE

THE THINGS ·YOU· KISS GOODBYE

LESLIE CONNOR

KATHERINE TEGEN BOOKS
An imprint of HarperCollins*Publishers*

Katherine Tegen Books is an imprint of HarperCollins Publishers.

The Things You Kiss Goodbye
Copyright © 2014 by Leslie Connor

Library of Congress Cataloging-in-Publication Data
Connor, Leslie.
    The things you kiss goodbye / Leslie Connor. — First edition.
        pages   cm
    Summary: "High school junior Bettina Vasilis is trapped in a relationship with
her basketball star boyfriend when she meets Cowboy, a car mechanic whom her
traditional father would not approve of" — Provided by publisher.
    ISBN 978-0-06-089091-9 (hardback)
    [1. Dating violence—Fiction. 2. Love—Fiction. 3. Greek Americans—
Fiction.] I. Title.
PZ7.C7644Th 2014   2013043191
[Fic]—dc23   CIP
                                                                        AC

Typography by Michelle Gengaro-Kokmen
14 15 16 17 18 LP/RRDH 10 9 8 7 6 5 4 3 2 1
❖
First Edition

For Judy and Jerry—
Thank you for your love.
Thank you for sharing the pond.

February

THE NIGHT I CUT OFF MY HAIR, MY MOTHER TOLD MY father to leave. That's when it hit me. Somehow I'd reached the mud at the bottom the pond. The scissors making it through my braid was just the landing.

I had hair that was a lifetime of long, and it was the kind of hair you *tame*. (My Greek genes made it wild, coarse, and curly.) Momma's remedy for my mop was olive oil with rosemary—Old World conditioner, but it worked. She'd massage it through the strands. Then she'd weave me a thick and perfect braid that was so long, the tip brushed my waist.

I had always liked the scent of the oil and the feel of her hands. But this night, I was on edge because of Cowboy, and

Momma and Bampas were on edge because of me. After my mother left the room, the braid seemed heavy down my back. In my bed, it made my nightgown damp, twisted around me—*tugged*. Then came the bad memory.

I don't remember reaching for the scissors. But I do remember how hard it was to close the blades over the braid—I realized it somewhere in the middle. But I finished what I'd started. I looked at that rope of hair in my hand. There was an elastic band on my night table. I twisted it onto the chopped end and let the whole thing drop.

I turned off my lamp and slid back between my ice-clean sheets, tucked my knees to my chest and begged for a dream—even a bad one—if I could just find Cowboy there.

My light came on again later—a brutal burst of whiteness. Oh, how my mother screamed when she saw what I had done.

One

I MET BRADY CULLEN IN THE LAST QUARTER OF OUR SOPH-
omore year. Back then, he was just a sweet, skinny kid. Before
we ever spoke, I'd seen him smile at me in the hallway—a
bunch of times. Each time, he'd dip his head and look at his
feet. Each time, I'd looked over my shoulder to see if maybe
he had his eye on someone else. I didn't think boys like Brady
were interested in girls like me. To be sure, he was different
from the boys I'd been messing around with. Come to think
of it, if he'd known about those guys, we might have never
happened.

If you stood us side by side, this is what you'd have seen:
Brady in a game jersey, the cuffs of his khakis scrunching

over the tops of his basketball sneakers; me in combat boots, a black leather mini, low-cut sweater, and a long whip of braided hair running down my back. Add a Steampunk choker, and maybe a henna tattoo wherever there was a patch of bare skin, and you're done.

Yeah, yeah—it's all fine and PC to say that what you wear doesn't matter, that anything goes and it's what's inside that counts. That should be true. But come on, who doesn't judge a book by the cover? Besides, it wasn't just our clothes. Brady also had a crowd to hang with. I was an outsider at my school, though not so much by my own choice.

I was also a dying breed, and it was my own parents who were killing me. Their weapon? Our Greek heritage, which, in my case, came loaded with dusty ideas about what I should be allowed to do and *not* do—and I am talking about everything from curfews to dating to life. If you asked me, my parents were about a century behind the rest of the world. I was constantly trying to crash through to this millennium. I wanted to bring Momma and Bampas with me—but only as far the front door, where I'd say something like "Love you. Don't wait up."

Yeah. In my dreams. That was the biggest drag—trying to get out of the house. My little brothers had longer leashes than I did. I had pulled out of my collar and had a good run in recent months. But that was over. I was reeled in tight again and not because I was in trouble. Not grounded. Not even fighting with Momma and Bampas. It was really all because of Julia.

She was my awesome, bold and crazy, kick-ass friend and fellow "dancerina." We had met in the kinder class at a studio across town. We took lessons together for years. By the time Jules and I turned fifteen, we were the pirouetting diehards of the advanced classes. Everyone else had left for high school sports or theater. So Julia and I took ninety minutes' worth of lessons three days a week—just the two of us. Then we helped with the beginners' classes, being "Miss Julia" and "Miss Bettina." We were serious dancers. But Julia also became serious about stripping off her tights in the dressing room after class, zipping into her mean-heeled boots, and pulling on a miniskirt so she could go down the block to mingle with the local free-range kids. Loyal friend that I was, I unpinned my coiled braid and I went with her.

I began to be semi-honest with Momma about class times, and she didn't question. She didn't confront me about the cups of coffee I sometimes had when I climbed into the car. I wasn't trying to be bold by showing her what I'd been up to; I was trying to be a little bit forthcoming. I always made it back to the steps in front of the studio by 5:45 for my ride. Momma made sure that if Bampas was coming to get me instead of her, I knew it. She had small ways of going to bat for me; she'd won me the right to wear mascara. "Three swipes and you're out the door," she'd said. Of course I'd add a few layers once I was on the bus.

My coffee cups were also a diversion. Julia and I did not sit still in iron-backed bistro chairs drinking lattes after dance class. We wandered. I smoked my first cigarette behind that coffee shop. My first French kiss happened in the city cemetery just across the street—and so did my second and third. I think Julia might have had another first with her back up against a granite monument; she never really confessed.

I did some parent-free shopping on that block. I netted a leather jacket at the Goodwill store, and an armful of sweaters that zipped up the chest (or *down* the chest) and a few T-shirts to slash up. One of the free-range girls sold me a pair of vintage combat boots for fifty bucks. I was so psyched to get them I threw in a pair of earrings I had made from vintage beads and glove buttons. I snuck my treasures home in my ballet bag and revealed my purchases slowly. Often, I came out of my room late for breakfast on school mornings so there would be no time to change. I thought my look was funky; Momma and Bampas called it "filthy." There was yelling. There was drama. I learned to leave the house looking "respectable." Then I'd fix that either on my way to school or in a stall in the girls' bathroom.

Julia also met the fringy friends at night. I only made

it out a handful of times—snuck out through my bedroom window at the back of the house. (You have to love a sprawling Mediterranean-style ranch.) Then I hiked it through the garden, past our little horseshoe of rabbit hutches, and along my father's property all the way down to River Road to catch whatever ride Jules had arranged. Little did my father know that the very swath his mowing crew kept cut so that he could walk to the river and "do his thinking" had become my escape hatch. Never mind my inappropriate clothes; for this, Momma and Bampas would have grounded me for a year. I tried to be courteous. I even left them notes to say that I had not been kidnapped just in case they discovered that the punched-up pillows under my covers were not really me. I also had my younger brothers, Favian and Avel, in my pocket. They had caught me the first time. Scared the snot out of me.

I'd heard the sucking sound as the window of the bedroom next to mine slid open. Both boy-heads had appeared. "Bettina! Hey! Where are you going?" The strains and giggles of one ten-year-old and a seven-year-old can fill the air like a damn chorus.

"Hey! Shush! Shush!" I'd pointed a finger at them to shut them up. It was only because Momma and Bampas had music playing in the living room that my cover was not instantly blown. "Don't tell! I'll owe you one. Think of something you want," I'd strained in my loudest whisper.

7

"You have to let us stay up *way* late next time you baby-sit!" Avel had returned.

"Double dishes of ice cream, with the works—"

"Fine! Now close the window, you dorks!" My mistake—they both loved being called names—don't ask me why—and they'd howled with laughter that night. I'd wasted a beat wondering if I should turn back. But I'd wanted to be out so badly. I'd turned to go up the garden steps. I'd slipped and touched one hand down and kicked one leg up behind me.

"Underpants!" Favian had taunted.

"Shh! You bad little boys!" I had hissed at them. I'd thumped my finger off my lip. "Shut the window!" The window had sucked closed and I'd faced it just long enough to see two plaid pajama butts pressed up against the glass. I'd marched away, snorting with laughter.

My parents never caught me, not that night, not any other—I was that good. I probably should have tried to get out more often because by January of my sophomore year, my free run was over. Julia's family moved away as suddenly as a door bangs shut. There went the bolder half of the advanced dance class. I got crammed into the new "advanced" dance class, which seemed not very advanced at all. It had more bodies in it, but they were twelve- and thirteen-year-old bodies. I felt big and bored. The coffee shop scene didn't have the same draw for me, not without Julia to lead. I wasn't even sure how to hang with those kids now that she wasn't there.

With Favian and Avel getting older and going to activities of their own, Bampas soon started complaining that my dance studio hours were disruptive to the family. He also began to grumble that he wasn't getting enough for his dollar anymore. So, before he could insist on it, I quit.

Bampas, and even Momma, seemed to forget that Julia had been my only real friend, and the dance studio, my only place away from home. For weeks, I stood in my combat boots, lonely as hell. That's about the time Brady Cullen started flashing grins at me. Then damned, if one day, he hadn't somehow learned my name.

Two

Brady had a signature way of saying "Bettina." The *B* sounded more like a *P* and the rest was clipped. "Y-you're P'teen-uh, right?" I looked up from my locker to see him standing beside me. He was blushing like a stoplight.

"P'teen-uh." It took me a second to hear my own name inside that pronunciation. Then I hid a smirk, and instead of saying, "Uh, not really," I nodded and said, "Yeah." *Yeah, okay. I'll be "P'teen-uh."* It was hardly worse than Bettina, which I had always thought was a prissy mouthful of a name—not to mention I'd heard myself called "Bettina Ballerina" way too many times.

Anyway, a few more "Hey, P'teen-uhs" and a few weeks

later, Brady introduced me to an upperclassman, also draped in a basketball jersey.

Brady said, "Hey, Spooner, this is P'teen-uh Vasilis. She's a friend of mine."

A friend. Was I? Already? Spooner took me in—full ride up with the eyes—but he seemed more curious than lust filled. I gave him the warmest hello I had in me. I suddenly liked being Brady Cullen's friend.

Meanwhile, Spooner smiled and tilted his head at me and I knew he was going to tease me. "Huh. So what is your deal?" he said. "Got a little 'girl-from-the-dark-side' thing going?" He did a little bobbing and nodding. "You've got your mean boots on. . . ." Then he flicked his own earlobe. "You like spiders and snakes, huh?"

I reached to hold one earring. "Serpents and tarantulas," I said. A blush bloomed from my insides to my cheeks. Then I broke into a grin.

"Oh! Oh! She's dark . . . but she *smiles*," he said.

I laughed and stamped a foot down. He sort of had me; I was always self-conscious about letting myself be cracked open that way. I had a giant mouth, full lips— like, take-up-your-whole-face full—and big teeth. I'd gotten all of that from Momma. Her smile was warm and appealing. I wasn't so sure I had Momma's grace.

Spooner was nice enough to gauge my embarrassment.

He knocked me gently on the shoulder. "I'm messing with you," he said.

Brady Cullen was encouraged. He obviously looked up to Spooner, who had, in his own way, given me his endorsement. After that, Brady kept turning up at the art room door and beside my locker, which were one and the same place, really. I started to look for him to be there. Then one afternoon after the last bell, he caught me lightly by the arm in the hallway. He stammered, "H-hey, what are you doing now?"

"Um . . . getting on the bus," I said.

"Could you miss it? 'Cause I never get to really talk to you for long."

"I could miss it if I walked slowly," I said.

"Well then, come on. Slow down." Another shy smile spread across his face.

So, I did miss the bus that day. Brady and I went to the upstairs hall where it was quiet. We leaned on the glass-block wall. He led with jock talk. He seemed surprised when I didn't know that he'd been top scorer on the JV basketball team.

"Well, I don't get to the games," I told him.

"How come?"

"Hmm. It's my parents," I said, and I rolled my eyes. "I don't get out unless I sneak out."

"What about after school? What do you do?"

"I go home to a tiny, turreted room," I said, and we both laughed. "I'm kidding. I used to take dance lessons right after school but they kind of ran out of classes for me."

"I go to dances," he said. "I don't dance. But I go." Again we were laughing. "So, you sort of don't *look* like you have strict parents. I saw you with a spider tattoo one time." He opened his hand wide and pressed it into the thigh of his khakis, indicating exactly where he'd seen the tattoo on me. "I get that it was a temp. But still, that doesn't seem like strict parents." He shook his head.

"Yeah, like I said, I sneak around." I ducked my chin just a little. I didn't know what he'd think of me if I started confessing my deceptions. But it wasn't like Bampas was going to let me date this boy—or any other boy. Having nothing to lose is a pretty cool headspace. I looked right into Brady's pale blue eyes. "I get into school on an early bus and I . . . do stuff. In the girls' room before the bell."

"You *do stuff*?" He opened his eyes wide as if to tease. I shrugged in return. *Nothing to lose*, I reminded myself.

"Yeah." I cocked my head a little. "I put that spider tat on in there one morning. Sometimes I change my clothes in a stall. Whatever." I tried to sound dismissive.

Brady Cullen smiled. Then in a voice just above a whisper he asked, "Will you go out with me?"

Suddenly, I flashed on all my kisses in the graveyard, how

13

fleeting all of it had seemed. I was pretty sure that Brady was asking me to be his girlfriend. Had he ever had a girlfriend? I wondered. More than one? It didn't seem like it. He was a little bit awkward and innocent, I thought. But man, his eyes were bright and his lips were full and perfect. I could *so* try kissing those. . . .

"Oh, God," I said, and his eyebrows bumped up just the littlest bit. I shook my head. "Sorry, but no. I cannot go out with you. My father is so old-fashioned. Prehistoric. I'm basically not allowed to date. We'd have to sneak around. It wouldn't be much fun for you."

"Oh. Wuh-well . . . uh, okay then." I watched the air go out of the boy.

"I'm sorry. Really. Look, I should go down to the office and use the phone," I said, though I didn't really want to leave him. "They'll wonder at home why I'm not off the bus yet. I'm supposed to call for a ride if I miss it."

"You don't have a phone?" He twisted up his face as he dug into his pocket. "Here." He held his phone out. I took it carefully. I *loved* phones. They were sleek and shiny and responsive—all in a package like a chocolate bar. And this one was warm from being next to Brady Cullen.

I dialed home. I got my father and, aware that Brady was listening, I tried to keep it simple.

"Bampas? Yes. Sorry, I missed the bus. I was slow getting

out of the art room," I lied. "Yep, okay. See you down in the circle—" I looked at Brady while Bampas scolded me. I was sure that he could hear everything.

"I do not understand it, Bettina! What keeps you in that art room too late for a bus? You will explain at supper tonight. When you take the time of others, you disregard them. And when you are late, you make them worry—"

I mouthed the word *sorry* at Brady and rolled my eyes while I continued to use his beautiful phone. "Yes, Bampas. I will. I will. Yes. Bye." When the call was over, I held the phone to my chest for a beat and sighed. "And there is a little sample of my life for you," I told Brady.

"So, are you in trouble now? He sounds kinda *mad*. Will you be grounded?"

"No," I said. "Well, not any more than I usually am. I'm kind of grounded as a way of life." Again, Brady and I were laughing together. "And sometimes, there just has to be a lecture and then it's over."

"So, wait . . . is *Bampas* your father or your grandfather?"

In truth, Bampas was old enough to be my grandfather. But Brady didn't need to know that. "'Bampas' is Greek for father, or dad," I told him. "Like Papa."

Brady reached for my hand and didn't so much take it as give it a timid sort of tug. "Is it okay if I walk you out to the circle? Or is that a bad idea?"

15

"Even Bampas doesn't get to say who goes out to the circle," I said.

On our way through the lobby, Brady and I leaned together. I gave him our home number and watched as his long fingers quickly tapped it into his phone. *I should not be encouraging this boy,* I thought. But it'd be so nice if he really did call.

For the next few weeks, I missed the bus about every other day. Bampas would pull up and see me standing with Brady. Finally, he dug down for the monotone and asked me, "Who is the boy, Bettina?"

"His name is Brady Cullen, Bampas."

Without taking his eyes off the road, my father said, "Do I need to tell you—"

"That there is no dating until *you* tell me there will be dating? And not to ask before I am at least sixteen? No, you don't."

"And do you know why?"

Oh. This part had not come up before. I looked at Bampas and tried to read his profile—stern as ever—as he stared forward.

"It is because you are not mature enough for a relationship, Bettina."

I suppose I could have said what I was thinking—that I wouldn't mind *practicing* a little bit before anyone called it a "relationship." But that wasn't a good way to deal with

Bampas; he'd ground me for being fresh. So, I dropped it.

Then one day around the end of May, after I had missed the bus some more, Brady walked up to the car with me. He leaned in to the window and introduced himself to my father, all the while holding my hand on the outside of the car where Bampas could not see.

"Oh, yes. You are the boy who has called the house?" Bampas said.

"Yes, sir. That one time, it was during your dinner. I apologize for that."

Bampas progressed from a shrug to a nod, saying, "No, no. This is okay."

"Mr. Vasilis, I was hoping Bettina could come to Shoot for a Cause with me on Friday night. It's a cookout and basketball free throw contest, down in the park. We have sponsors and the money goes to disaster relief."

I stood outside the car, linking pinkies with Brady, and thought about what a nice try that had been. Then damned if I didn't hear Bampas say *yes*. And damned if Brady didn't stand up, smile, and brush me a little kiss for the first time, there above the roof of the car where Bampas would not see it happen.

Brady Cullen became my beacon. He was the boy my father would let me go out with. Brady picked me. Bampas picked Brady. I flew free—a couple of times a week.

Three

IN THE BEGINNING, BRADY WAS WHAT ANYONE WOULD call a *good* boyfriend. He waited for me between classes, and he sat with me at lunch on the days our schedules allowed. He bought me little books of cartoony tattoos and left funny cards in my locker. Once, he brought me a lemon-poppy cupcake in a box from the best bakery in the city. He'd gotten up early just to have it at my locker when I arrived in the morning.

I made Brady ugly little clay creatures with big ears, snouts, and toothpick horns on their heads. I pinched them together toward the end of art class and handed them to him while they were still wet. He'd take them from me knowing he'd end up with mud on his fingers, which I found hilariously sweet, and put them on the top shelf of his locker to dry. He gave me discreet kisses in the hall. I had told him no tongues in school. Couples that did that grossed me out. He honored that.

He seemed oblivious to the fact that other than Spooner, who was about to graduate and be gone, his friends hadn't exactly warmed to me—especially the girls. They eyeballed the clothes I wore, my henna inkings, heavy-metal jewelry. I didn't think of myself as an outrageous dresser. But I definitely clashed with their designer labels. No one was outright mean but they nudged each other in my presence and made faces they thought I couldn't see. No one ever said more than a perfunctory "hey" to me. I wasn't good at striking up conversations with them either. I couldn't shake the feeling that Brady's friends didn't get me. But Brady was steadfast, if shy, in his affection for me. That melted me over and over again and it made me want to be with him no matter who else was around.

Then, just before school let out for summer, he talked me into something I had never even thought of doing. "Be a cheerleader," he said. I stared at him. If the mere suggestion wasn't enough to make my eyeballs squirt out of my head, he gave my arm an encouraging pump too. "You could make it," he said.

I managed a shrug for his sake, but a resounding *no* bounced all around the inside of my head. "I don't think that's really my thing . . ." I tried to tell him.

"Aw, come on. Sure it is. All that dance stuff you did?"

"But they'll make me take my boots off. . . ." I whined. "I *need* my boots." I knocked my heels together and Brady laughed.

He pushed at me. "Come on, come on, come on. . . ."

"I don't know. . . . I guess I could try—"

"Hell, yeah!" he said. He popped his fist off his chest and did a big sidestep in celebration. He jumped up, shot a pretend ball at a pretend hoop. I had to smile as his cap of hair landed back on his head. "If you make it, you get into every game free. You can watch me play. . . ." He tried to begin a list but it seemed to end there.

I wanted to go to Brady's games and if I made that cheer-leading squad, Momma and Bampas would pretty much have to allow that—sometimes even on school nights. Oh. My. Gosh.

"Colleges like to see that too—the extra stuff—besides the grades," Brady added.

Colleges. A stone sank through me. Bampas wouldn't talk about college—not for me. I was all about art, and Bampas had always said, "You don't need to be at an expensive university for what you do." That would always catch me a sympathetic and pensive look from Momma. She wouldn't say it, but I think she felt we should at least talk about college. But when I opened my mouth to mention the possibility of scholarships, Bampas raised a finger and said, *"Siopi."* He was telling me to be silent.

I did try out for cheerleading. I wasn't as loud as the teacher-judges wanted me to be. But I learned routines in a snap because I was used to impatient choreographers. As for what little actual dancing the cheerleaders did—well, piece of cake. I could leap. Or jump. I could lift and be lifted—no fears about that. If anything set me apart from the others, it was that I arrived and left the tryout alone.

A day after tryouts, they posted the names on a list in the girls' locker room. Bad timing: I met a cluster of girls ushering out a slump-shouldered friend who was weeping her way along the tiled wall. "Who is *Bettina Vasilis*, anyway?" she choked between sobs. "She took my spot!"

"Oh, so sad for you, Jenna . . ." came a consoling voice. "I think she's that *art room* girl—the one with the long, long braid. She wears metal. . . . She's into grunge. . . ."

Then a redhead locked eyes on me and hushed her friends with a few nudges and the words, "Hey, you guys . . ."

I was Bettina Vasilis. Right smack there. I couldn't do much but give them all a "sorry" look. The group went on by, moving like a single organism, I couldn't help noticing. The

21

redhead doubled back to whisper to me. "This is just hard for Jenna. It'll be her senior year. She really wanted a spot on the squad. But, hey, no mean stuff intended, okay?"

"Same," I said, but I felt like I should apologize and hand over a pom-pom.

I'd made the winter squad, which, I learned, was more competitive than the fall squad in our all-about-basketball town. Who knew? With the posted roster was a message saying we would start practicing in September. That was months before basketball season began and that seemed excessive to me. But, hey, there it was: my legit reason not to get on the bus for home right after the bell and, if the team made the play-offs, we'd be hollering and jumping through spring vacation. So, except for poor, crying Jenna Somebody, I started to like the idea.

Brady was thrilled.

"It's going to go like this," he said, and he drilled an imaginary ball toward the floor. "Every time I take a foul shot, you watch 'cause I'm going to bounce it seven times for the letters in your name. *B-E-T-T-I-N-A.* It's for good luck," he said.

Of course, between making the squad in spring and starting practices in the fall, summer happened. Brady and I had our two nights a week together: the two that Bampas allowed, and I snuck out a handful of times. Brady didn't want me to use up my nights on his crowded summer league games in the park. "I want to really *be* with you on those nights," he insisted. My heart worked overtime, doing all the things a heart will do when it is letting someone close—the flutters, the swells. Nothing had ever felt so good as bursting out of the house and into Brady's arms—all summer long.

By then, I was sixteen. But since Bampas had not even thought of letting me learn to drive, he didn't know the rules. He didn't know that even though Brady was older than most rising high school juniors I wasn't supposed to be riding in a car with him, and Brady's parents didn't seem to care. So he'd pick me up and take me to his house in the village. From there, we'd walk under miles of twilight together, through village streets and around the town parks. Maintenance guys locked up gates behind us and we pretended to leave. But really, we lurked, and we squeezed past posts or climbed fences after they'd gone. One night when the orange trucks had bobbed away for the night, I sat across Brady's lap while we kissed by the base of an oak tree. Gently, he slid his hands under my shirt, touched my belly skin with his fingertips. A long time later, he'd gone no higher—and no lower—than my first rib. His tentativeness melted me. No more one-shot graveyard kissing for me. No jawing on each other like there was no tomorrow. I had a nice boyfriend. I had him before anyone else had him—I was fairly certain of that—and I liked it that we were taking our time. Every so often I remembered what Bampas had said and I felt like I was proving him wrong; this was a relationship.

On a starry night in July, Brady and I stood in a fort of rhododendrons not far from a darkened baseball field. Loose buttonholes made it easy and my shirt fell back over my shoulders. The skinny straps of a cami slid easily down my arms. He touched me so lightly. His breath went crazy and he told me, "Sweet Jesus, I'm gonna pass out."

"It's okay, it's okay," I giggled, and his forehead met my shoulder and together, we knelt safely down.

"This is so . . . *embarrassing*. How out of my league am I?" He lay back in the grass, hands over his eyes, and laughed at himself. I wedged up against him, felt his heart pounding through his chest. We lay nestled together, looking up through the leaves at the shining pinholes of light in the sky until he felt a little brave again. "I—I don't even know how to say it," he stammered. "I guess being with you like this . . . just blows me away, is all." I leaned closer and kissed his summery neck.

So summer went. Little step by little step, I was falling in love.

Four

COME SEPTEMBER, BRADY AND I WALKED INTO THE FIRST
day of school together, me solidly on his arm. I felt his slight
backward tug the second we hit the lobby and heard him
swear under his breath. He scanned the hall like he was looking for something more to attach to than just me.

Brady was not in love with the "school" part of school;
he had confided this to me. So on that September morning,
I tried to console him. But he pulled forward and led me to
a cluster of his basketball buddies. I stood outside the huddle, my hand still tucked in the fold of Brady's elbow. I still
hadn't gotten to know his friends and now I wondered what
my absence at all those summer games had cost me. The girls

seemed familiar with Brady in a way I did not remember from the spring. They'd look at me sideways and barely say hello. I felt like I had something that was supposed to be someone else's. I heard one of the guys say to another, "Guess that's still going on. . . ." while he cocked his head toward Brady and me. I was the girl he'd brought in from the outside. I shifted in the school lobby, turning myself a few more degrees away from the circle.

I wanted to move on to my locker and peek into the art room and see what Mr. Terrazzi had done with the art budget over the summer. But Brady kept on talking to his pack and I didn't have the heart to pry him away. This was the *good* thing about school for him, his morning pep rally. If he could have skipped straight to basketball season he would have. I had half an ear on them as they talked about the state trophy they were going to bring home at the end of the winter. How they could focus on something that was still such a long way off, I had no clue.

Under my feet, there was the large mosaic of our school mascot—the White Tiger. I traced an arc across it with the toe of my boot. It had been designed by a group of senior art students some years before. This wasn't the first time I'd studied it. The White Tiger wasn't just white. There were dozens of shades of pale blues and pearly grays in that pelt. *How had they done it?* I wondered. *How did they plan for such a large-scale piece of art?*

"Hey, Bettina!" I looked up—way up—almost to the top of the stairs. There was Tony Colletti breaking into a grin. I had the thought that from where he stood, I must look like the tail on a big letter *Q*, standing outside of the jock circle like I was. I suddenly felt like a Brady Cullen accessory—like his backpack or gym bag. I waved to Tony with my free arm. He descended quickly and came to stand beside me.

"Hey! How was your summer? I can't believe it—I never saw you," he complained. "And now it's over!"

"Oh, I know," I said. "The families just don't get together anymore." I flashed on old times—the block parties down in the little ethnic neighborhoods where we'd lived before Bampas built the house out near the river. Seeing Tony made me nostalgic for fat trees growing out of the sidewalks, for brick houses with white iron railings, and steamy bowls of pasta fagioli. I remembered the dozens of Virgin Marys watching over that neighborhood from turquoise-blue grottos in the narrow backyards. I cocked my head at Tony. "Actually, maybe all of you *do* still get together," I said. I gave him an embarrassed smile. "We're the ones that moved."

"Eh, we don't do that so much. You and me, we'll have to light a fire under everyone again, huh? We'll do something this fall. Bring your little brothers down for trick or treat."

"Sure," I said, but I doubted it'd happen. "How is

27

everyone? Your family?" I asked. He gave me a nod but his grin dropped in a dark sort of way.

"We should catch up," he said. "Soon. I'll look for you." The first bell rang while I was watching him walk down the hall. Tony Colletti had had that same bouncy walk all his life, I realized, and it made me smile.

Suddenly, Brady was in my ear. "That guy—he *always* has to talk to you, doesn't he?" The huddle of basketballers was dispersing. I stepped out of their way.

"Who? Tony?" I thought for just a second. *Always? More like he's the* only *guy who ever talks to me.* "Yeah," I said, "our families know each other from wa-a-ay back. We used to live two doors down fr—"

"Yeah?" Brady interrupted me, and looked down the hall after Tony for a beat. Then he gave me an intense stare. He thrust his jaw at me a hitch. "Come on, let's go," he said. I was afraid I had somehow hurt his feelings but I let it go since I also knew that Brady was in a mixed mood about being back at school.

Walking so close to him in the halls I noticed how incredibly "eyes up" Brady was—meeting gazes and giving and receiving little nods and hellos every step of the way. This was new since last spring when we had both been pretty much invisible. People knew Brady now—about twice as much as they *didn't* know me.

When we reached my locker, he kissed my forehead. "Maybe see you at lunch if our schedules work out, huh?"

"I hope so," I said. Then I added, "Hey, hang in there. Have a good morning."

"What?" he said, spreading his arms wide. "Are we some old farts getting up from the breakfast table, here?"

I tipped my head back and laughed.

Truth was, I liked that we weren't a new couple anymore. We had lasted the summer, and that was always a big question with couples that met up in the spring. If anyone had asked, I might have said our relationship had been cemented by equal parts freedom and longing. It would have been nice to have more nights together. But I had warned Brady that it was best to push gently against the force that was my father.

"You've already performed a miracle where Dinos Vasilis is concerned," I had said, and it was true. Bampas had noted offhandedly that he was surprised we'd lasted. He must have been solid in his belief that Brady was the right boy for me to date. After the first several weeks, he hadn't even checked up on us the way I thought he would. Sure, I had curfew. But usually it was Momma who met me when I came in at night. I was freer than I ever dreamed I could be.

Five

So, Bampas gave me some grief about going out that first Friday night after school began again. It was as if he had to. He rumbled about my homework and how the lazy days of summer were past and how I needed a schedule again. But I bargained hard to have that Friday night with Brady. He was so low about being in classes; I took it upon myself to try and keep him bolstered up.

I won out with Bampas, and Brady came to get me that night. We had to drop the car back at his house in the village so his mother could use it. Mrs. Cullen waved from the kitchen window. Brady held the keys up over his head, jangled them for her to see, then threw them onto the seat of the car. She acknowledged, and Brady took my hand.

"Let's walk to the park," he said. "Then maybe we'll come back here." He was giving me a potent sort of look, and I felt like I was missing something—was it about the car? His mother? Or more stuff about the start of school? "I was just thinking we could hang a while," he added.

"Yeah. Sure," I agreed. "Let's just have a kick-back night."

We ended up making a quick loop that evening, rushed along by a metallic scent in the air and a sky full of rain clouds and then trees shaking in the wind. Half a block away from Brady's house, he paused to point to a brick school building.

"See, Alcott Elementary," Brady said. "My first and favorite place ever to shoot hoops," he said.

"Really?" I asked. "Even now?"

"Yep. That's where it all began. That's where I found out I could sink six, then eight, then thirty in a row."

I started to tell him how curious I was about Alcott—the school I had *not* gone to. But the rain began to come down so Brady took my hand and we started to jog.

That run in the rain was exactly what I would have planned if I could have, to keep Brady feeling light. He took us shortcutting across the last few lawns. We jumped little fences and avoided flower beds.

"This way, this way." He hustled me along the narrow side yard at his house. He stopped us at the cellar door—the kind that looks like a slide for little kids. He pulled it open and said, "Go ahead down. Careful."

"Okay . . . but why? What's down here?" I said. Was this the way in from the rain at the Cullen household? I two-footed my way down the cement stairs. Brady came in behind me, tucking himself below the door. He eased it down so it wouldn't slam.

"Why are we here?" I whispered. The rain pattered on the metal door. I waited for my eyes to adjust to the darkness. I had that excited, "safe inside" feeling. I grabbed Brady's shirt and pressed my nose to his chest, giggling.

"Come on," he said. He guided me along the cinder-block wall to a place where just a little more light came in through a ground-level window.

My toe bumped over something. I looked down and saw the raw edge of a big carpet scrap, then an old futon mattress covered in a worn *Sesame Street* sheet.

"I set us up a little spot," Brady said. I sighed. It was rare that we had a private place to be together. He wrapped me in his arms.

Holding me close and kissing me, he pulled me down and laid me on my back. Quickly, he peeled off his T-shirt. He slid my sweater up, undid the catch on my bra with a flick of his fingers. Our skin was damp from the rain and I shivered. He hovered over me, as if to warm me for a moment. But then

32

he sat back just enough so he could slide his hands up under my skirt. I felt his fingertips curl around the thin elastic at my hipbones. "Brady . . ." I whispered. He eased me out of my panties. "Hey, Brady . . ." I whispered again.

I guess I wanted to say that I thought we were skipping a few steps. But he didn't want to talk, and now I seemed not able to. A few seconds later, a condom wrapper with the corner torn back lay curled near my shoulder.

I never saw what he looked like that first time, and I can't describe what I felt. Not pain. But not nothing. When I twisted underneath him, he pressed closer. He whispered, "It's okay, it's okay."

I braced, and for a second or two, I turned my face into the sheet underneath me. I saw the yellow of Big Bird's beak, the white, cartoony eye with the black-dot pupil. The thought of my little brothers—their TV shows and stuffed animals— flashed through my mind. Was that even appropriate? Wasn't I supposed to be perfectly, completely, and passionately linked to Brady right now? And what was he thinking and feeling way up there above me? How could I be this close to him yet feel like he was far away?

He gasped several times, grunted, then rested heavily on top of me. I squeezed my eyes shut. I'd once watched our rabbits mate—the buck had fallen off the doe at the finish but he'd clung to her, wheezing once or twice before he'd righted

33

himself. I wished for Brady to roll off, roll away.

The Cullens' basement ceiling whirled. I was shaky. Brady knew it. He started kissing me and hugging me. He tried to cajole me with huge, handsome smiles shining in the dim basement light. "I—I'm so glad we did this now." He pressed those words into me—his hands on my face. "I love you *so* much. I do. So much." Finally, he thought to ask, "You okay?"

"Yeah, I am." I slid out from under him. I began to grope for my clothes.

"Hey. Come on." He pulled me back against him but I sat forward, clutching my sweater in a ball at my chest. My head swam with thoughts. I felt surprised and weird and maybe scared.

"I—I just want to know that—" I swallowed hard and began again. "That you . . ."

"What? Tell me."

"I—I don't want everyone to know."

"Uh, well, people are going to figure," he said, and I could tell he meant it. "We actually waited kinda long. People hook up all the time—"

"No," I said. "No. This is *us*. This is *ours*, what we just did. I—I'll feel sick if you race out of here and tell your friends as if it were nothing—"

"You think I'm going to do that? Really?"

I felt bad then. "No . . . but please, Brady. I didn't know we were *here* yet. I mean I thought eventually . . . b-but I didn't think we'd do this *now*."

"Well, I kind of know what you mean. But I think you were just . . . nervous. It'll be better the next time," he said.

Well, the next time was a few days later—same place. We'd cut a lunch period together. I went willingly—didn't think he'd go for it *all* in the middle of the day, though that sounds idiotic even to me now. Anyway, it was worse. I was tense, still trying to catch up to where Brady felt we were. I'd gotten a look at him this time, and that made me even more apprehensive.

"Jesus, P'teen-uh! Stop making that face," Brady finally said. "Christ! I can't do it if it's gonna be like this." He stopped and stripped off the rubber. "Do you know how much these things cost?" He shot the empty condom at Big Bird's head. "You have to *try*," he said. "And be glad I protect you! Not all guys are that good about this stuff," he told me. All I could think was, *Hey, protection is a* given. But of course I didn't say it. In fact, I was speechless. Again.

It was bad. Really bad. I thought we might have ruined every good thing we'd had. Dressing again and hurrying back to school for the afternoon was horrible. I felt like crying, and he wouldn't speak. This was worse than the first time. His angry tone had stunned me. I was heartsick. I spent the next hours at school asking myself what happened to the sweet, shy boy who'd nearly passed out the first time he'd touched me. I was desperate to have that boy back.

By late afternoon, Brady had flipped. He tracked me down before I got on my bus to go home. "I'm sorry. Man, I am so, so sorry. I was a total shit." His eyes pinked up as he spoke. He buried his face in my neck. He called to apologize again before I went to sleep that night.

Rough starts, I thought. This had probably happened to other couples. The next morning, he brought me flowers. We hugged in the hall and fought off tears. We told each other everything was okay, and I knew we'd go on.

When the next opportunity came, Brady made sure it was better. He slowed down, gave me time. We'd had a bad patch, Brady Cullen and I. But now he wanted to learn how to make it *good* for me.

"Don't be embarrassed, just tell me," he said. At first I couldn't. But he just kept encouraging me and finally, one afternoon in Brady's basement, I got to the good part.

Six

So, I HADN'T HEARD FROM ANY OF THE CHEERLEADERS over the summer—no time to become friends. I was worried about fitting in with them but I'd been so wrapped up in Brady that it didn't seem so important. I was aware that they were comprised of a pair of cliques that brushed up against each other and traded members. Our first gathering of the school year took place a few weeks in. It was not a practice but a meeting to set the schedule. After that was done, there was some socializing that had nothing to do with me—until I felt them circling up. The redhead from spring tryouts asked, "So, hey, Bettina . . ." (Ah, someone remembered me . . . and was that going to be good or bad?)

"How was your summer?"

I played it friendly. "Great!" I said. "Except for too much hanging out at home. I'm so glad school has started again."

"Oh, you didn't work?" another girl asked. She skewed her jaw, twirled her hair around her finger.

I shook my head no. I had wanted a job. But that was another never-ending bone between my parents and me. Momma was a broken record: "Your bampas provides for you, gives you money when you need it. In return, you'll babysit when we ask." To me, they were keeping me home and keeping me from having much money of my own. But it was okay. I had been so happy all summer. I'd been allowed to go out with Brady.

Then someone said it. "So . . . you're still *with* Brady. . . ."

"Yeah. I am." I smiled.

"Ooh, that's Brady Cullen, right? He's *adorable*!" one girl blurted, then giggled in a genuine sort of way. I had noticed her before. She was little and sort of hyper, bouncing about the open lobby like a free satellite.

Before I could nod at her, someone squelched her, saying, "Emmy, don't be a freak. . . ."

Emmy bit her thumb, closed her eyes tightly, and said, "Okay, I'm being quiet now," and she laughed again. I pegged Emmy as the most cheerful cheerleader right then and there, and I began to think of the rest of them as the

Not-So-Cheerleaders. They weren't done with me yet.

"So, that whole thing is all good? You and Brady?"

"Real good . . ." I said, and all of us laughed, and I felt one little second of warmth. I very nearly blurted something non-detailed about that recent bad patch. But I caught myself. That was between Brady and me, and we'd worked it out.

"But how come we never saw you at summer league games?" they wanted to know. "*Everybody* goes. . . ."

"Right. Well, it's complicated but, um . . ." I was not going to try to explain the uncool style of my upbringing to these girls. "Brady and I saw each other a couple of nights a week. Just not basketball nights," I said.

"Oh. I guess if I had a boyfriend I'd want to see him play. But you did see him? And he really doesn't see anyone besides you?"

"Well . . . n-no," I said. There was a roaring moment of silence in which I could almost feel Brady's fingertips on my skin—new inch by new inch. *We were close, close, close all summer. Shed our shyness, shed our clothes . . .*

I wasn't sure what those girls were getting at but it seemed like something was up. I looked at their faces. Most of them looked either down or away. "We had an awesome summer," I managed to say. There was another stretch of dead airtime. Then somebody chirped, "Well, that's *good*!"

Something about that high note stuck in my craw.

So, in the late afternoon, as I was pulling my head back through my shirt down in Brady's basement, I asked him about it. "Hey," I said, and touched his arm so he'd look at me and listen, "we're all good, right? I mean, have you . . . has there been . . . anybody else? You're just seeing me, right?"

"What? You mean have I been going out with other girls?" His head drew backward like he'd been knocked in the nose. "Sheesh! P'teen-uh! What the hell?"

"W-we didn't ever talk about whether this was exclusive. Someone said something—basically asked me if you had cheated on me this summer."

"Oh, who's going around saying that stuff? Who the fu—" Brady didn't finish but he plowed into me with a teeth-banging kiss—his only answer to my question.

As the weeks passed, I couldn't ignore the feeling that between June and September, while I'd been falling all over Brady, I had missed something—and maybe it wasn't even *exactly* what the cheerleaders had hinted at. But now I could see a change as we walked through the school together. Brady Cullen wasn't a shy, skinny guy bouncing a ball just beneath everyone's radar anymore. He was a nodding, fist-bumping "jock machine," working the hallway like it was his job. Younger girls were baking him brownies and he was mugging for phone photos with them. *Everyone* knew him, and everyone prized him. For all I know, that's exactly what turned him—exactly why he started to do bad shit to me.

Seven

IT'S HARD TO REMEMBER EXACTLY HOW THE BAD STUFF began . . . or when it turned from amusement to malice. One of the things Brady and I liked to do—when it was just the two of us—was play. In the beginning I'd bump off his shoulder to jostle him and he'd jostle me back. We would end up laughing and holding hands. As he got more comfortable around me he'd dump me on the ground— always protecting my landings—and maybe subject me to a raspberry on the neck. We ended up hugging and kissing every time.

In school, he started to make a game of coming up behind me, grabbing my braid tail, and wrapping it around my head so it covered my eyes. Harmless enough. But there were times that he pulled a little too hard, or kept me blind for too long—with other people watching and laughing. I didn't love it but I wouldn't make a scene. A couple of times he made me late for class. Once, I was about to get written up. But Brady popped through the door to the classroom and took the blame. He talked the teacher into letting him take my half hour of detention, which made him legend in the world of boyfriends.

I guess one day does stand out. We were at his locker just before lunch. One of those little clay figures I had made for him back in the spring fell off the shelf of his locker and broke into crumbs except for the head.

"Oops," I said, looking at the dirt by our feet. It was a little sad. It was our favorite, the one I had named Sputnik for its cap full of toothpick horns. When we'd emptied our lockers before summer break, I'd carried Sputnik into the art room and had found him a shelf to spend the summer on.

I looked at Brady in a mock-solemn way. "Here lies Sputnik . . ." I began an epitaph. "Hold on . . . I'm trying to come up with a rhyme. . . ."

Brady picked the clay head off the floor. "Save me!" he squawked, and I thought it was funny. "Fix me!" He waggled the head at me. I played along.

"No, no. You are beyond repair and must accept your

43

fate. I shall return you to the bucket of clay from which you came—"

"No! Save me, bitch!" Brady jabbed the spiny head at me and caught me in the forearm.

"Ow!" I drew back. "Brady, you just *clawed* me with Sputnik!" I let out an incredulous gasp. I pushed up my sleeve. A pair of stinging red welts were rising on my forearm.

"I *toothpicked* you," he said, and he laughed out loud. Then damned if he didn't come after me for a second swipe. Thing is, I'm not sure how it would have stopped if it hadn't been for several teachers who came down the hall. I slid my sleeve down over the scratches. They told us to clean up the clay crumbs and move on.

Brady didn't feel bad about it. Plain and simple. But I needed a minute, so on the way to lunch I ducked into the silence of the girls' bathroom.

"What the hell?" I muttered to myself. I took a squirt of soap at the sink and spread it over the marks. Some blood came up—enough to turn the suds pinkish. I heard a toilet flush, and freaked out. I was not alone. Bonnie Swenson came out of one of the stalls.

Big Bonnie—everyone called her that—was not really my friend. I knew her because she was a fixture in the art room. She was, well, *big*. Probably five foot eleven, and not fat, but large. She had dry, kinky hair the color of curry, and it seemed

44

to sit on her head in drifts rather than have roots there. Her skin was always chapped and ruddy. I started thinking *emollients* every time I saw her.

Bonnie was nice and that meant that other people dumped on her. They left her to get vats of clay soaking—a huge job—and she loaded the kiln for every firing.

"Oh, hey, Bettina," she said.

"Hey," I said back. I cupped water and rubbed it over my soapy arm to hurry the rinsing along and hide the evidence. Too late.

"What happened?" Bonnie leaned toward me. Her hands were in her own sink. I wished she'd stay over there. "Cripes. That's nasty. Is there a cat loose in the building?"

"No, no." I grabbed for a paper towel and slapped it over my arm. *Think fast, think fast*, I thought. *You're not going to tell her, well, Brady friggin' stabbed me. . . .* "I caught myself on a pin back. The dangers of jewelry making," I said with a little art-girl to art-girl trill. Sickening, but I guess I pulled it off because Bonnie laughed.

"Oh, bummer," she said. "You know, Mr. Terrazzi keeps a tube of antibiotic goo in the cabinet over the art room sink. Save you a trip to the nurse." She shrugged.

"Oh, thanks." I patted my arm a final time with the paper towel. "See you in class," I said, and I was out of there.

I felt low walking down to lunch with Brady. I was used to

sucking it up when it came to little wounds—Bampas had me trained for that. But Brady had done this on purpose. Did he just not know any better? Something else was bothering me more; I realized that in lying to Bonnie about it, I had lied for Brady. There's a first time for everything.

Eight

I WOULD HAVE NEVER MET COWBOY IF I HADN'T RUN from Brady Cullen. We, the junior class, had picked up our class rings in the morning—a milestone marked with a chunk of "Siladium." It was not the kind of thing I really cared about but Momma really wanted me to have the ring. Bampas had written the check with the comment that he approved of our school taking delivery of the rings so early in the year; the longer I could wear it, the more he got his money's worth.

I'd chosen the smooth, white stone—no starburst, like most of the girls. A bunch of us were gathered on the bleachers in the gym after lunch, everyone comparing rings. When Brady saw mine he started to joke. "Oh, baby!" he said. "So *ugly*! I'm so sorry for you." He put on a show grabbing my arm and shaking it to make my hand flap up and down. "So ugly!" he repeated. His friends laughed at that, and so did I. I liked my simple ring—the way it mixed up with a dangly bracelet I had made from little rusted keys, old watch parts, and a few faux pearls.

As the end of fifth period drew closer, Brady got it into his head to cut school and he wanted me to go with him. His house was only three blocks from the high school and his parents weren't home during the day. So, well, another "opportunity," and I had come to like opportunities. But I had an art class I didn't want to miss, and I didn't want to put Mr. Terrazzi in the position of having to write me up for the cut either.

Brady whispered close in my ear. "Come on . . ." he urged, secretly brushing the outside of my thigh with his knuckles. I shifted away from him mostly because his breath was tickling me.

"I'm not going," I said. "Not today. I have art—"

"Art, *schmart*! So what?" He grabbed my hand, full wrap, and pulled on me—just fooling around at first. But he had my fingers all bunched together and he was squeezing too hard.

"Ow! Brady!" I pushed against him with my other hand. He tugged me.

"Come on, come on!" He laughed, and squeezed harder.

I felt metal digging into flesh, my finger bones rolling over one another. It hurt so much I couldn't make a sound. I actually panicked about how to make him stop. Finally, I let out a cry. I pounded his shoulder with my fist. He let go. I bent forward, gasping. I pressed my throbbing hand between my knees and shook the other uselessly in the air.

"What?" he said. *"What?"*

I shook my head. Couldn't answer. I wanted him to shut up. I squeezed my eyes closed and huge, hot teardrops spilled. It got quiet all around us. People were watching.

"Are you *crying*? What! You're faking it." He gave me a push.

I had to stop it. Had to stop him. I got up, climbed down the bleachers, and started to walk away. Fast. Faster. Then I ran—right out the back door of the gym. Brady called after me in that husky voice, "Hey! P'teen-uh! What's the matter? What the hell? Get back here! You're making a big deal out of nothing!" I heard him swearing, and then the sounds of the outdoors filled my ears.

I ran through the back parking lot of the high school. Air rushed into my lungs. I crossed the pavement, then the long, green ball fields. I ducked under the bleachers and slipped through a break in the chain-link fence that backed up to Hammer Hill Industrial Park. I coughed hard. More tears came. And snot. That seemed to be everywhere. My fingers stung and throbbed in a way that made it hard to tell exactly which ones hurt the most. I tried to breathe.

I met with a Dumpster—something to lean on. I pushed the heels of my boots into the gravel and sank down against the cold metal. When I could look at my hand, I did. I had to blink to see it, but the little White Tiger mascot from the side of the ring was imprinted—*with amazing detail*—into my skin in shades of red and purple.

It hurt. It *really* hurt. I closed my eyes and swore over and over again. I was just beginning to breathe through it, when I felt someone standing there. I saw the blur—western boots and blue jeans. A man. He reached for my bad hand. I drew away. I tried to get to my feet but didn't quite make it. I started to fall back and thought I'd land on my ass. The guy caught me by my wrist saying, "Hey—hey! I'm not gonna hurt you."

I blinked and tried not to be obvious about needing a tissue. I suddenly worried that he could see up my skirt. I snapped my knees together and let him help me up. I wiped at my eyes and stole a quick look at him. He had sandy hair and a square jaw. He was long and skinny. A thick belt rode low on narrow hips—chunky buckle. His smokes were rolled up in the sleeve of his T-shirt. He looked a little retro, and like some kind of cowboy or a motor-head. Or maybe a carny. I wasn't sure. I knew he was just like *something*, but I also knew he wasn't like me. And he wasn't like Brady Cullen, either.

"How'd you hurt your hand?" he said.

"I—I'm fine." I shrugged. But my jaw shivered.

He took my hand in his, tilted it a bit, and checked the damage. "Looks crushed," he said.

Well, yes. Exactly right. Crushed by Brady Cullen.

"Come here," he said, and I have no idea why but I followed him right in through the open overhead door of Unit 37. Inside, I saw at least two clean-and-shiny car carcasses—and many, many parts of others. (Apparently, I had been right about the motor-head thing.) The smells of gasoline and motor oil were thick on the air but the place was spotless. He turned to a shelf on the wall behind him and brought down a tube of something that smelled like Vaseline but was greenish black. He squeezed a dab of the greasy stuff in underneath my ring. I muffled a gasp.

"I know, I know," he said. "Sorry. Try not to fight it." I sucked a breath. He turned the ring around and wiggled it gently over my knuckle. I watched him palm it.

"H-hey, what are you doing with that?" I asked. He tossed me a clean rag.

"Wipe that grease off," he said. "And be careful." In my own mind, I added three words: *It's gonna hurt.* And it did.

While I shivered and dabbed, the guy kept his back to me

doing something at his workbench. "I—I just got that ring."
I took a step toward him and craned to see what he was up
to. When he turned around, he had my ring strung on an old
shoelace.

"And you thought I'd steal it?" he asked. "Because it's
such good luck and all?"

I snorted a laugh and a new river of snot humbled me. I
tried to recover my tough act. Meanwhile, he let one corner
of his mouth curl up, and I had the crazy thought that, oh my
God, he was cute.

"No worries," he said. "Class rings are nothing but *bullshit*
to me. But I was never into anything about school." He dangled the ring in front of me and I brought my good hand up
under it and closed my fist around it. "Those fingers are going
to swell up on you," he told me, sticking his chin toward my
hand.

What was he? Some kind of authority on crushed hands?
I looked at my fingers. The tiger impression, though tiny,
was still amazingly clear, and stamped well into the tender
skin inside my middle finger. My pinky looked like someone
had taken a potato peeler to it. Just like he'd said, both were
swelling.

"You should ice those. I don't have any here. Maybe go
back to the school."

I bunched the shoelace and the ring together and stuffed

52

them into the tiny pocket at the top of my skirt. I turned to go, but the guy caught me by the arm. I flinched. He met my eyes with a funny squint. "Wait a minute," he mumbled. "Better come here."

He led me to a rough but clean bathroom, sort of pushed me inside the door and half closed it.

Oh no, he's a weirdo. What have I done . . . ?

He opened the door back up and handed me a roll of toilet paper that I'd seen stuck on a nail just outside the door. "You're a mess," he said, tapping two fingers beneath his own eyes.

The door closed again, and I dropped the hook-and-eye latch into place. I looked into the cloudy mirror. "Jesus," I muttered. Inky streaks of mascara were drying on my cheeks. I dabbed at my face with a piece of the tissue. I blew my nose and instinctively reached for my backpack—which wasn't there. Damn, where had I left that?

I peed, not because I really had to, but more because he'd handed me that roll of toilet paper. It seemed like as long as I did something bathroom y, I could leave afterward—no more questions about how all of this had happened. I sat there for a few seconds. I held the roll of bulk-buy toilet paper in my good hand and thunked it against my forehead a few times. I whispered to myself, *"Bettina? What the hell are you doing?"*

I had to get back to school and into the art room, and I

didn't want to see Brady on the way. And how was I going to get past this guy—this *cowboy*? I washed my hands in the cold water, letting it pour over my bruised fingers—still killing me. Then I swung through the bathroom door, stuck the toilet paper back on its nail, and headed out.

"You're welcome," I heard him call after me.

I kept on walking.

I didn't see the nurse, didn't get any ice. I found my backpack on the bleachers and went right into the art room without drawing attention. (Mr. Terrazzi overlooked tardiness whenever he could.) As I slid into my chair I felt the bundle of the ring on the shoelace press my hipbone from inside my skirt pocket. I pulled it out and put it around my neck. I didn't do much work. My fingers hurt just from the blood moving through them. But the rest of the day I kept holding my ring and looping that shoelace over one thumb and holding it under my nose. I smelled the garage on it, whiff after whiff. I liked that smell the same way I liked pigments and turpentine. I thought about the motor-head guy. He was sort of scary on the one hand. But he'd been nice too. Nicer than . . . a lot of people.

Nine

WHEN BRADY SAW MY FAT FINGERS AND THE TIGER embossing he seemed surprised. "Ooh, I didn't know I had ahold of you that hard," he said, and he stuck his bottom lip forward. "I never thought about the ring. I was wondering why the hell you ran away like that." What he said seemed perfectly true. His pout had faded to a natural grin. So I wondered, *Can I blame the guiltless?*

Oddly, I thought about Bampas, and his lifelong instructions for me: *Fili antio.* Kiss it goodbye. When I was little, if I cried or fussed because he'd denied me something, or gone back on a promise—or even if I'd gotten hurt somehow—he'd give me about a minute. Then, firmly and evenly he'd say,

"Fili antio." He'd present me his cheek. I was supposed to kiss him. Then I was to bury my pain or disappointment on the spot. Stop crying. Let it go.

All of that flashed through my mind as I stood looking at Brady. He hadn't meant to hurt me. Hell, he didn't even know that he *had* hurt me. Should this really be a big deal?

"I missed you after you took off," he said, and he wrapped me in his arms, rocked me back and forth. Then he laughed in my ear. "And you saved my ass because I would have missed a pop quiz in math if we'd cut." He hugged me tighter, kept his lips pressed to my head. Then he held me back and looked at me. He said, "Hey, there's that party in the glider field tomorrow night." His eyes were bright and flirty. Those parties were legendary but, of course, I'd never been to one. "I want you there with me," he said.

A party, and the words *I want you there with me.* Boy, did that sound good.

"Okay," I said. "We'll make a plan."

Mangled fingers would heal. I made a choice. *Fili antio.* I kissed the incident goodbye.

Ten

BUMPER TO BUMPER, CARS LINED THE SIDE OF THE ROAD.
I stepped out of the passenger's side of Brady's car. The
gravel on the shoulder crunched under my feet in a satisfying
sort of way.

"Over to the left," Brady said. "I think I see everybody."

Of course, "everybody" was his group of friends. We
stepped onto a sea of long, yellow grass. The strands seemed
to lie down at our feet for as far as a person could run. I stole
glimpses at the full moon over our heads. It was alternately
bright, then lost, behind fast-moving clouds. So this was the
famous glider field. I had never wanted to be anywhere more.
Or maybe it was truer to say that I craved being out in the

wild, and I felt crazy-glad to be at the first big party of the school year.

It had taken two lies to get me there. First, my crushed fingers were obvious enough that Momma had noticed. Instantly, I'd known that my freedom was in jeopardy. But the way I had seen it, I had a whole art room full of possible hazards to pick from. Even though I wasn't in a clay class, I'd chosen the mixing vat. "I was doing a favor for Mr. Terrazzi, mixing clay for the basics class," I'd told her with a shrug. (Well, I had watched Big Bonnie Swenson do it from the corner of my eye.) "I should have taken the ring off before I went digging under thirty pounds of red clay."

"Ring? Oh! That's right, your class ring! It came? Oh, where is it?" Momma's eyes were full of light. I liked the rare moments that she played girlfriend to me.

I pulled the ring out of the neck of my shirt by the shoelace string. I drew the whole thing over my head, freed it from my long tail of hair, and handed it to her.

Momma turned the ring over in her hand. "It's a pretty stone. Ooh . . . the polish," she said. "But this shoelace! So grubby!"

Oops.

"Bettina," she went on, "you should put your ring on the gold chain Bampas and I gave you for your birthday until you can wear it on your finger again."

"I should," I agreed, but I knew that I wouldn't.

My second lie was to get out of a dinner with my family at my father's restaurant; I was getting good mileage out of my spot on the cheer squad. Tonight, for example, we were having a pizza party and planning a pep rally. Right. My family dropped me off at Minio's Pizzeria in the village, where I tucked myself inside the entry next to the gumball machines, until Brady picked me up there ten minutes later.

So I had made it to my first party in the glider field. Historical. I stood with Brady, doing my imitation of the tail on the *Q* once again. This night, Brady's circle was full of guys and girls, including some of the Not-So-Cheerleaders. And as usual, I felt the vibe: *What the hell is Brady Cullen doing with that girl?* But we were a couple. I was proud of that, and I trusted that time would take care of the rest. Meanwhile, my spot on the periphery was giving me a crazy-good view of the night and that moon.

I could also see about fifty kids, and not nearly enough beer for all of them. There were a few other bottles of this and that and some smokes—various aromas rising. A beach ball kept popping into the air for a sort of dark-blind game of volleyball. I saw multiple attempts to get a little bonfire going. (I started to count the matches.) Another group of kids was singing, changing the words to familiar songs and having huge laughs. Me, I guess I was "being with Brady," and keeping warm against his side. I looked upward over and over again. The night was beautiful—that active sky above. I was a sucker for anything celestial.

Brady leaned down to tell me, "Hey, we're going for a smoke." I was a little surprised. All we'd ever done before was split a beer in his basement after sex once or twice. It just wasn't how we spent our precious minutes together, and besides, I couldn't see me dumping myself drunk or stoned back in through my bedroom window late at night. Still, I'd smoked with Julia and the free-range kids. I was game to get a little high, especially if I could do it with Brady. I nodded and started to follow. But Brady unhitched me from his arm. "Maybe stay here," he said, lifting his chin just slightly. "I'll be right back."

I'm sure I stood there giving him a dumbfounded look, at least at first. But I shrugged and said, "Oh. Okay." So he wanted to have a "guy smoke." No problem. I watched them move off under a stand of pines about a hundred feet away. Soon, a haze rose over their huddle. Off my mooring, I felt cold. I tucked my hands up into the sleeves of my sweater— still being careful of my wrecked fingers—and looked up at the moon. Music was drowning out the silly singers now. Something danceable filled the air. I swayed a little by myself, tamped down some grass, and fantasized about getting Brady to dance with me. Does *anyone dance out here?* I wondered.

What a great place for it. I stretched my arms out.

"Nice night, huh?" Tony Colletti was suddenly next to me.

"Tony! Oh, hey! Yes, it's awesome. I'm so glad to be out like this—oh, but never say that you saw me here. *Please*. You know how my father is."

"*Ooh*, yeah," Tony said, and nodded. "He hasn't let up on you?"

"Are you kidding?" I said. "I lied about where I was going tonight, so . . ." I let it hang. I trusted Tony Colletti. Then I distracted him. "Hey, look at that silvery edge that runs all along the tree line." I pointed up at the moonlight as I stood shoulder to shoulder with him. "It's like liquid metal."

"Like solder," he said. I laughed. We'd had an industrial arts class together the beginning of sophomore year, and Tony had spent two whole periods helping me put a seam on a metal napkin holder. (I'd been afraid of the torch.)

"Hey, Tony," I said. I tilted my head at him. "Is everything all right? With you and your family? When I saw you the first day of school, well, I just had a feeling . . ."

"Yeah. Well. I guess I kind of blew you off that day. Sorry." He sighed.

"No, no. I didn't mean that you had," I said.

"Well, you remember my nonna Regina?"

"Of course," I said. The notion that anyone might

forget Regina Colletti was laughable. I put a finger in the air and spoke. "We could call her Regina but we were *not* allowed to call her 'Nonna' unless she *was* our nonna." Tony laughed. But I remembered my mistake as a little girl. I had thought Nonna was her name so I had called her by it. She'd grabbed me by my wrist and she'd set me straight in front of a room full of people while I blushed like a cinnamon candy. After that, I had been equally scared and mesmerized by her.

"Does she still live upstairs from you?" I asked.

"She does. She's real sick though."

"Oh, Tony." I hesitated then asked, "What is it?"

"The big C. She's fighting. But it's not going so good," he said.

"Oh my gosh. I'm sorry. Regina? Really?" I said. "It doesn't seem possible."

Regina Colletti was beautiful—*never* vulnerable. I'd sensed that even as a little kid. Instead of a Madonna statue, Regina had a statue of a little pissing boy in her yard. He filled up her fountain where the neighborhood cats came to drink. She'd been both queen bee and rebel of that old neighborhood.

"Hardest part is keeping her cheered up," Tony said.

"Hmm . . . well, she always liked a crowd." I was thinking aloud.

"You're right. And she doesn't have the energy for big parties now, but she likes when people visit. Hey, why don't you come by?" Tony faced me. "She'd love that!" he said. "Walk home with me one day. I'll take you up to see her."

"Oh, Tony, of course I will." I heard myself say it, and immediately wanted to backpedal. Regina didn't even like me. I didn't want to see her. "I don't know when—"

"Hey! Hey, P'teen-uh!" Suddenly, Brady was coming across the toppled grass like his ass was on fire. When he reached us, he put on the brakes and gave Tony a pseudo-convivial nod. "What's up, man?" he said in that way that lets the person know you don't really expect an answer. Tony extended his hand, and Brady eyed him before he gripped it.

"Just catching up. Old friends," Tony said.

Brady cupped my elbow. "Come on. Let's take a walk," he said. I gave Tony a weak smile and Brady pulled me away, my boots catching on tangles of long grass. He stopped abruptly and gave me a big, territorial kiss.

My face went hot and my hair prickled. I wiggled out, whispering, "Stop it!"

"Stop it? Oh, that's nice. I can't kiss you?" Our breath mingled in the cold.

"Not like that."

"Like what?"

I glanced back toward the spot where I'd been talking to

Tony Colletti. I lowered my voice way down and hissed at Brady. "Like you're trying to drench me in piss!" I tried to take a step but it was like that damn grass had me tied down. I swore under my breath and ripped my foot free. I put a few paces between Brady and me. Found a little breathing space of my own.

Well, Brady got quiet after that, and I guess I did too. We didn't stay much longer at the glider field. I never got to ask him if he'd dance with me. As we drove along the dark roads toward home, he asked me if I was okay.

"Yes. Fine."

But Brady pulled over and shut off the car. He turned to me. "Look, the thing is, you act so shy all the time," he began. "It's like you never talk to anybody. Then you finally do and it's a *guy* . . . and it's *that guy*, and I don't know. I don't think I get that."

"Well, first, if you haven't noticed, I am just a little outside your circle of friends. So, yeah, around them, I feel shy."

"Aw, you just have to keep coming out with me. Get to know them better." He brushed my shoulder with the backs of his knuckles.

I nodded. "And I will," I said. "But about Tony, he is an old friend. I already told you that, and now he's told you that, too—"

"So what? That means you're going to talk to him no

matter what?" Brady stared forward, maybe looking hurt, I wasn't sure.

"Listen, Brady . . ." I thought for a second. "His nonna— his grandma—is super sick. That's what he was telling me tonight. He just wants me to come see her. It's nothing more. You and I are rock solid."

I leaned across the split seats and got as close to him as I could. He sighed and took my hand—the good one. (Protecting my mashed fingers was automatic for me.) He looked into my eyes and we kissed. I remembered summer, and my throat ached for wanting to roll in reverse, to go back to the way it was when Brady and I had kissed under the rhododendrons in the park. I tucked my face into his chest, breathed him in. He said, "I better get you home before *Bampas Dinos* sends a goon after me."

I broke a little grin. "He doesn't do things like that," I said.

"I wish we stayed longer at the field," Brady said. "Felt like half a party. We could have found a little camping spot, you know?" He slid his hands inside my jacket, took a tour all over the front of my sweater. He laughed. "You're cold!" he said. He turned on the car and cranked up the heater fan. "Man, I want you. Did I ever tell you, I'm *always* wanting you. . . ." he said. "Always, always."

Eleven

I CALLED TONY OVER THAT WEEKEND AND MADE A PLAN to see Regina on Tuesday. I dreaded it in at least a hundred ways. Surely having cancer was making her even crankier than ever. The one good thing about the pending visit was that Momma and Bampas had agreed that this was a "lovely" thing for me to do. I was released from going straight home one more afternoon.

But before I had to face Queen Regina on Tuesday, there was Monday. I lied about using the library after school so I could hang with Brady. He asked me to go with him to Jumpin' Joe's—best sweet potato fries in town, and walking distance from school. We went Dutch. Brady never had a lot of cash and I had never thought that guys should always buy.

I thought it'd be just the two of us, but it ended up being six of his friends too. I ordered somewhere in the middle of the pack, behind Brady. I turned from the counter, balancing the little cardboard boat of hot fries and a root beer, all while thumbing the change and a receipt against the palm of my bad hand. I glanced up to see where Brady was. Instead, I laid eyes on my motor-head, finger-fixer guy—just coming in the door.

Our eyes locked. I felt a split-second rush of something good, like when I am instantly glad to see someone. I might have even started to smile. He raised his chin a hitch as if to say he recognized me. In the next rush, I was *not* glad to see him. I swallowed hard. He was looking at my hand, of course. No hiding that behind my back—not when what I really needed that day was a third one to carry everything.

He went up to the counter to order. I took my balancing act to the condiment table. I set it all down, pocketed my change. I broke open a salt packet and shook it over my potatoes until it was empty. Then I looked toward the counter again. He had a coffee cup and at the same second that he brought it to his lips, we caught eyes a second time. I looked away quickly.

Come on, Bettina, just get to a table, I thought, and I gathered everything up again. Then Brady came up behind me

67

and knocked his knees into the backs of mine. My legs buckled and my drink sloshed onto my hand and into the fry boat. "Oh, don't do that!" I said. His friends were laughing and I could feel my face flush.

"Okay, I'm sorry," Brady said, tilting his head at me like a contrite little boy. Then he nudged me with his elbow, and my drink spilled again. He had this loud, high-pitched laugh, so there he was, crowing and gathering attention.

"Brady, come on." I kept my voice low and tried to give him a good-sport sort of grin. "Stop it," I said. "Seriously."

"What? I didn't do it again. I did something else!" he teased.

We sat down and, with my hands in my lap, I used a stack of napkins to mop my sleeve. I went carefully over my swollen fingers, trying to be invisible about it. I looked toward the take-out counter. No cowboy guy. Phew. And yet, I found myself scanning the lot outside the plate-glass window to see if he was getting in a car or just walking away. But he was gone.

Twelve

Now that I had seen him again, that cowboy stuck
to me like crazy. The light had been strong coming through
the glass at Jumpin' Joe's. His gray-green eyes were intense,
set deep behind an uncommon froth of pale lashes—or
that's what I saw in those few seconds. It was a long way
to travel up to those eyes, and it seemed that not just anyone got to go there. My sense of that was moony; I wanted
another look. The thought of him passed through my mind
every hour or so. He'd been nice. Well, sort of "pissed-off"
nice, if that was possible. Even that was interesting. I still
had my class ring on his shoestring. I fiddled with it often. I
thought about the way I'd walked out of his garage without

saying thank you. What a mess I had been.

So, the next morning I stood, hesitating, in the doorway of the auto shop with a coffee in each hand. I heard a hissing sound and followed the trail of an orange air hose across the cement floor to a car. I could see only his boots until I squatted down.

"Hey!" I called, and then again more loudly. "Hey!"

The hissing stopped and the guy rolled out from under the car. He squinted at me. "Hay's for horses," he said.

I rolled my eyes. "So original."

He shrugged. "So, what are you doin'? Cramming for exams and now you need two coffees to get you started?"

I smirked. "Naw. I thought one could be for you. If you want it. But I didn't know how you take it. One's black, one has cream. You can have either." I showed him two sugar packets as well, but he ignored those.

"I'll take black." He sat up and took the cup from me. I watched him peel the lid back while his dusty-blond head bowed forward. He took a sip and said, "Ahh. Thank you." He put his cuff to his bottom lip as if to catch a small spill. All I saw was the perfect, roundish dimple in the center of his square chin. I watched him stand—again, it was a long way up somehow. He was older, but boyish-looking, and cleaner than your usual motor-head, I thought. I should stop staring and remember what I came for.

"Uh . . . thank *you*," I said. I looked down at the clean cement floor. "I should've said that. The other day." I looked back up at him. "You were . . . nice to me."

He nodded, switched the hot cup from one hand to the other and rubbed his palm against his thigh. "I saw you yesterday," he offered.

"I saw you too."

"Yeah. Well. I saw you first."

I took a drink of my coffee so I could hide an idiot's smile from him, but instead I laughed and I burned my mouth. Then I tried to hide that too. It didn't work. He winced for me.

"Be careful now," he said. "So . . ." he said. He glanced up at the fluorescent lights above us, then eyed me pretty hard. "That guy you were with at Jack's yesterday, is he the one who hurts you?"

"Hurts me? *Pfft!*" I pulled my chin back, then put the coffee to my lips again.

He gave me this all-knowing nod that kind of pissed me off. Then he asked me, "How's the hand?"

At my side, I flexed my fingers and felt the ache, the thickness from the swelling. "It's better. That was a dumb accident," I said.

"Uh-huh." He let it go. "So, you got a name?"

"Yeah. A terrible one," I said.

"Come on now. How terrible?"

71

I pointed to myself and enunciated: *"Bettina."*

"B-buh-*what?*" He opened his eyes wide and pretended to choke on his coffee.

Oh, he was quick. I had to smile.

"Yep. I know. It's awful," I said.

"So, what do your friends call you?"

"Bettina." We both laughed. "Yeah, I keep wishing for a nickname but . . ." I held my shoulders to my ears in a suspended sort of shrug.

He tilted his head at me. "What could we do about that?" He took it on. "Buh-buh-Betty? Bette? Tina? Ugh. Change a letter? Drop a letter? Bettina, Betweena . . ." He closed one eye at me.

I shook my head and thought, *Oh, please don't let him say "P'teen-uh."*

"B-bah . . . Bay . . ." and then as if striking a match, he said, *"Beta!* Second letter in the Greek alphabet." He probably had no idea how relevant that was. But he looked very satisfied. "May I? May I call you Beta?"

"Depends. What *may* I call you?"

"What do you wanna call me?"

I looked him over for about a nanosecond. "Cowboy," I said, and I didn't bother to ask if that was okay.

All through that day, during homeroom, morning classes, and then lunchtime with Brady sitting right next to me, I

72

thought about this nice guy—this Cowboy who'd called me Beta—oh, I liked that. He'd done it in a matter of seconds; I'd been waiting for a nickname most of my life.

Just before I'd left the garage, he'd said, "You know I was kidding, right? It's not really that bad—your name." But I wouldn't let him take it back.

I wished the Not-So-Cheerleaders would call off afternoon practice so I could go back across the parking lot and playing fields, and through the chain-link fence to see him again. But I had no reason to go see some guy who was, for one minor thing, older than me *by years. . . .*

Brady poked my shoulder. "Hey. You spacin' out?"

"No." I straightened my back. I watched him draw a chunk of bread through the gravy on his plate.

"You want my salad?" he asked. I shook my head. He gave me a handsome grin, put an arm around me, and pulled me close. I went all soft and just a little guilty inside.

Thirteen

"**I** CAN'T TELL YOU HOW MUCH MY FAMILY AND I APPRECI-
ate this." Tony Colletti bounced along beside me through the
crosswalk. I listened to my heavy boot heels making contact
with the street. *Tony's shoes must weigh nothing,* I thought. "I
hope I'm not making trouble for you," he added. I knew that
he meant trouble with Brady.

"No, I'm glad to do this," I said. It was at least a half lie,
maybe more. I was up for seeing the old neighborhood. In
fact, it seemed ridiculous that I hadn't been back before
this. But the prospect of having to hang in Regina Colletti's
apartment this afternoon was making my stomach roll. I was
already thinking of ways I could leave.

But Tony was talking on about the fall mums he was putting into the garden for his nonna to look down on from her bedroom. His voice and his bounce carried me along the increasingly familiar rows of homes and garden Madonnas.

There was a place in the sidewalk that looked like a broken cracker where the root of an enormous oak had pushed on it for years. That root had been our "home free" spot during games of tag and hide-and-seek. Tony laughed when I took an extra-wide stride to plant my foot on it. The crack also marked the place to turn into the narrow passage between the two-family houses—"up and downs," I had called them when I was little—and to the stairs that led upward to Regina Colletti's door. I gripped the white iron railing and followed Tony. With every step, I wondered what I'd find for skin and bones and attitude at the top. Bampas and Momma would want a report at dinner.

"Nonna? I brought an old friend," Tony called as he pushed the door open. "Can we come in?"

I wiped my feet on the little carpet of fake grass that covered the decking while I waited. It would be just like me to piss Regina off at the start, though maybe if I did, she'd want me to leave and all would be done. Hmm. I felt one of my eyebrows pump upward.

"In the bedroom, Tony," Regina called, and he ushered me in.

There it was—the garlicky air in the kitchen, and the eye-burning scent of seashell soaps everywhere else. In the hall outside her bedroom door, I smelled her lilac perfume—the same one she'd worn how many years ago? Eight? I thought so. I reached out and touched Tony's elbow. I don't even know why, perhaps a reflex. He turned quickly, and we stood there staring at each other for a moment.

"Don't be scared," he whispered. "It's not so bad."

"Who'd you bring for me?" Regina asked in a gravelly voice. I expected Tony to call out: *Sacrificial lamb!* I came around the doorjamb. Regina squinted at me.

"It's Bettina Vasilis, Nonna," Tony said. "Remember?"

"Dinos's girl?"

"That's right."

Queen Regina sat high on her wide bed. Her hair and makeup were perfect but she looked tired—like someone had come along and hollowed her out somehow. She adjusted a seed-stitched afghan over her legs. She had the same velvet pillows on her bed, the same crystal water carafe and tumbler on her nightstand, and a few snow globes from a collection that she kept out year-round. I'd seen them all before. She would have slapped me if she'd known how I sneaked around at the Colletti parties. I'd shaken up every one of those snow globes—had a contest with myself to get them all snowing at once.

"I haven't seen you in years. Look at you! Gorgeous! You have your mother's mouth—those lips!" Regina raised her eyebrows at Tony. He blushed. So did I. "I saw that coming years ago," Regina claimed. "And those weird, wonderful golden eyes—now those are all your own. Always were."

"Nonna, you need anything? Tea?"

"Yes. Black tea for me."

"And for you, Bettina?" he asked. "Tea?"

"Of course she'll have some. Go get it!" Regina told him. She made a whisking motion with her hand as if to get rid of him. I felt panicked, not wanting to be left alone with her. "Sit down." She patted the bed. I reluctantly propped myself on the very edge—in that bad spot where you need to be either more on or more off.

"So tell me about yourself," Regina insisted. "You got a boyfriend?"

Interesting she should start there. I still had a bad taste in my mouth from the scene Brady had created in front of Tony in the glider field. Was there any chance that she knew about that? Or could I try lying?

"Y-yes, there is a boy I date," I said.

"So . . . it's serious?"

I shrugged and felt another blush coming on. I didn't want to talk about Brady—not there—and suddenly the thought of Cowboy came swimming through. *Cowboy!* He had nothing

77

to do with any of this.

"Oh, for the love-a-God!" Regina squawked. "You're a shy one! Fine. You don't want to talk? Then you can listen to me, girl.

"I am sick as a dog," she began. She told me how the cancer had spread from her lungs to her brain, and when she said *brain*, the whole thing sounded so final to me. I winced and wondered how she could be so matter-of-fact about it all. "One thing I'd change, let me tell you. It's the cigarette smoking. I don't regret much, but I do regret that, Goddamn it. You don't smoke, do you?"

I had smoked. A little. And mostly I hated it. But there were times that I wanted that hate. . . . Did those times count? I shifted on that lousy perch at the edge of her mattress. I was a good liar. I should be able to lie about cigarettes, with a lilt. Instead, I kept glancing out the door, looking for Tony.

Finally, he came in with the tea and he stayed to drink a cup with us. Regina wanted to know about my family, and so I tried to catch her up on everyone. I told her about the boys mostly. They were a safe topic.

Regina remembered my little brothers. "The pride of Dinos and Loreena Vasilis!" she said. "The sun, it rose and set on those two little bumbies."

"Did you ever hear the story of how they got their names?" I asked. Oh, yes! This would take a while to tell. I felt brilliant. I launched.

"Bampas always said that a baby boy will tell you his name in time. Maybe you remember that Favian came home from the hospital without a name. Bampas was watching him that first week and he saw him stick his fingers in his mouth. The baby scrunched his brow, looked right at Bampas, and sucked those fingers *hard*." Tony and Regina both laughed, and I went on. "Bampas thought the baby looked like he was concentrating, trying to understand. Favian means 'man of understanding.'"

"Ohh . . . I had forgotten." Regina tapped her fingers against her teacup.

"That's how it went," I said. "And then Avel did not breathe right away—"

"Oh, now *this* I recall," Regina said, looking rather serious. "The doctor, she sucked something out of his nose. The mucus. And just in time!"

"That's right . . ." I slowed my speech. What were we to talk about when I was done? I sipped my tea, took my time to swallow. "That's why they called him Avel. It means 'breath.'"

"So, where does Bettina come from?" Tony asked.

I shrugged. "Bampas says you should name a girl the way you make a wish. Name her what you *want* her to be. But I'm not sure anyone knows what a Bettina is," I said. That sent both Tony and Regina into laughing fits, and then she coughed wildly.

"Your parents were very proud of their family," she said when she had recovered. I nodded. It was hard to hear. Of the boys, yes, and maybe they had once been proud of me. For something. Or maybe they never really even looked to be proud of me. I toed the rug, fidgeted.

"Tell me more about Dinos? One of the handsomest men ever," she said.

"He still has the restaurant," I offered mildly.

"Yes, yes, Loreena's Downtown. I remember. My Salvador helped him move the ovens in. What a chore! Dinos and Sal were the same age when they both came to the States. When Sal died, Dinos was there to carry the coffin. See that? Sal carried Dinos's ovens, and Dinos carried Sal."

Tony let out a quiet laugh. "I didn't realize Grandpa knew Dinos from so far back."

Regina pointed a finger at him and she shook it. "That's *Mr. Vasilis* to you," she said firmly. "You know better than that."

Tony gave me a sideways grin and said, "You're right, Nonna."

"I'm always right." Regina set her cup on her bedside table and leaned up slowly. "Right now, I have to use the toilet." I took the opportunity to stand and get off my uncomfortable perch.

80

"You need help today, Nonna? Want me to walk you there?" Tony was careful—no doting, just offering. This, I thought, this must be the way the old lady wants it. I was betting Tony didn't get too many of Regina's wishes wrong. She'd been training him his whole life.

"No, no. You sit," she told him.

I felt impolite standing there watching so I moved away to the window. I looked down to the tiny garden where Tony had planted the mums. They were like clusters of fuzzy embroidery all around the fountain—the pissing boy—who, I noted, did not appear to be doing his job. *Too bad*, I thought. I'd always liked him for the bit of sass he brought to the neighborhood. He was no Madonna and neither was his owner. Queen Regina had a reputation. She was, at the very least, a flirt. I knew that without knowing how I knew it. I had probably overheard something. My own parents loved her, but rumors were that she'd slept around with neighborhood men—not while her husband was still alive. But after he died fairly young. Whatever she'd done, Regina had developed a tough crust that kept her from caring what other people thought of her. *Maybe*, I thought, *that's how one gets to be queen.*

Tony startled me. He whispered, "She's doing good today."

"She looks the same," I whispered back. "Just tired. She told me it's the treatments."

81

"Hmm, it takes a lot out of her but then she recovers and she's almost herself."

"Nice job on the flowers," I said, poking a thumb toward the window.

"Hey, she told me what she wanted. From there it's just hoping I get it right."

"Yeah," I whispered. "But you *did.*"

"Yeah, and in a month it'll be time to change to those purple cabbage things," he said. "Anyway, thanks again. It's nice you came to see her. She does better when people come around. Her energy picks up. She likes the attention and—" He clammed up then, lips in a tight smile. The queen was returning.

Regina sat back on the bed slowly. She was only some-what careful not to let her gown ride up as she settled one leg and then the other in front of her. I could not help but stare at her legs, stretched bare from her knees to her toes. Her skin was that beautiful, coffee-with-cream color and it fit smoothly over her toned muscles. "These legs," she said as if she could read my mind, "are just too much. Like honey to the bees these legs are to men."

"Nonna!" Tony shifted and laughed but in an adoring way.

"It's true! And it's a Goddamn good thing I'm taking these legs with me. Not another woman alive who'd know what to do with these. Look at me." Regina pointed her painted toes. "These legs are sixty-six years old and they're almost the same as when I'm sixteen." She settled against her pillows.

"Let me see *your* legs." Regina was looking right at me and I opened my eyes wide. It just so happened I was wearing jeans. She waved a hand at me. "Go ahead. Drop your pants," she said.

I shot a glance at Tony.

"Uh . . . Nonna! Bettina is our *guest*," he said.

"Yeah, and you've seen a lot more than her legs."

"*What?*" I gasped.

"He's seen a lot more than your legs," she repeated. Tony sat back in his chair and briefly hid behind one of his hands. "You two used to go bare-asses in one of those little swim pools out back. Or maybe in my fountain. Hey, one of you kids made a poopa in it one time. Was it you?"

"Nonna!" Tony protested again.

"Oh, all right, all right. Never mind. I'm getting tired anyway," Regina said. "It's not the disease, ya know, it's the Goddamn cure that'll kill you—this radiation." Regina slouched down, and reached for her afghan. "They do my head 'cause they see some little spot or shadow up there and then I get Goddamn diarrhea from it. Who can figure that out? You come see me again, Bettina. And leave him downstairs." She flapped a hand at Tony. "You and I will talk about legs and your boyfriend and good stuff beyond that." She yawned while I forced a little smile and nodded.

"Tuesdays," she added, her index finger coming at me like a dart. "And you, Tony, you're going to look at my fountain next, and fix it. Did he tell you what happened?" She looked at me and I shook my head. "My pipi bambino got his winky knocked off. No happy spray. It runs down his leg instead. For a year now!" she added.

"Not quite a year . . ." Tony said. He began to explain. "Halloween night. Somebody tipped him and, well, like my nonna says . . ."

"Broken winky," Regina said. She yawned again. She nestled into her velvet pillows, pulled the afghan up to her chin. "Tuesdays," she said, and she closed her eyes.

Fourteen

THE THING I NEVER SAID OUT LOUD WAS THAT EVEN though I looked for reasons to stay after school, I liked being home for dinner. It was the one time of day I felt connected to my parents. Setting the table was something I could do without being criticized, and I knew how to help serve the meal. Momma was a good cook and, on busy days when she had to run the boys here and there, Bampas brought home something fabulous from his restaurant. It crossed my mind that if I were still going to dance lessons now, we'd be racing home from three different directions and have absolute chaos at the dinner hour.

Sometimes though, I just had to do it—stop and risk a

high, steady arabesque right in front of the china cupboard. I'd watch for the reflection in the glass as I tried to point my toe inside my stiff boot. Bampas caught me in just such a pose the night after I'd seen Regina Colletti, *and* I had a basket of warmed bread balanced on the fingertips of one hand, no less.

"Bettina, my dining room is not a dance studio," he muttered.

I drew down to a curtsy and set the bread basket gently on the table.

"How did Mrs. Colletti seem?" Momma called from the kitchen doorway.

"Oh, yes," Bampas said, remembering. "You saw her today?"

"Yes. Hmm . . . she seemed less than she once was," I said. I told them about the radiation sickness, the way Tony was pitching in to care for her. "She liked visiting. She wants me to come again," I said. "On Tuesdays."

"Tuesdays?" Bampas held the *s* on the end. "*All* Tuesdays?" He scowled. He stood beside the table and began to count my life off on his fingers. "So then you are cheerleading on all the Wednesdays. You are with Mrs. Colletti all the Tuesdays. You want to see the boyfriend on Friday night and Saturday night." He was beginning to drone on. "Soon you are gone from home more days than not."

"Well, do you want me to tell Regina—I mean, Mrs. Colletti, no then? Because, actually, Bampas, there's something else. The cheerleaders are adding a practice on Mondays. And sometimes Fridays, too." (Okay, I was accelerating things. But it would be true at some point, and I needed to get him used to the idea.) Bampas shook his head and put on a frown.

"No, no. You'll come home."

"Bampas, remember, I told you when I made the squad, it would eventually be every day after school?"

"Dinos, she did tell us this," Momma said softly as she came in from the kitchen.

"Yes, and if you remember, Loreena, she did not ask permission to join in the first place," Bampas said.

"Well, just the same . . ." Momma's broad lips made a gentle smile.

Why does she always sound like she is apologizing to him? I wondered. She set a heavy, steaming dish of lamb and lentils down on a trivet and motioned at me. "Bettina, your bampas will need the serving spoon from the sideboard." She touched my father's sleeve and said, "I'll call the boys."

My father turned to me. "Perhaps you should stay late once winter comes and the basketball begins," he said, "but it is not even October yet." He set to filling plates and handing them to me. I adjusted place settings as I put each one down.

"Well, it's not really my decision," I said.

"No. It is *mine*."

"You are going to tell the cheerleaders when to practice, Bampas?" I tried a coy smile but he missed it.

"Don't be fresh," he said calmly. Neither of us had missed a beat with the supper, and I set the last plate at my own spot. The boys came rushing in and slid into their chairs.

"Hey, never have to call you guys twice, huh?" I said.

"Lamb!" Avel said, and he rubbed his palms together. "I knew it! I smelled it!"

Momma handed me the water pitcher and I started around the table with it. "Bampas, I wasn't being fresh. Just saying that practice is a school decision." He did not respond. He looked at the table as if checking to see that everything was in order. I knew these moments. This was when I had little to lose. "Bampas?" I said. "What I really want to ask is if you will just allow me to stay after school every day?"

I felt Momma watching this. Sometimes you just know when someone in a room is holding a little bit of breath for you.

"No!" Bampas scoffed. "There is no reason."

"But I will always have something to do," I suggested. "If I am not cheering, I'll be in the art room or the library, or over at the Collettis' on Tuesdays—"

"Collettis'? You meant Tony?" Favian asked. "Aw, we never see him anymore."

"Or visiting with Brady before his practice," I went on. I

had not and would not mention that possibly hanging out at Unit 37 once in a while was also on my mind.

Bampas clanked the serving spoon into the dish and stared me down. "You are asking for your momma or me to do extra driving all over here and there to pick you up every day? Look around the table, Bettina. How many family members do you see?" Avel gave me some help, slowly opening up one hand with five fingers spread wide.

"I see everyone," I said, trying not to laugh at my brother. I explained to my father that I would be on a loop that pretty much coordinated with Favian's and Avel's activities. At this, I saw my mother nod slightly. If only she would pipe up! Instead, I was on my own. I told Bampas, "I can always borrow someone's phone if we need to be in touch, and Brady will drive me home, or Tony, and maybe other kids can—"

"Oh, no, no, no! You won't be in cars with just everyone," Bampas said firmly. "I will look at my schedule and let you know what I decide. Let us eat our supper now."

"I can also walk," I couldn't help adding. "I actually like walking. I'll get myself wherever you or Momma say—"

Bampas knocked his knuckles against the table. *"Siopi!"* Something actually flew from his lips when he said it. He seemed even more flustered as he gathered a napkin over his mouth.

I knew to do like he said and shut up.

Fifteen

IT WAS A LOUSY TIME, LOUSY DAY FOR ME TO VISIT THE dentist. First, leaving at 12:45 would mean missing the end of art class. Second, I had to check in at the office first thing in the morning, get my excuse confirmed with a phone call home, and wait for a med pass. There was always a line. That meant no time to take Cowboy a coffee. I had been trying to get back there. This day, I'd only just catch Brady at my locker. He told me something was up for Friday night, and once again, he wanted me there with him. "We'll work it out," he said. He gave my braid a gentle tug and took off.

That afternoon, Mr. Terrazzi presented the new project for our Commercial Graphics class. He had created a company—something to do with garden sheds. We were supposed to come up with a logo first, then a complete graphic design package. As he put slides of examples up, I listened to comments and wisecracks alike. I'd figured out that when it comes to any kind of art, you get information from every reaction.

When he brought the lights up, my head was already swimming with ideas. The art room was the one place at school where I spoke up. I put up my hand when Mr. T called for questions.

"So, the graphics come before the product, right? I mean, as far as what the public sees. The logo gets the first reaction."

"Exactly!" Mr. T tossed a marker into the air and caught it again.

"Okay, so I'm wondering . . . will you let me do my own company instead of the one you made up?"

"Ack!" He pretended to stab himself in the chest. He feigned pain. "I have three kids of my own and they bargain with me all day long, Miss Vasilis."

"But I have this idea. . . ."

"Fast food for vampires?" He bit the cap off the marker and had everyone laughing. "No, wait . . . a drive-up tattoo parlor?" More laughing. "Okay, okay. Tell me what you are thinking."

"I want to mock up a coffee shop," I told him, "but something out of the ordinary." Across the room by the door I heard Big Bonnie Swenson let out an envious sort of sigh. "I'm picturing a Steampunk theme—with paintings on the walls of machines that grind the coffee with big wheels that go around," I added.

"Well . . . then we have to adjust the assignment," he said slowly. He thought for a moment. Then he glanced up at the whole class. "That means the same opportunity is open to any of you. Fair is fair—"

"Yes!" I heard Bonnie say. "Oh, so cool!"

"But, but, but! If you choose to go your own way, I want more. And you have to get it right." He began to address me for the benefit of others. "So, for a coffee shop, you still need a logo, but let's also see you design a menu, a paper cup—and signage for the front of the shop. It's more work," he warned. "Think it through. But also, feel free to go the extra mile on this." He gave me a nod. "By the way," he said, speaking just to me, "I think that's 'gears' on the grinders. Not 'wheels.' Just a thought. I like it," he added.

I had only minutes to start before I had to leave for that stinking dental appointment. I began to mock up a menu. I didn't get very far. I flashed my med pass at Mr. T and he nodded. Big Bonnie tagged my arm as I headed out. She whispered, "You just made this project a ton more interesting."

I paused beside her chair with my backpack over one shoulder. "Oh . . . good."

"I can't wait to see what you design!" she squeaked.

"Yeah, me either," I said with a laugh. "I'm probably a fool."

Halfway down the hall I realized that, in truth, I couldn't wait to see what Bonnie came up with. I wished I'd said so.

I thought Momma was all set to pick me up and take me to the appointment. So, when it was Bampas who met me in the school office, I was surprised.

"I have quick business in the area," he said, and punched the button for the automatic door. "How was your morning?" he asked in a perfunctory way.

"Fine," I said. "We have a new assignment in Commercial Graphics and we—"

"Hold," Bampas interrupted, and that's when I heard the buzzing sound. He thrust his hand into his pocket and drew out his phone. He was on the line all the way from school to the dentist. I was used to his business calls. I often wrote the dialogue for would-be conversations between Bampas and me inside my own head. This time he might have really been interested. Business and design coming together—that would be his thing. Oh, well. I watched the buildings go by and wondered which ones I could turn into coffee shops.

In the hygienist's chair, I kept running ideas. With my mouth wide open, I watched the overhead lamp on that impossibly cool swinging arm. I imagined ideas beaming into me and I had to try not to laugh.

No cavities. Good hygiene. Rinse. Spit. I was out of there and back into the car. Two short blocks away from the high school on Green Street, Bampas pulled up in front of a tiny, mustard-yellow building. "I have to take a look," he explained. I was not surprised. He often stopped and peered into empty buildings while we waited in the car. But this time he pressed a key into the lock and went inside.

I sat looking at the place. It looked like a toy that someone had left outside—misshapen with its bumped-out windows, the mismatched clapboards. The old brick chimney had a tile with the number 66 set into it. *So, 66 Green Street*, I thought. A metal stack popped through the roof with a top-hat cap that made it look like it would cough a puff of steam at any second. Out loud I said, "The Steam & Bean at 66 Green." I hopped out of the car.

"Hey, Bampas?" I called to him. "May I come in?"

"Yes, yes," he said, but he sounded irritated. At first, I thought it was because of me, but then I heard him say, "They leave it such a mess. They want their security deposit returned. But they give me no choice. . . ." He went on talking, more to the slightly rotten-smelling air than to me.

"That's too bad," I said. "So, Bampas, you own this building?"

He didn't answer. But if he was arguing about security deposits, he must be the landlord. I tried to remember what I had seen here in the past. I followed him into the tiny kitchen at the back. It was not fancy—a little stove and bake oven, a dishwasher, a fridge, and a chest freezer. With all the empty shelves—no pots or dishes—the place looked stripped. It was grimy right up to the dull silver vent pipes along the ceiling.

My father poked around the kitchen in disgust. "People have no pride," he muttered. He swore under his breath—something in Greek.

I peered into the serving area from the pass-through. I could imagine it—a small glass-front display out there, and half a dozen little tables with random chairs. There was one windowless wall—*For a mural*, I thought. Something fabulous in a perspective that would alter the space—make it look like a deep train platform where people were being served coffee and tea from fantastical windup machines. I could see mechanical arms made of brass and nickel gears scooping beans and dipping tea bags into steamy china cups. Oh, I was nearly out of my mind with the possibilities.

"Bampas, what are you going do with this place? What happens to the building now? What if it wa—"

"Agh! Damn it!" He'd put his hand in something

disgusting. He turned to the sink. The faucet coughed and splashed on his suit jacket as he rinsed. "Bettina, it's *not* your concern," he said.

"But wouldn't it make a good coffee shop?" I pressed. My father would know this sort of thing. "I mean, hypothetically. I have this art assignment—"

"Bettina! Enough! Now, come. You're already late back to school. I should have dropped you off first," he said. "Then I would not have all your questions, would I?" He shook water from his hands and motioned toward the door. I wanted one more look. I tried to turn around. But Bampas was on my heels and he wanted me out that door.

Sixteen

BAMPAS NEVER ANSWERED ME ABOUT STAYING AFTER
school every day. But a few mornings after my trip to the dentist, he brought what looked like a new phone to the breakfast
table. He put it just above his place setting. It stayed there
through his toast and coffee. When I moved to clear my place,
he made a sound in his throat that stopped me. He put two
fingers on the shiny phone and pushed it across the breakfast
table. He stopped just before the phone reached my plate. I
looked up at Momma.

"For you," she said, and she smiled in a way that blanketed the room.

"Bampas? You got me a phone?"

"It is yours. . . ." Bampas cleared his throat, and I knew more was coming. "Yours to *use*."

"Dinos," my mother sighed. He'd taken something out of it for her.

"The phone belongs to me," Bampas said. "It is for us to stay in touch."

"Okay . . . what does that mean? What are the rules?"

"It means it is for our convenience and your safety. Be clear," he said, "it is *not* a reward for the way you have complicated our family schedule. The plan is limited." He held up a finger to make the point. "Do not think you can talk to friends for hours and hours. No endless messaging the way I see your friends doing in your school yard."

Okay, I thought. *He didn't say* no *talking and he didn't say* no *messaging.* "But I can give the number out? To friends?"

"*Judiciously*," Bampas said. "You'll give it to your boyfriend, of course. But you have the phone so that we can discuss all of your constantly changing plans, Bettina." His note of resentment was crystal clear.

From that moment on I felt ambivalent about having the phone. I worried that Bampas had his thumb on me; he could call me and say no to anything now.

But one thing had not changed. My best shot at getting him to yield was to go about it gradually and not shine too much light on it. So, my plan for staying after school was the same; I would jump and squeak with the cheerleaders on Wednesday but meet my ride right on time afterward, and then go straight home on the bus both Thursday and Friday. It wouldn't be so bad. I was throwing myself into the Steam & Bean project and I could work on that at home.

Friday morning, I did a little research inside the coffee shop by the school. I stood on my toes, craning for a peek behind the counter while the girl poured my medium-light. She slid the cup my way. Then I did what I suppose I knew I was going to do all along; I ordered a second cup—black. That gave me another couple of minutes to check out coffee shop décor. I noted the orange walls with the pink and brown stripes; I took a picture of that. The colors seemed more like an invitation to leave than to stay and I wondered if that was done on purpose. I paid. Then I stepped out into the late-September morning sun.

Morning was *mine*, especially since Brady had started arriving closer and closer to the homeroom bell. I could hang in the girls' room or I could deliver coffee without feeling like he was waiting for me. The sun felt good on my back as I hustled toward Unit 37. I walked in pursuit of my own shadow, I noticed. I watched my dark pavement-self stretch its arms out. Coffee on the left, coffee on the right. I twirled once around, did a salsa sidestep—an old dance move.

As I got close to the industrial park, I slinked back a little.

Should I really stop in on this guy again? I already had his coffee in my hand. I made a deal with myself: If I didn't see him right away, I'd leave. If I found him working under a car again, I wouldn't bother him. I'd disappear. I took a wide path to the door and stopped in my tracks.

He had a sign—a brand-new shop sign. It wasn't even up yet. It was leaning on one end against the block wall just outside the overhead door. A loose dressing of bubble wrap still clung. I walked right up to the sign and tilted my head. It read: SWS CLASSIC AUTO. I stepped closer to look at the crisp edges on the cobalt lettering. *Sharp*, I thought. Being careful with the coffees, I used one elbow to push away a drift of the wrapping. An arching, gray band at the very top of the sign narrowed like a stretch of road receding, and on it, a simple silhouette of a classic car looked like it was driving away.

"Well, hello again, *Beta*." Cowboy used an easy drawl, but he startled me something crazy.

"Hello, *Cowboy*." I did my best to parrot him. "Sweet sign," I said.

"Hmm. I'm happy."

"Happy? Hell, yeah! Kick-ass graphic. Great typeface. It's beautiful," I said. He held his bottom lip in his teeth for a second and tilted his head at me.

"So, kick-ass, like a tattoo?"

"No, kick-ass, like a really good logo for a car restoration

100

business. I mean, look at it. It says we fix 'em here and then you're back on the road."

"Well, okay then."

"We must drink a toast. Cup o' joe?" I offered. He took the black coffee with a smile that about dissolved me at my knees. *That*, I thought. *That right there is why this guy stays on my mind. That smile. The way he takes the cup. Lowers his lids. Puts his lips to the rim—*

"So, Beta, this is nice. But you don't have to keep bringing these." He looked at me over the cup. "You could just come by." He headed back into the shop and since we seemed to be having a conversation, I followed him.

"Good to know," I said. "But you're helping me with some research this morning."

"Whoa!" He swallowed. "What did I just drink?"

I laughed. "I had a reason to go to the coffee place today."

"Are you job hunting?"

"Eh, no. Wouldn't that be nice," I mumbled. "No, I just wanted to know some stuff about the business for an art project. So, what's in here?" I asked. I poked a finger at a pan full of dark liquid that sat on his worktable. A few nuts and bolts rattled inside it. "Screw soup?" I asked. We both laughed. "Breakfast of champions?"

"I have to brush the gunk off of those. It's not done because it's tedious."

"Hmm. Ten minutes," I said.

"How's that?"

"I have ten minutes. Can I try it?"

He shrugged. "Not much *trying* involved. It's just a pain in the ass." I picked up a wire brush from the bench. "Wait, wait." Cowboy swiped two rubber gloves out of a dispenser box and tossed them my way.

"I love the smell," I said, leaning over the pan.

"Me too." Cowboy laughed. "It's a good thing. I live with it all day, and I take it home with me every night." He disappeared around the far side of a silver car and went back to work.

While I brushed, I thought about what he'd said. Taking the smell home. I loved it when I caught a whiff of the art room on my clothes at the end of the day. And of course, I loved the scent of SWS Classic Auto that lingered on that shoelace that Cowboy had put my class ring on. I looked over my shoulder at him, and saw him curled over the silver car. His home. What was it like? *He's older than me*, I thought. *Damn, he could be married.* I wasn't used to looking for wedding bands on men's hands. Maybe this was weird—me bringing him coffee, and now *brushing his bolts*. I laughed right out loud.

"What's tickling you?" he called, his head still down inside the car.

"Nothing!" Just being sophomoric. "Hey, it's getting late.

102

I probably better split," I called. I peeled off the gloves and peered at the clean bolts. "I think these are done."

"I'm sure they're beautiful," he said.

"Do I leave them in the tray?"

"Yes. Thanks."

At the overhead door I gave the new SWS CLASSIC AUTO sign another good look. I glanced back at Cowboy too, but he didn't look up. Weird or not, I liked hanging out at Unit 37—and he had said I could come by. I could have stayed there all day.

When I reached the playing fields, I could see that the back lot of the school was busy. Kids were swarming toward the entrances. I was on the late side. So I jogged. I still got to my locker before Brady did. But, oh, what a wash of guilt I felt when he handed me a short little stem of purple mums and brushed his lips across my forehead.

"Don't forget, we're on for tonight," he said.

Friday afternoon found me running again, this time through the hallway at school. I had to get into the art room before I got on the bus, and pick up my portfolio, which had the Steam & Bean project in it. I wasn't going home for the weekend without it. I wove my way between the desks and stools to the back of the room where the storage drawers were. Big Bonnie suddenly rose from the floor, her curry hair tied into a little tuft at the top of her head. She wore a blue check mark of glaze dust on one cheek. In her chapped hands she held a clay pot.

"Oh, hey," she said.

"Hi, Bonnie," I said. I was breathing hard.

"You're in a hurry. Going to see Brady before the bus?" She grinned.

Brady. I felt sad hearing her say his name. This was a girl that Brady would never, never have given the time of day to, though he did probably know who she was—everyone did. Her height and her fuzzy yellow hair made her stand out. But Bonnie also served on student government, and her family ran the main funeral parlor in town. There were jokes about everyone ending up over at the Swensons'. I once heard some of that escalate into some sick, sex-with-the-dead stuff. But Bonnie had great comebacks ready: "Yeah, well, when it's your turn we'll be sure to ice your sheet and put a mint under your slab," she'd said.

"I'm actually not going to see Brady," I finally answered her. "I'm grabbing my work for the weekend."

"Ah. The coffee shop." She was still holding the piece of pottery with both hands and she took care of a nose itch with her upper arm. "How's that going?" she asked.

"Actually, I'm having a pretty good time with it. What about you?"

"Ooh . . . I have to put in some more work on mine. . . ."

She grimaced. "But it'll come together. One thing at a time. Right now, I have to concentrate on this." She nodded toward the kiln and turned back to her work.

"You're loading for a firing?"

"I am."

Dumb. Of course she was. She was always the one. I'd had a Clay Basics class with her sophomore year—all pinch or slab work. I'd always felt like I'd missed seeing a major step of the process because I'd never loaded or emptied a kiln. Mr. T wanted that done after school when the room was empty and the forms could be moved safely. He'd asked for sign-ups. But I was always on the bus at that hour, and other kids begged off, and that left Bonnie loading the kiln by herself.

"Hey, Bonnie," I said. "I'd have to make a phone call, but if it works out, could you use my help?"

Her eyes lit up. "Yes! You can hand me these pieces so I don't have to keep bobbing up and down like a doofus."

So Bonnie pretended not to listen in while I handled Bampas. (Her scrunched brow betrayed her.) He accused me of misusing the phone. I explained to him about the kiln. "I just wanted to see if staying late would be all right today, Bampas," I said. In the end, he let me.

Big Bonnie took pot after pot from me as she crouched before the kiln. She scrutinized every piece before it went in. She had me clean glaze drips off a few pot bases. Looking at all that clay, I suddenly remembered about a certain special part of Regina Colletti's little-boy fountain that needed replacing. My eyes went wide. Maybe I could help Tony fix that—

"I would *die*," Bonnie suddenly piped, "if I ever set up a firing that went wrong. Like if something became fused to something else."

"Hmm . . ." All I wanted to do was ask her how I could *get* something fused to something else and if she thought anyone would notice if I snuck a little plug of clay while I was not officially in a class. Mr. T was fussy about materials—especially clay. But how much could I need? A pinkie finger's worth? How would I get it fired?

"It'd be a nightmare," she said.

"What's that?"

"Like if a lid got fused to a pot."

"Oh, right."

"Are you taking any clay classes this year?" she asked.

"Next semester. The wheel class."

"Oh, good! I'll be in that with you."

We were nearly done when she thanked me for staying. "But listen, don't you want to go catch Brady—just in these few minutes before your father comes? Practice is about to start." She glanced at the clock. Why was it that everyone seemed to know the basketball team's schedule? "I think the team is going to have an awesome year, don't you?" Bonnie added.

"Seems possible," I said.

She would be there in the stands, I thought, cheering for Brady and his mighty White Tigers come winter. I got it that everyone loved the basketball games. But something seemed unbalanced about all that attention. I couldn't imagine Brady and his bros standing about in admiration while the White Tiger mosaic was being cemented down. Quirky example— art is not generally a spectator sport—but it did come to mind.

"Really. If you want to split, I'm all set here," Bonnie said. I had the thought that it was really Bonnie who wanted to be down in the lobby. But she probably didn't feel invited. God knows, I knew what that felt like.

"Brady thinks I've already gone home on the bus," I told Bonnie, "and besides, right now I'm doing this with you."

Seventeen

B<small>RADY'S PLAN FOR</small> F<small>RIDAY NIGHT WAS FOR US TO MEET</small>
up with his friends and "take a drive out to the sticks."

"Don't I already live in the sticks?" I asked.

"No, no, we're heading way the hell out where they grow
apples and cow shit."

That should have been resistible even to me. Nonetheless,
I folded myself into the minivan packed with Brady and a
half dozen of his friends. They probably didn't even want me
there messing up their guy-time, I thought. Brady was doing
this so that I could get to know them better. But it was weird
that I was the only girl out with a carload of jocks—*and* these
were the guys who snidely referred to me as "Cullen's wife,"

and that's when they were being polite. I sat pressed between the window and Brady and waited for the orchards and dairy farms to come into view. Mostly, I saw darkness falling over the roadside ditches.

I figured we'd trespass onto the corner of some field, and maybe Brady's homeboys would break out a few beers and build a campfire. Or they'd steal some apples and do something dumb like cross a brook on a slippery log in the dark. One of the guys had brought along a bag full of hundreds of rubber bands. He started handing those out all around the car. "We're making a rope," he said. "This is going to be *hilarious*. So just tie as many of them together as you can."

Whatever. I took a handful. The guys were fumbling. They were actually trying to *tie* the rubber bands in knots rather than chain them. I was beating those boys to a pulp. I made it through a lapful of rubber bands in no time and grabbed another bunch. Brady nudged me.

"What the—? How are you doing that?" he asked. He punched the switch on the interior light. "I don't know how to do friggin' *macrame*. I'm not an *art girl*." He let go of one of his loud, high laughs.

"Thread it, loop it, tug it," I said. I showed him while a couple of other guys leaned around to watch.

"Oh. Yeah! Yeah! She's right. I get it."

"Thread it, loop it, tug it," they repeated, and that

became a little car-ride mantra. Imagine that, my words, their song—until they changed all the *T*s to *F*s. "Fred it, floop it, fug it." Then they sounded more like themselves. Soon we had a chain of rubber bands long enough to . . . well, to stretch across a dark country road.

"Wait until you see this." I watched the Rubber Band Kahuna tie a bandanna on one end of the string. He gathered it all up like handfuls of spaghetti.

We left the van on a dirt pull-off and started walking along the open roadside. I didn't ask questions. I followed. The night air was awesome. Brady held my hand and swung my arm. I listened to the guys joking up ahead of us, their dark forms sliding left and right as they changed places. When the language got crude, someone said, "Hey, hey! Watch it. Don't forget, we got Bettina here tonight."

Another silhouette turned back toward me to say, "Oh, yeah. Sorry . . . sorry."

Huh. So polite. Maybe a tide was turning. I pressed a smile into Brady's shoulder in the darkness, and he said, "See that? They're good guys."

We must have walked a mile when we reached an orchard. We split up, half on one side of the road, half on the other. I made sure I stayed with Brady. Two guys stretched the rubber band chain across the road. We crouched in the ditch, hiding from the headlights. We waited. A car finally came and the guys shot the bandanna right across the front windshield.

Oh . . . my God, I thought. *This is* not *a good idea.*

Yet, nothing had happened—nothing at all. But the next car swerved when the bandanna flew. The taillights glowed. The brakes screeched. I crouched lower and covered my ears, as the car fishtailed. It slowed, but then drove away.

Brady and his pals laughed in loud whoops. They dashed across the road, changing sides and taking turns being the shooter. My heart pounded. The road was long and lonely and sometimes it seemed like an eternity between cars. But they managed to pull the prank six or eight times until finally, a car snagged the bandanna on its antenna and sped off.

Good. We'll pack it in now. I was ready for that. Instead, I fidgeted in the ditch while a new plan was hatched.

We moved up the road and they found a spot to fix the rubber bands between a post on one side of the road and a tree on the other. I strained to see the string but it was invisible in the night.

I was glad. The first car along would surely snap the thing.

I heard the loudest whisper in the world. "Everybody down!" We hid again, kneeling in the grassy ditches. It was then that I realized I'd lost track of Brady. A pickup truck came down the road—going fast. (The answer to my string-busting dreams . . .) It came squealing to a stop just in front of the strand. I dropped but I got hung up on the side of the ditch. I needed to get lower but I was afraid to move. I heard the pop of the door handles, people getting out of the truck. I froze.

Two men held flashlights, and they stood no more than twenty feet away from me. They walked up to the string.

"My God! It's a bunch of rubber bands all stuck together!" I saw them strumming it with their hands. One man's voice carried over the hum of the truck's engine, the other, not so much.

Close to me, I heard rustling, felt movement. Seconds later, I saw figures ducking and running along the orchard across the road from where I hunkered. The men from the truck stayed focused on the string.

The louder man spoke. "Hey, Shep, you got your knife? I'm going cut it down before someone drives right off the road. Goddamn! Dangerous as hell!" he yelled. I heard a snapping noise. "You see anyone?" he asked. His boots thudded on the road.

"Aw. No." His friend replied much more softly.

"Must be around here . . ."

I pressed myself harder against the damp grass and leaves. I smelled something sweet-sour. Then I saw it—a rotting apple right next to my shoulder.

"Well, take a good look around. I'd love to catch them, the shitheads."

Oh, I don't want to be here. This is not *me. It's* not. *And where are the guys—those* dumb-asses? *Where is Brady?*

The wide beam from the quieter man's flashlight moved over the roadside with a casual sweep. His footsteps came nearer and nearer—as if he had directions right to me.

The light hit my eyes. I squinted. Quickly, he raised the flashlight high so that it shone down and I could see him and he could see me. His face glowed out of the shadows. So surprising. He looked kind and sweet like the man in the moon from a little kid's book. But he was *not* smiling. He looked sorry—as if he wished he hadn't seen me at all. But I was caught in his light. *Should I stand? Give myself up?* Say I was sorry, or could I lie and say I was just out walking in the night and that it was their truck that had scared me? Suddenly, he turned and walked straight away from me. The light fanned over the road as he crossed back toward the truck.

"Whoever it was must be long gone," he called to his friend. "Come on, let's go home." I heard him open the door of the truck. "Let's go!" he urged. "Beer's getting warm and the game won't wait."

"Those *jackasses!*" the other guy fumed. "They could've *killed* someone!"

I had the sickening thought that he was right.

One door slammed shut. Then the other. The driver gunned the engine, and they were gone.

113

I lay still. Seconds ticked. A blanket of exhaust drifted over me. Was I alone? Had all the boys run? Had Brady left me here? Finally, I heard thumps. Footsteps. The swish of the grass.

"Hey, Bettina! Bettina?" the whispers came.

I could not answer. I stayed pinned in my ditch beside the rotting apple.

"Where is she? They didn't take her, did they? Did she get busted?" Heavier footsteps pounded near me.

"P'teen-uh!" Suddenly, Brady came up on me and yanked me up by one arm. "Holy crap! I thought he had you!" he said. He gave me a shake. "Why didn't you answer us just now? Huh?"

The rest of the guys were gathering around us. They uttered a chorus of *holy shit*s. I looked down the road in the direction the moon-faced man had gone. I tried to step away from Brady but he kept his thumb pressed hard on my muscle.

"What the hell? Are you *deaf*, P'teen-uh?" Brady went on. His spit hit my cheek. "Didn't hear me calling you? You scared the shit out of me just now."

"Well, I—I was scared too," I finally said. My voice quaked. "I—I thought you left me—"

"So you just don't answer?"

"Hey, come on. She was just scared." One of the other boys came over and patted Brady on the back. "Shake it off, man." So there they were trying to console him. But Brady was bent on getting the last word.

"I should've never brought you out here in the first place." He waited, sneering at me. Disgusted. "Get back to the car," he said. He turned me, gave me a shove. In case I hadn't gotten the message, he grabbed the end of my braid and threw it at my back.

I slipped on the bloated apple as I stepped out of the ditch. That sour smell stayed on my boot all the way home.

Eighteen

ALL FRIDAY NIGHT AND INTO SATURDAY MORNING, I kept picturing the man who let me go. Asleep or awake, I'd picture his kind face—the sweet, sleepy eyes—and think, *He could be dead because of me.* In some horrible, dystopian layer of my own thinking I believed that he *was* dead, and it made my breath halt. I told myself, *But that did not happen; he's okay.* But the next moment found me running the same little mental movie of that night, and feeling another big wash of guilt.

Brady called on Saturday. I lied and told him that my parents weren't going to let me go out. He was mad that I wouldn't sneak out. He reminded me that he'd included me in a night out with his friends, as if I could forget that. But I knew he blamed me for the bad turn the night had taken. If he brought it up, I would never be able to forge an apology. We'd end up fighting. I held fast. I was staying home.

Saturday afternoon I climbed into a hot shower, fixing to scrub away my bad feelings, I suppose. I drew the bar of soap along my upper arm and *wham*—something hurt like hell. There, I found a blue bruise with a lump in the middle of it, the very size of Brady Cullen's thumb. And now it was throbbing. Well, served me right for being a miscreant, I thought.

I dressed in cruddy sweats and a hooded fleece after my shower. Staying-in clothes. I did all the homework I hated most. I even studied for a math test. Then I stared out my bedroom window, watched the sun beginning to settle on the treetops. I longed for the scent of petroleum. Unit 37. Cowboy.

You're an idiot, I told myself. *The only place you know to find him is the auto shop, and he won't be in there on a Saturday night. He probably has a date. He's heading out to a bar. He's a grown-up and you are a dope who plays road pranks with stupid boys. Stop thinking about him.*

There had to be something I could feel good about, something to be in charge of. I hauled out the newsprint pad with my dozens of sketches for the Steam & Bean at 66 Green. I split away the pages and stuck them on my wall. I stood back and looked. Not bad. I began to think and work, and finally, I felt a normal, quiet breath make its way through me.

A while later came our household war cry. "Hoya! Hoya! Hey-yah-hey-yah!" My brothers came flying into my room and threw themselves into handstands on my bed, then came bouncing down on their knees.

"Ack! Mini-man alert!" I pretended to protect my art-work, arms spread wide.

"Bampas says to tell you they're going out. You have to babysit us tonight," Favian said. He began to jump on my bed, hands making swipes toward the ceiling. My bed pillow caught air and landed on my night table, which was always piled with art mess. Magazines, glue stick, and a big pair of scissors all slid to the floor.

"Ack! Enough!" I said. I restacked my materials.

"Yeah. And you owe us," Avel reminded.

"Not *still*," I said. "That was months ago."

"We can still tell on ya. For all the times we saw you sneaking out."

I stared them down. It seemed my duty to pretend to believe they'd actually rat me out. "Well, *stink* me," I said, and they burst into fits. They were so easy; all I had to do was say the sort of thing neither of my parents would ever say and my brothers would practically pee themselves.

"So, let's hear it. What do you want?" I put my hand on my hips.

"Double servings of ice cream, and we walk to the river," Avel said.

"Is that all you got? So lame," I said.

"Ice cream *while* we walk." Favian upped the ante.

So after Momma and Bampas went out, I made fudge parfaits in the fluted-glass dishes, just to give the boys a sense of living dangerously. Avel strapped one of those spelunker's lamps on his head. "So I'm hands-free for the parfait," he said.

"Yeah, well, we're coming back before dark," I warned. "This is dessert and a sunset. Not a walk under the moon."

Then, because they insisted on it, we all climbed out my bedroom window instead of using the back door. We headed through the garden and spooned ice cream as we walked the swath to the river.

I thought about stopping my brothers before River Road, but then found myself following them across to the riverbank. They headed down the wooden stairs, then off to play at the water's edge.

"Just a little while, you guys. The sun drops fast now. Try not to muddy up your shoes," I added. I made a mental note to hose them off before we went back into the house.

I sat down on the last, weathered step next to a pair of empty parfait dishes. I hugged my knees. My father's piece of riverfront had a scary, abandoned feel to it, even while a gorgeous, pink sun melted on its waters. Off and away, upriver and down, were homes that actually celebrated having water-front. The gardens and patios seemed to reach toward the river and frame the view. But Bampas's stretch was long and empty. Not welcoming. Or maybe it was just me. He'd never brought me to the bank the way he'd brought the boys. They were used to it here, with their boats and skipping rocks. For me, the mud and stained grasses made it look like a place where you could lose something, or someone—the slip-in-and-never-be-found-again part of the river.

"Hey, boys!" I leaned forward to see along the bank. Fave and Ave were pushing sticks into the mud at the shore about a hundred feet away from me. "Back this way! Now!" They hopped a few steps toward me. I gave them a few more minutes to play.

I was the first one back up the stairs. I held three parfait glasses with spoons clanking inside of them tucked against my chest with one arm. We stopped at the edge of the road, checked traffic, which was never much. Yet, sure enough, a pickup truck was coming. A glint of pink sun popped off the chrome. I could tell by the way it was slowing down that the driver could see us and would probably wait for us to cross.

"Hold on. Let's make sure we're safe. . . ." I warned the boys.

"We know, we know. . . ." Favian complained.

The truck came closer and closer, then stopped in front

of us like a school bus coming in for a pickup. Instead of a door folding open, a window rolled down. My heart spread beneath my ribs. I broke into a grin.

"Well, what are the chances?" Cowboy said—in a voice that could melt butter. He hung an arm out and drummed the side of the truck with his fingers.

"Hey," I said back. "Where are you coming from?"

"A sunset."

Apparently alone, I could not help noting.

"And what are you doing out here?" he asked.

"We took a walk," I said. "And same as you. The sunset." I glanced at my brothers, all round-eyed and curious, and maybe even nervous in that don't-talk-to-strangers way. I felt Avel take hold of the back hem of my hoodie. I rubbed my hand over his head to let him know all was well.

"So, everybody's okay?" Cowboy asked.

It was so good to see him. And that was such a *nice* question. And outside the garage, he was different somehow—not under a car and not distracted. His face was giving back the last little glow of the sun, especially along the bridge of his nose and the tops of his cheekbones. How good it was to have time to look at each other here in the road—and *oh*, here I was in my ugly sweatpants. Awesome.

"Hi, guys," Cowboy addressed Favian and Avel. "Hey, I'm a friend." He put his thumb to his chest. "Not some creepy dude. You get that, right?"

"That's right," I said. "We're all good here." Maybe I should have thought up an introduction. But I was totally thrown, running into Cowboy this way. He was a secret of mine. I didn't want to give that up.

"So, where're you heading with your . . . *ice-cream dishes*, is it?" Cowboy squinted.

I laughed a little and Favian piped up. "Home. We live across there."

Cowboy craned for a peek out the passenger's window. "Down that path?"

"That's right," I said.

"Oh. Okay. So you're not lost and you don't need a ride?"

"Nope," I said. He was making me wish otherwise.

"Okay." He hung a second, grinning at me. He checked his rearview. "Why don't you go ahead and cross now then?"

"Thanks!" Favian called. Both boys shot ahead of me.

"Well," I said, feeling a little awkward. "Nice to see you." I took one parfait glass in my hand and walked it along the hood of the truck as I passed in front.

Cowboy leaned toward the passenger's side window and said, "Good night, Beta."

I started slowly back along the swath. The boys criss-crossed ahead of me as if lacing the path like a shoe.

I sniffed a laugh. *Saturday night and I got to see Cowboy,* I thought. *And*, I realized, I had forgotten to feel so bad about everything else that had happened in the last twenty-four hours. I turned to look back at River Road, noted the narrowing of the path—the perspective.

"The bad stuff goes away when I'm around you." I whispered it. Suddenly, my eyes burned. Tears surprised me. Oh, oh, and why? What was this? I shook my head. I didn't have time to cry. I had to catch up to the boys—with their muddy shoes. I tucked the ice-cream dishes closer and switched from stroll to stride.

"Hey, dorks!" I called, and I heard them laughing out of the dusk. "Wait up!"

Nineteen

THE LIGHTEST RAIN WAS FALLING ON MONDAY MORN-ing—the kind where you don't think you are getting wet until you feel the dryness of stepping indoors. It was like that for me as I arrived at Unit 37. As soon as Cowboy saw me he said, "Well, that was a day-topper."

"Day-topper?" I asked. I handed off his coffee. He set the cup on the hood of the silver Chevy—the one he called "the '57." He reached into his back pocket, pulled out a twenty, and held it toward me. "For the coffee fund."

I didn't want his money but he flapped the bill at me and I took it rather than getting into a thing over it. But I gave him an eye-roll to say, *Ridiculous.*

"What's a day-topper?" I asked again.

"Oh, that. I'm not sure. I might have made it up. But seeing you out on River Road on Saturday evening—it was a nice way to top off the day."

I steeled myself not to go all smiley and dopey. "Yeah, for me too," I said, and I sounded wistful even to myself. I recovered. "Well, because otherwise Saturday night was just another night of babysitting. I mean, I like my bitty bros and all."

"They seem like good men," he said.

I grinned. "*Men*. They'd like it if they heard you say that about them. Sorry for not introducing them. Favian is the big one and Avel is the little one. I call them Fave and Ave."

"Well, you'd have to," he said, and we both laughed. Then suddenly, Cowboy's face changed. Dead serious. He was looking at something behind me, outside the door. Before I could turn around, he spoke.

"Hey, Beta, duck in, will you? And just stay inside while I do this. . . ." He took a couple of huge steps to get by me. One of his hands closed over my shoulder for a split second and he tucked me gently to the side of the doorway. I heard tires on the pavement outside, a car arriving.

I stood stock-still. When I heard voices, I leaned just the littlest bit so I could peek between the sections of thick, metal track that carried the overhead door. There was a patrol car out in front of the shop. No lights flashing. But there were two cops in it, and Cowboy was leaning down by the open passenger's side window to talk to them. The cops had their once-in-a-wipers going to clear the windshield. I watched the spritz hit Cowboy's shirt sleeve.

I flashed back to the day I had met him, the way he'd been helpful, but also peevish, about my crushed fingers. I remembered that I'd gotten creeped out in the shop's bathroom for a moment. But I had been wrong that day. He *was* nice. The *nicest*.

So, why were the police here?

Dozens of thoughts flooded my head. Maybe they were his friends. But they were both older with salt-and-pepper hair. Maybe there had been a break-in at one of the units. Maybe this one. Old cars were valuable and parts were hard to get ahold of. I'd learned that much. But Cowboy hadn't mentioned any trouble, and things looked easygoing out there. He rose slightly and I slipped back into the recess. I listened as the patrol car drove away. I stayed against the wall and waited for Cowboy to come back inside.

"What was that about?" I asked.

"Aw, nothing, really."

"But why were they here?" I pushed for an answer. "Cowboy?"

He took a big breath in. "It's not a simple story, Beta. My

family . . . is kind of broken."

"Okay . . . so, what do you mean?"

"You know, problems." He sounded annoyed. Again, I waited. "There was this bad night," he said. "Been a while now, but there was trouble at my ma's house—"

"And what? You got arrested?" I tried to sound unconcerned.

"No." He sighed. "But I took the heat."

"For what?"

"Doesn't matter. Those two guys answered the call and now they kind of check up on me a bit. It's friendly . . . well, as friendly as cops get, I guess. But it's better if they don't see you hanging around here. I don't need them thinking I'm into jailbait."

That stung. I guess because suddenly I felt like a thing and not a person. Cowboy lifted the hood of the '57 Chevy and leaned toward the engine. I knew it was his way of letting me know he was done talking to me.

Twenty

"HA! I KNEW IT!" REGINA COLLETTI SAT FORWARD IN her bed. "Great legs—almost as alluring as my own," she said.

I stood before the queen in my leather skirt, having forgotten that she'd recently tried to make me drop my pants. While she gave me a good looking over, I wished I'd worn jeans. I wished I'd skipped the visit. I wished I were at SWS Classic Auto.

Tony Colletti shifted over by the door, embarrassed by his grandmother's gawking. "Nonna, can I get you anything?"

"Yes, *mio nipote*, you can get *out*," she said. "Leave Bettina and me alone. We want to talk, and you are a fox in the hen house." She motioned at me then, patting the bed

128

beside her. "Come. Come sit."

I glanced at Tony. He shrugged apologetically. "I'll come back in twenty," he said, and I thought, *Ten, please.*

Regina told him, "Make it thirty."

So there I was on that damn uncomfortable edge of the bed again, feeling like a sucker—make that a sucker in a very short skirt.

"Closer, closer!" Regina reached and tugged on my bare thigh. "Oh, feel it! That's a good, firm leg!" She held her hand cupped on my quads. "I remember now," she said. "You're a dancer."

"I was," I said. I was surprised when a little wash of longing filled me.

"No more?"

"No."

"But don't I remember that you were pretty good? Yes." She answered for herself. "Little medals on ribbons, and shiny trophies." She squinted like she could see them lined up on the windowsill back at the old house.

"I guess I was good," I said. "But it was Bampas who loved the prizes. I loved the dancing. But it's funny," I added, "I didn't realize you even knew I danced."

"Me? I knew everything about everyone," she said. "You should go back to the dancing! You are young with your beautiful, strong body. You've got to keep doing these things while you can." She stopped and said, "Oh, poopa! Did I really just say that? I sound like a sick, old woman—someone I don't want to be." She sneered at the notion. I felt obligated to distract her.

"I sort of outgrew that studio," I said. Then I babbled, "There was only one other girl my age. My best friend, Julia. She moved away. Bampas started to say that maybe it was time for me to stop too. You know, it was a trip across town for my momma, and the boys were starting Little League. Bampas had the restaurant sponsoring their teams so he had to be at all the practices."

"Ha!" Regina laughed. "Leave it to Dinos! Thinks they want *him* when his money would have been fine."

She caught me off guard there. His money? Oh, yes, that's what sponsoring is. But the way Regina said it felt loaded to me, as if Bampas had some terrific amount of money. "Well, anyway," I said, "if I'd kept up with the lessons the family would be separating all the time now."

"Well, that would teeter Dinos's boat," Regina conceded. "But what about you? Don't you miss the dancing?"

"I do. But I have more time to be at school—do some social things."

"*Boyfriend!*" Regina fired that one into the air. Her eyes widened. "Now this I want to hear more about."

I drew a blank screen right then—I actually had to think,

who? *Who* is my boyfriend? Regina was waiting. . . .

"Um . . . oh, he plays basketball."

Regina waited again. When I didn't add anything more, she screwed her mouth all to one side. Then she blurted, "So . . . *basketball*? That's who he is?"

"W-w-well . . . it's his biggest focus. It's important to him."

"*Pfft!* Well then, how are you supposed to stay entertained if he's all busy with a bouncy ball?"

"I—I don't mean *just* basketball. He has tons of friends all over the school. And I am allowed to see him on weekends. . . . That's important to him too. . . ." *Could I sound any dumber?* I wondered.

"So . . . is he *it*?" Regina asked. "Because I get the feeling he's not enough for you. Keep your side-view mirrors adjusted. Maybe something else will come along."

I popped up off the bed.

Regina let out a hoot. "You act like I goosed you! I must have hit a nerve."

I should not listen to her sass. I crossed the room to look out the window. Down in the flower bed, Tony had Regina's little-boy fountain upended. He was stripping a length of plastic tubing out of the fountain—part of the demolition phase, I suspected. I hadn't talked to him about it, and I hadn't done anything about getting that lump of clay that might complete the aesthetics. How hilarious; I was trying to come up with a *penis* for Regina Colletti! A convulsive laugh formed at my core. I hugged myself to keep it from rising. As I cupped my hands over my upper arms, I found the place where it was still sore from the bruise Brady had made with his thumb. *Brady. My boyfriend.*

Just an hour earlier at the school he'd stood over me while I'd spun the combination to my locker. As soon as I'd gotten the door open, he'd slammed it shut on me. I had to snap my hands out of the way. He'd done it twice in a row. I'd been a good sport; everyone who'd seen us had laughed. Brady was so quick and so cute, apologizing and even kissing me in between each door slam. He looked playful. He looked good to everyone. . . .

"What's the matter with you?" Regina asked.

"Pardon?"

"You're all scrunch-brow and puss-face."

"No, no," I said. I shook my head. "There is nothing wrong. Look, if you don't mind me rummaging in your kitchen, I'd love to make you a cup of tea," I said. "I could drink one with you, and then I should really go."

Regina gave me a look that said she was letting me off the hook. "Bring me a cup of the raspberry pekoe," she said. "Upper cupboard, right side of the sink." She must have been watching me as I left the room because she called out, "You know, I used to have a walk like that too. Foxy."

132

In the kitchen, I tugged down on my skirt. I made a note to at least wear tights or leggings next time I came. Waiting for the kettle was a curse and blessing. If the water boiled quickly, I'd have to go back in that bedroom. On the other hand, once my cup was empty, I could split.

I leaned against the countertop, watched the flame under the kettle. Regina annoyed me with her prying remarks and snap conclusions. But part of me wished I could fast-forward my own life just to try it on. What if I could be blunt, ask questions, and be sure about everything? What if I could be older for a day?

Suddenly, I remembered myself as a noun: *jailbait*. Cowboy didn't want the cops thinking he was "into jailbait." But how was I jailbait when nothing had happened? Did he ever think—

"God, stop it," I snarled. I saw my face reflected in the shiny kettle, distorted and ferret-like. "You *have* a boyfriend," I hissed at myself. The kettle hissed at me. I poured water. I dunked tea bags. I splashed on Regina's countertop.

I should have been able to say something substantive about Brady Cullen. Then again, can it ever be anything but awkward to go listing the things that make you care about someone? We went for walks all summer long. He's funny. He has a hundred friends. He's handsome and has great lips. Oh, no. I would never leave an opening for Regina to ask me about sex. I was afraid she'd swing that door wide on her own one of these afternoons.

I guess I could have told Regina how I'd met Brady. That he was a shy boy who Bampas approved of, and that later he—what? Became un-shy? Became popular? And now he was confident and he joked loudly, and played too rough sometimes. Was any of that a crime? People *liked* Brady. He made everyone laugh, *and* he could be with any other girl, yet he chose me. We were a couple. I was committed to that, so if there was something not working. . . .

I just had to steer him around so he'd be funny *and* tender. But was it wrong for me to think that he needed changing? Was I just being terrible? Anyone else who knew Brady could have come up with a long, long list of all his charms—on the spot. No *but*s. My head was a lumpy knot of questions. Regina had wanted to know what was wrong with me, and now, I wondered the same thing. Maybe I was the problem; maybe I wasn't much fun.

Twenty-one

THAT CONVERSATION WITH REGINA COLLETTI DID SOME-thing to me. For the next week or so, I committed myself to making things better with Brady. Every time I felt him cranking up to do something I knew I wasn't going to like, I'd reach for his hand to hold, or I'd drop my head against his chest and hope he'd put his arms around me instead. If he embarrassed me, I got quiet, but I smiled and willed myself not to blush—or not be *seen* blushing. My face fit perfectly into my own bent elbow where I pretended to laugh—and I'm pretty sure I sold that move to Brady and his crowd.

I let every good time we had together be the thing that I clung to. Alone on a Friday night in Brady's basement we lay, facing each other, the Big Bird sheet rumpled underneath us. Mostly bare and entwined, we rested. Sex wasn't the only thing that made these nights the good ones; Brady was easy to be with when he didn't have an audience. I pressed closer to him. A tiny thought floated in—something about how there was no space here for anything to come between us. He kissed my shoulder, traced a line to my breast with his lips. I felt his breath ride over my skin.

In the quiet of the basement, a loud *tick-a-click* sounded. A whooshing noise followed—like something inhaling before an enormous sneeze. It sent me into a whole-body spasm. I was scared to hell thinking it was the door sucking open at the top of the stairs—his mother about to catch us—and I would've rather the earth swallow me whole. Brady took me up tighter in his arms, saying, "No, no! It's just the furnace turning on! It's been getting cold at night." He hugged me. "It's okay. It's nothing."

With the rush of fear subsiding in me, I wanted to cry out and ask him, *Why? Why can't you act like this all the time? Why can't you ever buoy me up a little in front of your friends? What if you had hugged me instead of shoving me around out in that ditch full of rotten apples?* Instead, I didn't say anything. I just waited out my pulsing heart with my eyes squeezed shut and my face against Brady's warm chest.

When he drove me home later, he said, "Hey, I don't

know what it is, but you seem kinda different lately."

"Oh?" I said.

"Yeah, the way you've been at school. You're just . . . different."

Well, he was right. I was refocusing, and that spread over
to my dealings with the Not-So-Cheerleaders too. But it
wasn't easy.

It turned out that those girls had their sights on a trophy
just like the basketballers did. This news came up at one of
our practices—"making states," they called it—and there was
a very pointed remark made about how it would take commitment and perfect attendance from every one of us. Of course,
the not-so-committed one with lousy attendance was me.
Now they were talking about making up separate routines
and new skills for "making states."

Crap. What had I signed up for?

Okay, okay. This is like dance competitions, I told myself,
though I wasn't completely buying it—nor had contests ever
been my favorite part of being a dancer. I decided I'd better
start showing up at every practice, and I'd better remember to
bring sneakers, too. The trouble was the Not-So-Cheerleaders
didn't practice. They stressed out—*out loud.* One day, all they
did was argue. We never did a single jump, never cheered a
single cheer. I stayed mum, wet my thumb, and rubbed a fading henna on the back of my hand. I got that whole thing off.

I thought up an idea for a new one while they yammered.

Another practice came and it was pretty much the same. They discussed and re-discussed, and I shifted around on my bare feet. (I still hadn't remembered my sneakers.) I took a look at that wooden floor in the auxiliary gym, that long diagonal. I tested it with one toe—nice, dry slide. I lifted myself into a pirouette, knee turned out—oh, that felt *not* as familiar as it once had. I did it again. I circled once, twice. They were talking. Not watching. I stepped into a tour of twirls that took me the full length of the gym. I picked up too much speed. Lost my focal point. I ran out of real estate and hit the padded wall with a grunt. What a dumb-ass.

I got ten dirty looks and one wet-your-pants cackle. That laughter came from the cheerful cheerleader called Emmy, who doubled over and covered her own mouth with both her hands. When we took our break—and I guess that would be our break from not doing anything—Emmy told me she was sorry for the outburst. I shrugged and told her that I would have laughed too. "You're a dancer, aren't you?" she added. "I mean, the real deal. That was awesome, Bettina."

More than once that afternoon, I glanced at the gym's back doors—at the crack of light that leaked inward. Cowboy was out there, just a parking lot and a football field away. Damn. I wanted to see him so much. For all we were getting accomplished in that gym, well, double damn.

I couldn't help thinking of him. One Tuesday, Regina Colletti slept through my visit after a tiring day of doctors' appointments. Tony had a music lesson. I was alone with the dozing queen. I shook up a few of her snow globes. Most of them were tacky—puppy dogs wearing Santa hats—but a few were little masterpieces, like the one with the Russian rooftops in royal purples and golds. My favorite, though, had a Chinese boy inside, all dressed in red and flying a kite. It was full of tiny falling stars instead of snow. I sat down and listened to Regina's breathing. I opened a sketchbook and without planning to, I drew one of Cowboy's boots from memory.

So my afternoons were pretty swallowed up. Then my mornings changed too. I got semi-grounded for missing my curfew by *four* minutes on the weekend. Momma would have looked the other way but Bampas caught me and he clamped down. He granted me the two cheerleading practices and he insisted that I still see Regina Colletti. So, that wasn't bad. But the other part of my punishment was that either Momma or Bampas had to drive me to school for the week. Favian and Avel had to ride with us. We left late every day and I barely had time to stop at my locker before homeroom.

"Perhaps you see the hardship you put on your family," Bampas had suggested.

When he was well out of range, I had answered back,

"Yeah, yeah, whatever. You're choosing this hardship."

Well, one of those mornings my grounding fell apart because of car troubles. I took the bus. So, there I was with a half hour until the bell would ring. So, I did it; I bought coffees that day. But holy hell, I ran into Brady and his friends on the sidewalk just outside the shop. It was amazing it hadn't happened before. Brady walked to school every day, but rarely this early. I'd finally been caught coffee-handed.

"P'teen-uh! What the hell is this?" he asked. He pointed at the cups.

"Oh! Coffee," I chirped, and I held one out to him. He curled his lip so high I saw his eyetooth.

"I don't drink that shit. You know I don't." He shook his head.

"Oh. Right." I hunched my shoulders as if to say, *Oops.* "Well, anybody else want a black coffee?" I offered it to the huddle. No takers. "Well, I guess I'm going to be *wired* today," I said. Brady was busy acting offended, and nobody else was paying any attention to me. Pouring Cowboy's coffee down the art room sink that morning felt like a sad tiny act of betrayal.

At the end of that week, Momma drove me to school early while Bampas took the boys out to breakfast. I had three to-go containers of baklava to share with the Not-So-Cheerleaders and basketballers. They always gathered in the lobby after school, everyone hanging around in the vicinity of the White Tiger mosaic before practices began. Brady had wanted me there, so I'd been going. The girls had started bringing cookies and brownies. I got this idea to contribute. So Momma had walked me through her recipe for the baklava, and to my own great surprise, it looked gorgeous—flaky, golden brown, and running with honey. I stowed the stack of containers in my locker. I knew there was time—I could make that mad dash for coffees for Cowboy and me. He was always so happy to see that cup of joe and in fact he'd given me money for it, and now it'd been days since I'd—

"Hey, Bettina!" I looked up, and there was Big Bonnie standing half in, half out of the art room doorway. "I'm unloading a firing this morning. Wanna come?"

"Oh. Umm . . ." I did want to see this. I did want to help her. I wanted to see Cowboy too. But the kiln was ready now. I looked at Bonnie. Nobody ever helped her. I heard myself say yes.

From the moment Bonnie unlatched the hatch of the kiln and swung it open, I was mesmerized. Gentle heat left over from the firing rose into the art room. We listened to the quiet *tink-tink* of the warm surfaces as they cooled.

Bonnie put on a pair of oven mitts and reached into the kiln. I watched each piece come into the light. I made space on the shelves.

"I love this glaze. . . . Check out the layers of blue. . . ." Bonnie turned a pot this way and that. She settled it on a shelf and faced me. "Half the time people come in here and don't even recognize their own work after the glaze firing," Bonnie said.

"Oh, right . . ." I thought about that. "There's a sort of ugly-duckling phase first, isn't there?"

"Ha! That's a really good way to describe it," Bonnie agreed. "Here," she said, sliding out of the mitts. "You pull the next one out. You have to get low, make your arms kind of like a pair of tongs—"

"Oh. Yikes," I fretted. I clenched my teeth as I cupped a small bowl.

"You've got it," Bonnie said, unworried. I watched my padded hands set the pot down on the shelf. Slowly, I released it.

"Done," said Bonnie, and a broad smile broke across her chapped face.

"Ah," said Mr. Terrazzi, who had appeared out of nowhere. "The mistress of the kiln has an apprentice. It's about time."

I guess life was okay. I had things to do. But I was surprised at how much I missed Cowboy—and the *way* I missed him, like a boat unable to touch shore. I told myself that I belonged at school where people were my own age, and when I thought back to that little moment when Cowboy hid me away from the cops, well, if nothing else, it was a relief to be "not-jailbait." The days went by, there just wasn't the opportunity to get over to SWS Auto. I thought maybe I'd given him up. Maybe that was the way it should be. Or maybe it was the cause of the creeping, seeping sort of sadness that seemed to be making its way to my core.

Twenty-two

THE BEGINNING OF OCTOBER FINALLY BROUGHT ME A DAY
I was looking forward to pretty much no matter what else
was going on. Mr. Terrazzi had promised to hand back our
projects. I was dying to know how I'd done with the Steam
& Bean at 66 Green. Bonnie had settled on her topic for the
project late, but then she had kicked butt. She invented a
business called *Art~*Urnity—as in, creative *cremation* urns.

"I'm combining my love of pottery with my knowledge of
death," she'd said, "*and* I'm honoring the business that puts
bread on my family's table and will hopefully send me to college one day." That bit of melodrama had freaked out a few
people, but I'd split a grin with her.

I was invested in Bonnie's grade as well as my own; she'd asked me for advice on typefaces and layout. I'd spent a while with her. I suggested she italicize the "art" part of *Art*~Urnity and use the tilde to both separate and join the words. She'd liked the balance. Mr. Terrazzi had seen us working together and had said, "The kiln mistress becomes apprentice to the graphics mistress now. Oh, you're both so smart."

When I got to school in the morning, I peeked into the art room. I could see our projects waiting in folders on his desk. But I was going to have to wait until sixth period to see the grade. This would be a deadly long morning.

"What's that?" Brady leaned against the locker next to mine. He tapped a finger on a pair of to-go containers on the shelf inside my locker.

"In translation? This would be *cheese pastry*," I said. I flashed him a grin on the *cheese* part. "For this afternoon," I added. Brady shook his head at me.

"Ya know, you should just make normal stuff. That thing you made with all the nuts in it—that sticky stuff?"

"Baklava." I gave him the word.

"It seemed like there was something wrong with it."

"I didn't know you had tasted it," I said.

"Naw, I didn't. It was too much mess."

I sighed. It was true that my creation had resented its hours of warm storage and was a little less beautiful by the time I'd offered it to the masses. "Well, this is a totally different pastry this time. These are little sweet cheese pies—"

"P'teen-uh! I'm just trying to tell you, do cookies or brownies. Okay? Ya got it?" His face was turning red.

"Yeah, yeah. Okay," I said. I wanted to stop talking about it—maybe a little of Bampas's old *fili antio* philosophy at work. Besides, I had something more important on my mind.

The news in sixth period couldn't have been better. Mr. T gave me an A-plus for my work on the Steam & Bean. Then he'd written me a note:

> *Miss Vasilis,*
> *Your effort has been impressive. If I could hand out double A's, you'd have one for this work. Nice! Keep it up.*
> *T~*

From across the room, Bonnie flashed me a satisfied smile. She showed the large letter *A* Mr. T had put on the back of her cover page. Awesome.

As a class, we pinned the projects up around the room and had a free-flowing art show for the entire period. People were talking about everything from composition to computer enhancements. I made my way around the space twice. *This is my fuel*, I thought. *Making art, talking about design. This is what I want to do.* When the bell rang, we answered with a collective groan.

"Ack, people!" Mr. Terrazzi called out. "How did this happen? We're not going to have time to take this down but I will be pleased for the next two classes to see what you've done. Hey, hey!" he said, raising his voice above the buzz in the room. "New project assignment tomorrow! Be ready!" I think he meant to sober us with his tone. But actually, I felt invincible.

On my way out the door, I glanced back at everybody's work, and yes, my own, which, in a removed sort of way, caught me as rock-solid. "Miss Vasilis and Miss Swenson," Mr. Terrazzi said, "I've got a faculty meeting today. Any chance the two of you could come back here to take these down right after school?"

"I'm in," said Bonnie, and I echoed her.

So at the end of the day, I had to tell Brady I wasn't heading down to the White Tiger mosaic with him for the usual assembly. I was talking fast while I shuffled things around inside my locker. "I'm helping take down a bunch of art. Oh, and Brady, and I got an A-*plus* on this huge thing we just did . . . and all the projects were so cool . . ." I realized I was losing his attention. "So anyway, I was wondering if you could tell one of the Not-So—I mean, a *cheerleader* not to worry; I *will* be at practice. And will you take these to everyone?" I

147

pulled the boxes of pastries out of my locker. "By the time I finish up it'll be too late to—"

"No effin' way," Brady said. I looked into his eyes—ice-cold.

"You won't? Really?"

"You want be in the art room, instead of going with me. Fine. Do that. But I'm not taking your pie-turds down there. I'm not your delivery boy."

"I wasn't trying to send you on an errand. Never mind . . ." I turned back toward my locker. "I'll just leave them here and—"

"Whatever," Brady said. I looked at him. His jaw was set hard. He wrapped his hand around the edge of my locker door. He flung it backward on its hinges. It smashed into the locker beside mine with a loud bang. Then it bounced into me and knocked the pastry boxes out of my hands. There went Brady, striding away on khaki-covered legs. Lockers *always* bang in a crowded hallway. Not a soul had noticed. But my hands felt weightless and my knees felt weak. I shook it off. I straightened up, set the pastries back on my shelf, and went into the art room to help Bonnie.

"Bettina," she said. She already was holding several pages in her fingers. "I know Mr. Terrazzi asked us both to do this but I can handle it on my own," she said. "If you want to go join Brady and your friends—"

"I'm good here," I interrupted her. *My* friends? Did she really see them that way? "We can get it done before I have to go to practice," I said.

"Okay . . ." I could feel her looking at me. "Hey, is something wrong?"

"No." I gave a convincing eyebrow scrunch and swallowed the lump in my throat. I looked at the artwork on the wall. "So, hey, this is cool," I said. "We get to have another look at everything, up close."

We talked about the projects as we pulled out pushpins and peeled tape. I tried hard to forget about Brady's fit, but it weighed on me. Bonnie and I squared up everyone's pages and packed the work back into the folders Mr. T had left for us.

"More of a job than it looked like," Bonnie mused.

"Yeah—oh, hell! Is that clock right?"

"W-well, yeah, probably. Oh, your practice!"

"Is starting!" I added. I swore and tore into my backpack for a pair of gym shorts. Bonnie laughed, but not unsympathetically. "Oh, hell . . . They think I don't put in enough effort as it is. . . ." I mumbled.

"Here," said Bonnie, "I'm putting your project into your pack."

"Oh, thank you!" I stuck one booted foot then the other into the legs of my shorts. I pulled them up under my skirt then unzipped and pushed the skirt to the floor. Bonnie grabbed that up and tucked it into my pack.

"Turn, turn!" she said. I did, and she hung the pack on my shoulders. "Go!"

"Bonnie, thank you! See you tomorrow!" I said.

I shot into the hall and spun my combination as fast as I could. I grabbed the boxes of pastries and started running. My backpack clobbered me, the pastries bounced around inside the boxes. My boots struck the floor like hammers—

"Boots! Oh, no!" I said it out loud. I came to a halt and turned around. Sneakers! I had them. Back in my locker. So there I went clobbering and hammering back down the empty hallway to get them.

Again I trotted, this time with my sneakers slung around my neck by their short laces and kicking me in the face as I went. Those girls were going to hate me for stumbling in late—especially after all the talk about commitment. And here I was with these dumb pastries.

"Yikes!" I stopped just short of crashing into two guys who were coming out of the music room. "Sorry!"

"Whoa! Bettina!"

"Oh, Tony. It's you! Hi." I stopped to catch my breath. I was so late. What was one more minute? Tony had a friend with him, and the guy was giving me a dazed sort of smile. I

150

said hi to him too. Apologized again for nearly taking them out.

"Moti, this is Bettina," Tony told his friend. "She likes to run in big boots."

"I heard," the guy said. "I think the sound saved my life. I heard you coming."

That made me laugh. "I forgot my sneakers," I began to explain. "Now I'm really late and . . . oh, never mind." Then a moment of brilliance struck me. "Tony, take these! Please!" I held the pastries toward him. "Maybe Regina would like some, and your family. Sorry they're sorta broken."

Tony laughed. He had one box lid up and his nose inside. "Oh, I remember. Kali . . ." He closed his eyes tight, thinking. "Kalit-sou-nia."

"Yes!"

"Your mom's?"

"But baked by me," I said. I tapped my breastbone with my finger.

"There's nothing better than this stuff," Tony said, leaning toward his friend. "Except maybe my mom's cannoli."

"Right," I said.

"Can I share these? Like with Moti, here? And the band?"

"Of course!" I said. I clapped my hands on both his shoulders. "You're doing me a favor, Ton." I started away again.

"Well, thank you," Tony said. "Thanks a lot!"

"Sure!" I called over my shoulder. *Go, go, go,* was all I could think. I reached the end of the hall—a T where you must go either left to the main gym or right toward the auxiliary gym. I rounded toward the right and—*bam!* Something hit me in the side of my knee—and it felt like a bus.

Twenty-three

I DON'T KNOW HOW I STAYED STANDING. I YELPED LIKE A dog and went hopping to the opposite wall for support. I knew that no good thing had happened. A stray basketball rolled over my sneakers, which had landed in the middle of the hall. Brady came up to retrieve it. A handful of his teammates were gathered up not twenty feet away, waiting to go into the main gym. But they were talking, bouncing basketballs through their legs, spinning them on their fingers. Oblivious to the girl who been bowled down.

"You didn't catch it," Brady said to me. He drummed the ball into the floor a few times. Looked at me sideways.

"Oh, I caught it," I mumbled. I reached for my knee.

There was that bent-the-wrong-way feeling—an ache and a strain together. I circled my knee with both hands and held it tightly.

"Well, *bad* catch," Brady said, and he laughed. "I sent you an easy push pass."

Or maybe you whaled the thing at me. . . .

"You were running. How come you're so late?" He wedged the ball between his arm and his hip and waited for an answer.

"I was taking down that artwork," I said. I played the last few minutes in my mind. Then I realized what he must have seen. "And I just handed Tony Colletti those pastries," I said. I hoped I sounded as guiltless as I felt.

"Yeah. *Him again*," Brady said.

"He just happened to be there. Besides, what else was I going to do with them?"

There was only a second—just time for his eyes to soften the littlest bit—when a reprimanding sort of yell came from doors of the main gym. The basketballers were being called to the court. Brady was gone in an instant.

I tested my knee. It didn't feel great but it held and slowly, I started to the aux gym. It dawned on me how much I hated basketballs—had *always* hated basketballs. In gym classes, they were my nightmare; something my hands were too small to hold and my arms could never push up or away. It sucked getting hit in the tips of the fingers with them, and was there anything heavier, uglier, or clumsier than a basketball? I hate, hate, *hated them*! My eyes welled up.

I pushed on the door to the aux gym, heard the squad actually calling out a cheer. I stopped in the alcove and took a drink at the fountain. My knee throbbed.

Buck up and get in there, Bettina.

I did. I let myself down onto the lowest seat of the bleachers just as they finished their cheer. Of course I caught every eye in the gym. "Sorry I'm late," I said. I set my strangling sneakers down on the bench beside me. "And I just screwed up my knee, so I can only walk through our routines today. I'm sorry," I said, and as those words went off my tongue, in jogged Brady Cullen. He had an instant-ice pack, and he gave it a pump between the heels of his hands to activate it.

"For your knee," he said. Then, being quick and adorable, he swung a leg over to straddle the bench and scooted up close to me. He wrapped both arms around me and hugged me tight.

The cheerleaders all said, "Aww . . ."

Brady planted a bunch of mini kisses at my temple, in my ear, and again, the cheerleaders cooed, and even I could not squelch a ticklish grin all because of his breath in my ear. That made me madder. Then Brady jumped up again. He patted the ice pack onto my knee. "I gotta run," he said, and he did. Back to his own Goddamn gym.

155

Twenty-four

I DID NOT TELL MOMMA AND BAMPAS ABOUT MY KNEE. I'D had dancing injuries before, and I figured I knew what to do. Besides, I didn't want them to make me stay home. I retreated to my bedroom after supper as usual, where I iced and elevated. I dug a compression wrap out of my old ballet bag and wound that on there. For the next several days, I wore it under my jeans. Whatever had happened to the knee it was not so bad as to make me limp. I could put weight on it and I could bend it and the knee would only ache. But if I did both, it hurt like a bear.

In spite of the fact that I could not jump or lunge, it was my full intention to get through the day and go "be a cheerleader"

156

as scheduled, and to walk through every moment of practice and try to be loud. But in the late afternoon there was something waiting for me at my locker: Brady.

"Hey," he said, and he leaned down to kiss me.

"Hey," I said.

"What do you say we cut last period? We can go to my house."

I shrugged. "I don't think so," I said. I focused on the contents of my locker. "I need my study hall, and I'm conserving my mileage. My knee hurts, and I still have to get through practice."

"It hurts? Even after I brought you that ice?"

"Even after that," I said. "But I would like to see you. Alone."

"Yeah?" He brightened.

"To talk."

"Okay . . ." he said slowly, "that sounds some like heavy shit."

I shrugged.

"So, we'll talk on our way down to the tiger together after eighth and—"

"Not what I had in mind," I said. I kept calm as I shelved my books.

"Come on, P'teen-uh. What are we talking about here?"

I stepped back from my locker, not willing to be in the

way of that door should it suddenly swing. I was keeping one eye on Brady Cullen, and right now, he didn't look so good. His cheeks were slack and taking on color. His eyes darted and he adjusted his books under his arm.

"I was thinking we could sit outside the east entrance," I said. It was the place where no one ever gathered.

I watched Brady swallow. He stuck his chin in the air and said, "Yeah. Okay."

I think he must have stewed through the next forty-five minutes. He showed up at the end of the school day, looking hunched and miserable. We went out to the quiet side of the building, where we tucked ourselves around the side of a planting of broadleafs.

I remember I began with these words: "If you're ever mad at me, you need to tell me and we'll talk."

Brady got defensive; he accused me of accusing him of winging that ball into me on purpose. He wanted to know how I could suggest that. I took that to heart because—and this seemed to always be the case—I wasn't absolutely sure what had happened. I tried to take the basketball incident out of the equation.

"I think you were mad at me before that. Remember the cheese pastries? You said I was making you my errand boy or something? You bashed my locker."

"Okay, but I was just bummed because I wanted to be

with you." His mouth hung open, his palms faced up. "You're going to fault me for that? You're the one that didn't care. You wanted to go do art stuff. We had plans! We don't get that much time together, P'teen-uh! God!" He slammed his own fist into his palm.

We had to sit in silence while several people walked by. Then we stayed silent a bit longer all on our own.

"I miss the way we were before," I told him, and to my surprise, he dropped his head into one hand and let out a single, enormous sob. It was very real and it stunned me. He pressed his thumb and finger into his eyes. I noticed then how callused his knuckles looked. I'd seen him biting the backs of hands in a nervous way in recent weeks. Brady flicked moisture off his hand. He mumbled something about pressure and the team and not being able to hold it all together. I had no idea he felt so much weight. I turned to mush. My eyes teared up and my nose ran, though I refused to think of that as crying. I put my arms around Brady.

"Coach is reviewing grades already," he added. "I have a D in Spanish."

I told him I was a Spanish whiz—true—and that I'd help him.

"But what about us?" he asked, and he wrapped me tighter.

I went back to one thing I hoped he'd take away from an

exhausting conversation. "All I'm saying is, if you get mad, let's talk. All right?"

"But are we okay?" he wanted to know.

"Yes," I said.

We walked back into the school hand in hand. He headed for the boys' locker room and I ducked into the girls' room to check my face and fix my mascara rivers.

I hustled on my bad knee to my practice. I thought I was only a few minutes late but as soon I walked into the alcove, I knew the Not-So-Cheerleaders were already deep into things. I heard Emmy's voice first.

"Really, you guys, we should ask Bettina. She knows dance and I bet you anything she knows choreography—"

"Are you kidding me?" There launched a diatribe. I stood hidden in the alcove of the aux gym, listening.

"Even when she's here, she's not *here*. And now she says she's hurt her knee, and obviously Brady buys it but I don't. She's going to show up to practice in her jeans instead of shorts." (She had that right.) "And by the way, are we going to have to chip in to buy her a pair of sneakers?"

"She had her sneakers—" Emmy for the defense.

"Yeah! She finally remembered them on the day she couldn't work out. Hmm . . . what does that say?"

A new voice opened its cords on me. "What I want to

know is who's going to tell her to kill it with the freaking ho-stamps?"

"Seriously. That is *not* a part of our look."

"W-well, we don't all have to look the same. . . ." Emmy said.

"The judges for states want to see precision. Our look is part of our precision."

"Are we all going to get the same haircut?" Emmy asked. She laughed now, trying hard to be disarming.

"Hair. Now there's something Bettina has going for her. I have to say, that braid is beautiful."

"Yeah, her braid and her boyfriend. Both gorgeous. She'd be nothing without either one of them." I thought I heard snickering. Then someone being more serious.

"No. She's beautiful too . . ." the thoughtful voice conceded.

"Yeah, but what the hell? She always looks like she's on her way to a horror flick."

"She's just artsy," Emmy said.

"She's just so out of place on this squad. . . ."

I turned around and slid out the door.

Twenty-five

"Well, Beta!" Cowboy was smiling. How beautiful he was—the pair of deep dimples framing his mouth, the one in the center of his chin. How many people in this world got three of those? I felt my bad afternoon melt into the distance.

"Hey," I said and, as we crossed the auto shop floor toward each other, I almost reached out to hug him. But his arms were low and I ended up bumping him in the shoulder with my forearm. Ungraceful, but he laughed warmly.

"I haven't seen you in days." He squinted like he was trying to remember how long it had been.

"Yeah." I shrugged. "Just otherwise occupied. Oh, and

grounded," I offered with mock pride. "I was grounded for a while too."

"Well, aren't you a badass." Then he said, "Everything okay?"

"Yeah," I said. An unexpected swell of warmth rolled through my core. "And you?" I asked.

"Just fine," he said.

"I—I'm glad to see you. . . ." The words caught in my throat. Before I could turn things awkward again, I took a breath. "So, hey, I'm not here to bother you. But is it okay if I just . . ." I jabbed a thumb toward the workbench.

"Sure." He nodded. "I'm finishing something up." He nodded toward a car and left me.

I opened my backpack, dug in for my sketchbook. With it, out slid my folder from the Steam & Bean project. Something successful. That was nice. I set the folder up at the back of the bench in front of me, perhaps like a talisman. But I had no great art ambitions for this day. I'd be happy to stand at Cowboy's workbench and make lines or doodles. The smell of the shop, the feel of paper under pencil, and the clink of Cowboy's wrenches just a few feet away all combined to take the sting out of the things I had heard earlier that afternoon. I replayed what the cheerleaders had said. I was hurt but I couldn't be mad. Most of what they'd said was true.

I lay my head down on my arm on the workbench. I

looked across the sheet of paper as I drew and watched my pencil move from that perspective. *One-legged dancer on pointe,* I thought. I watched the page fill with lines of graphite.

"Beta."

I lifted my head and looked at Cowboy. He set a metal stool down beside me.

"Here." He scooted it closer. "You're standing on one leg," he said. His jaw was askew. "Something happen?"

I shook my head no.

"You look uncomfortable." He hesitated. "And you usually go bare-legged."

"Well, I guess you just proved you have two good eyes in your head," I said. I was shocked at how snotty I sounded. "Sorry," I added.

"You okay?"

"Yeah," I said. "And you're right. I did hurt my knee."

"How?"

I looked away. "I was running. Late for cheerleading—"

"Ch—*what? Cheerleading?* You, Beta?"

"Yeah, I don't even want to talk about that," I said.

"Me neither," he said. He leaned on the workbench, smiling with interest at the doodles I'd been making.

"Oh, don't look. I'm just being mindless," I told him.

"What's this?" He tapped the Steam & Bean folder with

a finger and it fell open, pages fanned forward one by one.

I picked up the pages and held them between us so he could see. "It was for an art class," I told him. "All the graphics for a . . . well . . . for a hypothetical coffee shop. I designed the menu and this one is the signage for out front." I flipped through the papers. "I didn't have to do the interior art, but once I got into it—"

"Wait, wait! Slow down!" he said. I let out an embarrassed sigh and handed him the whole folder. He turned the papers over in his fingers carefully like he didn't want to get grease on them.

"You can touch them," I said. "It's all in the computer. I can print more." I tried to shut up then, but I squirmed where I stood. There was something excruciating about watching him look at my work.

"Wow," he said. He looked at me. He looked at my art. "These are great, Beta. And they are so . . . *you*. I mean, it feels like you and looks like you, and only you could've— well, hell, what do I know?" he scoffed. He got to the page where I'd enhanced the exterior of the building. "I know this place," he said with a slight smile. "My brothers and I used to call it the 'potbelly building.' There was a business in there called the Sandwich Hole."

"Ew. That sounds fatal," I said, and he laughed.

"I think it was. They're gone." He turned to the back

of one of the sheets where Mr. Terrazzi had written me the killer-nice note.

"Oooh . . . and she gets the *big* grade—"

"Oh, don't look at that," I said. I was busy blushing, but then I saw that Cowboy was staring more intently at the page.

"What?" I said, leaning closer to him. "What are you looking at?"

Silently, he pointed to my name. Mr. T's handwriting was full of loops and a little hard to read. "Does this say Vasilis? Is your last name Vasilis?"

I hesitated. "Yeah."

"Not like Dinos Vasilis?"

"Just like that. Why?"

"Holy shit! Seriously?"

"W-why? Do you know my father?"

"Not exactly. I had coffee with him—once. I write my rent check to him every month." Cowboy let a breath out that lifted his wavy bangs.

"Rent? What? Where do you live?"

"I live at my ma's for the moment. But I'm talking about the check for the shop, for *this* place. Unit 37."

I looked around me, trying to take it in. "Bampas owns Unit 37?"

"Yeah, right." Cowboy laughed at me. "Just this *one* unit."

Then I realized how stupid I was being. Surely he meant that my father owned the whole industrial park. "Cripes, Beta, your father is a powerful man—self-made, too, the way he tells it." Cowboy slowed down as something dawned on him. "And boy, would he ever *not* like you hanging around me."

"What do you mean?" I asked, though I suppose I already knew.

Cowboy turned his palms up and looked around the garage. "I work *here*. And that's just for starters."

"You have a business. A *bona fide* business. And my father's not a snob," I said. I felt like I should tell Cowboy how Bampas did dishes in his own restaurant on holidays, and that he tended his own roses at home, carried rabbit manure in his hands. . . .

"No. I didn't say he was." He let a beat go by while he looked at me. "Where I work is the least of it. You know what I'm talking about," he said.

"You mean that 'jailbait' thing? There's nothing inappropriate going on." I shrugged. "I haven't even seen you that much. . . ." I let it trail.

Neither of us spoke for a moment.

"Funny." Cowboy looked at me sideways. "I hadn't pegged you for . . . hmm . . ."

"For what?"

"I was going to say that I hadn't pegged you for a rich kid.

Sorry, that's rude. Come to find out, your daddy owns half the town."

"Half the—what? *What?*" I shook my head.

"You do know that, don't you?"

I opened my mouth, then closed it. I took my Steam & Bean prints back from Cowboy. "Y-yeah . . . I know. I know what he does." I stood there tucking and re-tucking the papers into my pack, then messing with the zipper.

"Hey, did I say something wrong? I'm sorry."

"No." I shook my head. "I—I just have to go." I turned away.

"Beta!" Cowboy called to me. "I'm sorry!"

I put my hand up, faked a grin his way, and called back, "Thanks for letting me hang." Then I booked out of there, or tried. My knee made me slow.

I felt terrible. I even started to cry as I walked a wide, uncomfortable block around the school. Here I was killing time—time that I could have spent with Cowboy. Oh, so stupid. And over what? A Bampas factoid. *Half the town.* But Cowboy had said it so casually, as if everyone knew it. Well, not me, and how had I missed it? I flashed on the many times we had stopped at empty buildings while Bampas checked on this or that. Like the day at 66 Green Street, though apparently that was the least of all the places.

"My God, you are dense!" I told myself.

There were offices over the restaurant, and I think he had something going with the apartment buildings on either side of that. Oh, and there'd been buzz about the renovation of an old mill building. We were often interrupted when we dined at Loreena's. There were men, vaguely familiar to me, who would slide a chair up next to Bampas and tell him about a building or a business he might be interested in. I always thought Bampas was being polite the way he'd say, "Oh, yes. I'd like to see it." I thought it was his way of getting rid of them. Guess not. Guess he bought a lot of those buildings.

In my bedroom, I opened my backpack to look over my homework. The Steam & Bean project stared up at me. I stared back. I thought about how Cowboy had been admiring the pages and then the next thing I knew we were talking about my father.

I wanted Bampas to see what I'd done with 66 Green Street. This was some of my best work yet, and didn't it scrape up against the sort of things that he did and thought about all day long? If he could see that I was serious, maybe we could talk about art school.

I took the pages to the dinner table with me that evening. "Bampas," I said. (Bampas, who owns half this town . . .) "May I show you something?"

He took the papers. He slipped them one behind the other as he looked. "Very nice," he said. "Look at your sister's artwork." He waved the papers at Favian and Avel in a perfunctory sort of way.

"I got an A on the project, Bampas," I told him. I saw Momma give me a nod.

"That's good. Good girl. You should have A's for art classes," Bampas said.

"A is for art," Avel quipped. He and Favian both craned to see the pages.

"Oh, it's A-*plus*," Favian noted. "That sign is for *plus*, it is really cool."

We all laughed, even Bampas.

"It'll be a good portfolio piece," I said. I lost my nerve about mentioning art school but I thought of something else to say. "Did you see the address, Bampas? It's 66 Green Street? You and I stopped there—"

"Near the high school," he mumbled.

"One of *your* buildings," I said. I thought he might look up and wonder how I knew that, but he didn't. "Well, it's just an assignment, but I had the idea that a coffee shop would do well there—something with a little more to offer than the usual. Do you think so?"

My father dished some of my mother's fish and rice with grape leaves onto a plate and passed it down the table to her. "Yes," he said.

I was right!

"Possibly. But not like this," he said. He paused, serving spoon in hand, and browsed my menu page again briefly. He shook his head. "You cannot sell fine Greek pastries and expensive coffees to high school students, Bettina." He continued serving our meal.

I remembered my baklava debacle, the cheese pastries that had finally gone home with Tony Colletti, who could appreciate them. Maybe Bampas was right.

"Well, then it needs tweaking. What about lattes? Ice-cream bars, gelato?" I said. "I think high school kids would go to a place based on my idea, Bampas. I'd go."

"And you are not everyone, Bettina." He pulled in his chin and shook his head.

"Well, maybe not, but—"

"Att-att!" My father raised a finger at me. "*Siopi,*" he said. I looked at his fingertip, then his eyes, then down at my own plate. He reached toward my mother, then the bottle of white in his hand. "Some wine, Loreena? This is a good one. Very crisp." He paused to look at the label on the bottle.

"Yes, Dinos, thank you," Momma said. "It's beautiful work, Bettina," she added, and I suppose she was looking at me while I pushed at my fish with my fork.

"I'm adding this wine to the list at Loreena's Downtown," Bampas went on.

While I picked at my food, a green pea came rolling

across the tablecloth and bumped into my plate. I looked up at Favian, the shooter. Avel, the audience, let out a giggle. I gave them both a smirk. I imagined gathering them up after supper for a conference.

Hey, your bampas owns half the town. Did you know?

They probably didn't know, not yet. But Bampas would be different with the boys than he'd been with me, I guessed.

Another pea rolled past my place at the table and fell to the floor. Favian and Avel cracked up. I put a finger to my lips and opened my eyes wide at them. They were about to get in trouble.

Sitting there, under fire of green peas, a thought came out of the air: *You can get an A-plus and still fail.*

Twenty-six

I WAS AFRAID OF WHAT COWBOY WOULD THINK OF ME, leaving the way I had. So, the next morning before school, I went to Unit 37 again, two coffees in my hands.

"Ah, Beta. Bless you!" Cowboy dropped the hood on the '57 Chevy. He smiled and I felt my heart swell so much I was sure he'd see it at my throat. He'd been working on that same car yesterday—quietly cussing to himself underneath it. I thought it must be a lost cause. But Cowboy didn't give up easily on old cars, especially not the silver Chevy. That one belonged to him, he had told me.

I set the coffees on the workbench and sat down on the edge of a couple of stacked-up tires close to where he was working. "I guess I confess," I said. "I didn't really know about my father before you told me."

Cowboy wiped his hands on his shop towel, pushed his dolly over with one foot, and sat down in front of me. "I'm sorry," he said. I half expected him to take my chin in his hands. But the great thing—*one* of the great things—about Cowboy was that he didn't condescend.

"Or if I did know . . . well, you completed the picture for me." I swallowed hard and focused on a grease spot on the floor. "I know that his restaurant does well. I've even seen him deal." I shrugged. "We always have what we need. I know he helps other people. . . . He's like a human ATM, although—ha!—he'd never use one. He wants to go inside the bank and see a person to make his transactions."

"Yeah . . ." Cowboy seemed to get that. "He wanted to meet me in person before he'd rent this space to me. Most of the other places I looked at, the owner sent an agent."

"Well, Bampas will always choose the old way of doing things. Anyway, I don't even know why it bothered me," I said. "But can I ask you, how did you know?"

"Newspapers. I don't read everything but I read the land records pretty often. His name is always there—buying this and selling that. He's got apartments and renovation projects—all of it. Vasilis Inc. is one of the city's largest tax-payers."

"So why didn't *I* know?" I mused.

"You're a kid," he said, and he must have seen me wilt. "I don't mean it like that, Beta. It's just—you're not supposed to care about this stuff. Look, he's a good guy. He sent work my way when I opened up here. It's not like you just found out that he's a drunk or a drug dealer." Cowboy was always a little deadpan. He shook my shoulder gently, and I tried to nod my head.

"He's been stopping at these empty buildings all my life. A while ago I was with him, and I asked him about a place—actually, it was that potbelly building that I based my fake coffee shop on—and he just said, '*Never mind, Bettina.*'" I mocked my father's voice, his accent. Cowboy laughed a little. "He doesn't include me," I said.

Cowboy shrugged. "Because you're his daughter. He probably thinks about other things when he's around you," Cowboy said. I looked at him, puzzled. "Does he know about your boyfriend?" he asked.

"He thinks he does," I said. Then I realized how true it was, and I wished I hadn't said it.

"If he really knew him, he'd have the kid on a spit by now."

My core went rubbery. I didn't like hearing Cowboy talk about Brady.

"By the way, how's your knee?" Cowboy asked.

"Improving," I said, but I didn't look him in the eye. I stood up and checked the clock. "Oh, no! Is that right? I'm going be late. And I have a load of tardies already. I think I'm due for a detention." I shouldered my backpack.

"Yeah, probably because you bring me coffees. Here, let's try this." Cowboy dragged out an invoice pad. He wrote so slowly. I waited. He held the slip out to me. "It just says that you're late because you had trouble peeling a tattoo."

"Very funny," I said. I felt slightly self-conscious of the skeletal bird on the inside of my wrist.

"Beta, I'm kidding. Here, take it. It's worth a try," he said.

I looked at the invoice, which had the same logo as his shop sign printed at the top. He'd actually written:

Bettina Vasilis stopped at my place of business Unit 37 Hammer Hill Industrial Park to give me a key from Dinos Vasilis owner of the property.

What a joke. My father would never give me a key to anything. Yet there it was, stated in triplicate on Cowboy's invoice pad. (I couldn't help noticing that it was a wicked run-on sentence.) He had signed it with three initials: *SWS*.

On my way across the playing fields, I took one more look at the would-be excuse and jammed it into my pocket. I wasn't going to try to use it. If the school checked it out with

176

my parents, it'd screw up everything.

I sat in detention that afternoon, glad to be free of the Not-So-Cheerleaders. I rested my knee, and considered what to do about the squad now that I'd overheard them trashing me. But that draining discussion with Brady was still fresh in my mind. I had little doubt that he was still stressed over basketball. But he was trying hard with us; he'd been sweet and solicitous. If I quit the squad now it would seem like I'd just set out to piss him off. Also, without cheerleading, Momma and Bampas would have me riding home on the bus again after school every day. Miserable as it was, staying on the squad preserved my freedom.

The detention clock ticked. I pulled the invoice out of my pocket again. I held it to my nose and sniffed, wanting the scent of the shop to fill me. Cowboy hadn't signed his name. Just SWS. Maybe because it was a bit of a game between us. I didn't know his real name, and he'd only recently learned all of mine. But the letters must be his initials. What could SWS stand for?

Twenty-seven

REGINA COLLETTI WAS UP AND COOKING. TONY AND I both knew it the minute we reached the bottom of the stairs. He stopped and sniffed. I did the same.

"Pasta fagioli," we both said at once.

"She must be having a really good day," Tony added.

In her kitchen, Regina sat on a stool next to the stove. She pushed a wooden spoon around the inside of a saucepan.

"Ah, good," she said when she saw us. "Tony, carry that pasta to the sink and pour off the water. Bettina, take that knife. Mince that basil." She pointed to a cutting board on the table. "Grate us a nice little mound of that Parmesan, too."

"Nonna, what meal is this?" Tony asked. He glanced at the clock.

"What does it matter?" Regina asked.

I was just glad Tony would be staying, at least for a while. It was a walk back in time for me to sit in my old neighborhood with the scent of basil filling my head and the flavors of garlic and soft cannellini beans sliding over my tongue. Of course, Regina kept bossing both Tony and me.

"Put more basil on yours," she said. She pinched up the herbs in her fingers and reached across the table to sprinkle them in my bowl. She gave herself a nod of approval. This was the sort of Regina-thing that made Tony laugh in an acquiescent way that I found contagious.

Sitting in the kitchen with Regina and Tony, I forgot my real-world self a little more with every mouthful. But as soon as Tony and I had washed and dried the bowls, Regina told him to leave us.

"Go practice that horn," she said. As soon as he was gone, she leaned toward me. "Did you know," she began, "when I was a girl, I had a *forbidden* boyfriend?"

Nice opener.

"I think of it every time you come," she said. She reached forward and patted my hands. "You bring it all back, you make me remember."

Oh, great. Go me*!*

"I see you, and you are a young, gorgeous girl and it was the same time in my own life. Well, I was younger—fourteen. I was just in high school, and Ricky was just out," she said. "So, a boy, an older boy at that." She shook her finger. "Not allowed in my papa's house. Ricky had a job sweeping up and cleaning the johnnies at Saint Barnabas Roman Catholic Church and that's where I met him. We took a shine to each other, first glance. Sometimes it's just that way. That church was not a nice place to work. Ricky told me all he got was a scolding for every job he ever did there. He always wondered why they kept him, but they did. He was the oldest boy in his family and he was earning money to help out at home. Sad, because he was as smart as any of the boys who got to go to college."

Regina paused, looking out the small window over my shoulder. I saw the curved, square reflection of light shining in her cocoa-brown eyes. "He always saved out a little money from his pay to get me a handful of bubble gums or a Sky Bar. You know, I didn't need fancy presents from him to know that boy loved me. Those little treats were fine enough. He showed up at the high school every afternoon. Well, not right at the front door. Whoa! No! We had to keep ourselves a secret. So Ricky waited across the street, in his blue jeans and a clean, white T-shirt. That's all I ever saw him in besides the overshirt he wore to do chores at Saint Barnabas.

"Anyway, your friends helped you out back then. Because of course they knew. They'd be your lookouts, making sure none of the parents or their parents' friends were around. They'd help you on a Friday night so you could get to the burger place to be with your boy, or go canoodling in the park. Best kind of lying there is," Regina said, and she arched her eyebrows at me.

"I ran with Ricky all those months, always afraid someone would tell my papa. Oh, we were Goddamn careful. Then one Friday afternoon, I looked across the street to the place where Ricky always waited and there he was . . . but also, my papa. And they weren't speaking to each other. Just standing some ten feet apart, both with an eye on yours truly. Mother of God, I nearly wet my polka-dotties. Right away, I knew that Ricky didn't know he's standing next to my papa. Because his eyes were twinkling and he was looking right at me. Love isn't blind; it just wears blinders. Well, my friend Cherise— oh, that girl was something—she saved the day, or tried to. She came out of nowhere hollering, 'Hi, Mr. Paladina! How are you this afternoon, Mr. Paladina?'"

It was all I could do not to stop her there and say, *Wait, wait! You were* Regina Paladina? But the story was too scary to interrupt.

"So Ricky heard that name *Paladina* and of course he figured out that my papa was right there sharing the pavement with him. And real smart, Ricky straightened up from where he was leaning and he walked off."

"Well, why was your father there?" I asked.

"Good question," Regina said. "I didn't know either. I wondered if he knew something or just thought he did. But I figured I had to go to him, and when I did he told me to start walking home. He followed me, just a few steps behind me. Nothing warm about it, no father-daughter chat. And when we reached the park he told me to step off the sidewalk. He walked me another thirty feet into the wooded part. He knocked me flat to the ground on my belly and beat me on my back with a rock."

"Oh! Jesus!"

"Yep. That's who I cried for. But not out loud. No. I didn't make a sound, except maybe the breath he pounded out of me."

"But why? And didn't he say anything?" I could hardly bear to ask.

"Oh, yes. When he finished, he told me to dust myself off and he'd see me at home. He told me to see the boy and to show him my bare back—the price I'd paid for him dating me while I'm so young."

"Did you?"

"I was too scared not to. I did it that Monday. And I have wondered for years if my papa planned that. Beat me on Friday so the bruises would rise for Monday. I met Ricky same as usual and he wanted to know right away, was everything all right. I shook my head no and asked him to walk with me. I took him to the same place in the park where Papa had beaten me. Hidden away there, Ricky tried to put his arms around me but all I could do was squeak, 'No, no! Don't hug me! Don't hug me, Ricky, 'cause it hurts, it hurts bad!' Then I told him to look at my back. He stood behind me, I felt his fingers on my dress buttons—so careful. I still remember it—him gasping while he peeled my top off my shoulders, all the way down to my waist until he could see it all. I crossed my arms over my little breasts before I turned around because he'd never seen any of that. He was so good." Regina smiled gently. "I had offered him my virginity months before but he wouldn't take it. He had said not until he made something more of himself. Anyway, Ricky got down on his knees and hugged me around my hips where it didn't hurt me, you know, put his ear to my belly." Regina placed her hand over her stomach. "That's how we said goodbye."

She had me weeping. I drew my fingers under my eyes trying to trap tears. "It's awful," I said. "So sad."

"It was a long time before I stopped crying about it," Regina said with a tiny shake of her head. "I still think that this thing that was supposed to be so, so bad—my being with Ricky—well, it never felt wrong to me. *Never.* And I still believe it was my papa's big mistake."

"What about your mother? Did she know and—"

"Oh, I never told anyone what Papa did to me. He went to his grave without us ever talking about it again."

"How?" I asked. "How could you be silent after he beat you?"

"Times were different. He was my father." Regina raised her eyebrows and stared off for a second. "He was loving me the best he could. Fathers are complicated," she said. She took a little breath as if to bring herself around again. "Do you know, I was sixteen before I dated any boy again? With my father's blessing, of course. I went with half a heart because I still wanted Ricky. But that next boy, I had to knee him in his sausage. He tried to take what I wanted to give to my Ricky."

Twenty-eight

REGINA'S STORY STUCK TO ME. IN FACT, IT STITCHED ITSELF to my heart. Tony drove me home in his mother's car while a steady rain dotted the windshield. On the way I thought about Bampas. For all the ways in which I felt he didn't believe in me, I had never feared he'd hurt me. Never. I thought about things that were forbidden, and exactly how they became that way. Who put that judgment on them? How often did we as human beings get it wrong the way Regina's father had? Such a tangle. Not something I could sort out in a minute or a month, I knew that. But I was helpless for the way the thoughts kept rushing at me. When she'd put me out the door at the top of her stairs, Regina Colletti had said, "I don't tell

185

that story much. If you repeat it to anyone I'll find a way to feed you cat shit when you aren't looking."

"I believe you," I'd said. Then I'd taken a chance and I'd hugged her.

At home before supper, I received my desultory kiss from Bampas—that one he brushed on me almost every evening while on his way to do something else. But then I circled him with my arms and hugged him tighter than I had in months—or years. He noticed this stoppage with a slight double take. He quickly restored order, opening his mail. He asked about the quart container I had set on the kitchen counter.

"Regina sent me home with some of her pasta fagioli," I said. The cat shit comment flickered through my mind and I kept an alarmed smile to myself.

"Oh, my goodness," Momma piped, poking her head in from the dining room.

Bampas glanced at Momma and agreed, "Regina is too kind."

"She was so low last week and now up cooking," Momma said. "It's remarkable. But she puts me to shame. I should be sending meals to her."

"She had some of those cheese pastries I made," I said.

"Not enough. I will have the restaurant make several dishes. . . ." Bampas said. "Bettina, you have a table to set," he added, and we fell to our evening routine.

Throughout dinner, I thought about a particular thing Regina had said—that spending time with Ricky had never felt wrong to her. Cowboy was not my boyfriend, but he was still someone who I would not have been allowed to see had Bampas known. But seeing him never felt wrong to me.

I went on showing up at Unit 37 as many mornings as I could, always with coffee. I found my way there a couple of lucky afternoons a week, and yes, it always meant lying to someone—usually, the Not-So-Cheerleaders. Cowboy seemed happy to see me every time. We talked about his work and my work and we stayed off the subjects that went prickly on us—like Brady.

Cowboy taught me how to change a tire. I degreased, I polished chrome, and I treated interiors with conditioner, but only if I felt like it. Often, he needed to be underneath a car, and I'd do homework or fill a few pages of my sketchbook while I savored the oily smell of the shop.

Unit 37 gave me the same sort of feeling the art room did. Both spaces could be amazingly silent except for the sounds of work getting done, and maybe some music. I never told Cowboy, but sometimes I pretended that being in his shop was my job.

A few times now, we'd gone off in Cowboy's truck. We took back streets to escape being seen in the village. We hit the country road that took us to the Dairy Bar for milk

187

shakes. He'd buy or I'd buy. Except for the slight bittersweetness of spending lunch money that Bampas had given me to fatten up a friendship that he would forbid, those were the best afternoons ever.

One October afternoon I was striding my way toward Unit 37, and I looked up at a yellowish light in the sky. The trees had turned; leaves were falling. It was like somebody had flicked a switch. It wasn't just the landscape. People's faces were turning rosy over faded tans. They were wrapped in knits and fleeces. Change of palette, change of texture.

I gave the parking lot a cursory check for Cowboy's policeman friends. All clear. For the first time, the overhead door was not open. It felt a little different turning the handle on the small swing door; entering this way seemed more deliberate. I stuck myself half inside and called, "Knock-knock!" No answer. I walked in anyway. I almost leapt backward, thinking Cowboy was someone else as he rolled out from under the Chevy; he was wearing a gray zip-front coverall against the chill. As his head emerged, I said, "Oh, good. You're still you."

"Who'd you think I'd be?" he said. He grunted and sat up.

"It's just that you didn't look like you. In the . . . uh . . . *romper.*" I drew a line up and down in the air to indicate his attire.

"Beta, if you ever see me wearing a *romper*, you can kick

188

my ass," he said. I threw my head back and laughed. He pointed to his clothes and said, *"Coverall."* Then he added, "It's cold. I need an extra layer."

"Yeah. Everything's changing," I said.

"Guess so."

"If you have time I'll buy you a shake," I offered.

"Too cold for milk shakes."

"It's warmer in the sun," I said. I might have been pleading. I wanted to go for a ride. I was afraid he'd slide back under the car not to be seen again. I had a whole hour and a half before I needed to be back at the front circle of the school for my ride home.

He got up and rolled up the big door. He stood for a second, looking up to the treetops, the sky. "Hmm. How's that knee of yours?"

"I don't feel it much anymore," I said. I almost mentioned that things had been better with Brady. I guess I was longing to talk to someone about all of that. But not Cowboy.

"Yeah? What if we go somewhere different?" Cowboy asked. I nodded. A lot. "You're like my mother's Gordon setter," he said. "Always up for a ride in the truck—"

"Hey! Don't get personal!" I said.

"That's not personal. That's specific. My way of saying that I like your enthusiasm," he said. He peeled out of the coverall and pulled his boots on. He put his long arms into a big flannel jacket and he looked like Cowboy again.

I was surprised when he took River Road. We drove out past the place where my brothers and I had seen him back in September at sunset. A few more miles and he pulled off at the water company property. Cowboy was out of the truck so fast I had to scramble to keep up. "Hope you're game for a climb," he said, jabbing a thumb toward the steep, wooded slope. I looked up.

"Whoa. Sure," I said. I was never so glad to be wearing long jeans. "Are we . . . uh . . . supposed to hike here? I mean, allowed to?"

"Yup. It's a public trail. But I rarely meet anyone. A shame. It's so nice."

He led the way taking quick, broad strides. He caught handholds on tree trunks and rock outcroppings as he went. I followed his moves as much as I could. But my reach was much shorter and it wasn't the easiest climbing. I'd lost my dancing lungs. I kept falling behind.

"Hey, Speedy, are you *trying* to lose me?" I called.

He turned around on the next ledge four feet above me and reached down for my hands. We slapped grips together, I planted a toe, and he pulled me right up toward his beaming face. I landed, two-footed. He let go of my hands. "Sorry, I'm rushing us. But I know you, and up there," he said, pointing,

190

"is a view you'll want to sit with."

I know you. I heard it like an echo. Then I was chasing his plaid back once again.

Finally, we stopped on a scrubby overlook. Cowboy offered the view to me, with a sweep of his hand. The lemon-colored sky spanned the spaces both above and below us. I had that feeling of breath laughing its way out of me. We were in a place that was neither earth nor sky. "You were right," I said, steadying my breath. "Worth the race."

We looked down on a blaze of orange-and-amber tree-tops. Mounds of colors grew fuzzy in the distance. Closer to us, the sun came through the blush of leaves and lay bare the branching veins. I raised my hands and framed the sharp points of a maple leaf in my thumb and fingers for a moment. I gave Cowboy a grateful smile.

He lay back against the hill in a patch of sunlight. He sighed, tossed out a rock that bothered his back, and I listened to it thumping off the steep hillside on its way down to who-knows-where. He put his hands behind his neck. His knees poked up like a pair of matched mountaintops. I watched him: quiet, eyes closed in the sun. It was a rare chance to stare at him—to trace his lines—and I did.

I was between earth and sky, between two tantalizing views. We'd have to leave soon. I reached out and patted one of Cowboy's knees. He opened one sleepy eye at me.

"Hey," I whispered. "I'm going to take the trail a little higher."

"Hmm . . . careful. Leave bread crumbs. . . ." he mumbled, then settled back.

I stayed low—fingers touching down every so often. I stopped on my way to look across the treetops. Then continued up. I liked rising, rising, rising, while little balls of dry earth slid down the slope behind me.

Last plateau, I thought. I was out of breath. I wrapped my hand around a small tree trunk, rested my cheek on my knuckles and gazed out. *Frost.* I'd like to see this whole place covered in crystals. I stayed there, frosting the view in my mind. Oh, for sure, I was spending too long. I took a last look and turned back.

Going down was tricky. Every few yards I felt myself being shot forward—taking stupid, fast little steps along the steep path. I grabbed at the skinny trees trying to slow myself down and practically jerked my arms out their sockets. Then I launched on my feet again. The jarring made me laugh as it traveled from my boot soles to my jawbone. Down, down . . . I must be getting nearer to—ah—*Cowboy.*

He was standing below me. He was smiling, I was smiling and—oh God! Was I just bouncing down this hill in front of him? And was he watching? I pulled one side of my open jacket across my chest. I took another step and suddenly the whole hill beneath my boots was marbles. My head went back. My feet came up.

I hit the ground. *Hard.*

I slid. There was nothing to do—nothing to grab. I hit Cowboy, square in the ankles. He fell smack on top of me. I closed my eyes.

I heard him say, "Oops . . ."

Other sounds were coming from me. I was trying to get air back into my lungs. I realized I was clinging to him. I closed my fingers tighter on the cloth of his shirt while I squirmed for that breath that would not come in. Then it did, and the fight for the next one began.

"Beta . . . you okay?" His lips were near my ear.

I blinked. Focused on the gray-green eyes that were looking right into mine. I saw how crowded his lashes were, the white-blond tips. And he had freckles. Tiny, tan ones that I had never been close enough to see before. There was a thin, white line of a scar beneath one of his eyebrows.

He lifted off of me the littlest bit. "It's only my boot heel against a root keeping us from a six-foot drop," he said. "So we have to be careful here."

"Hu-uh. Really?" The words rode out on my jagged

breaths. At least a hundred little rocks dug into my ribs from the back. "S-sorry," I said.

"Well, *I'm* okay." He let out a gentle laugh, a puff of air along my cheek.

"But I hit you so hard."

"And I landed on you—so much," he said in a commiserative way.

He was still very much on me. I looked at him again. I uncurled my fingers from his sleeve and put my hand against the side of his face. I felt his beard—rough, but not spiny—on my fingers.

His eyes closed. He pressed my hand between his chin and shoulder. He huffed a laugh and said, "Beta . . . I'm going to get up now."

I didn't want him to move. But he did, slowly dumping himself to one side. He kept hold of my folded elbow, lest I go sliding again. I badly wanted to spring to my feet—to be perfectly fine, and damn sure of it. But this wasn't going to go like that. With his help, I sat up. I pulled my boots underneath me one leg at a time. When I was ready, Cowboy pulled me slowly to my feet. We stood close—touching—just a few seconds before we let each other go.

"You are all right, aren't you?" he asked. He looked worried.

"F-fine," I said. I was pretty sure it was true. I tried to

speak smoothly, like a person who could actually breathe. "Got the wind knocked out of me," I said.

"At the least!" he said. He wrapped his hand around a skinny tree trunk and rested his cheek on his knuckles—just like I had when I'd been up the trail, alone. Was that something universal or just something Cowboy and I both did? No way to know and too strange a question to ask out loud, especially in a silence like this one.

"Hmm . . ." he said, looking me over. "You look like you went ten rounds with a mean mountain." He came up close again and began to dust me off. He was gentle, sweeping dirt from my jacket cuffs, flicking little stones from their impressions on the underside of my forearms. He held my braid in his hand and picked little sticks and leaves from it while chills rippled through me. Then I couldn't stand it.

"Stop," I said. I stepped back. "D-don't." He kept trying anyway. "It's too much. . . ." I stepped away from him. I pulled my braid to my front and swiped at it. Then I swatted dirt off my jeans.

"Too much?"

"Yes." I faced him. I felt helplessly honest. "Cowboy . . . I *liked* holding you. I *liked* you holding me. I didn't want to let go—" I stared at him, my eyes pooling.

He waited, lids down so I couldn't read his eyes. Then he picked up his chin and said, "We better head back to the truck." He started off down the trail.

I followed him, legs wobbling. "Hey. Do you understand what I'm saying?"

"Nope."

"Cowboy . . ."

He stopped and turned to face me. He took hold of my shoulders. "I hear you," he said. "But I don't understand because I don't want to understand. Do you get that, *Bettina*?"

What a punch. He never called me Bettina. I hated the way it came off his lips.

He stared at me as if he had something more to say. But he took too long. I boxed out of his grip. I hugged my own body—trying to pull together. My ribs felt like a cracking cage around my heart, and my heart felt like an exhausted bird. I sucked it up. I began to march. I went all the way down the slope ahead of Cowboy.

Alone in the truck, I dialed Bampas. Thank God I hadn't smashed his precious phone up on that hill. I picked a lie and steeled my voice. "Bampas, I—I'm going to be late coming out to the circle. Sorry." He launched—started giving me nine kinds of shit through a signal that was full of hiccups. While I listened to that, I thought about how stupid it was that I couldn't just get out of the truck on River Road a few miles from here and walk the swath to our back door. But that would raise deadly questions. "I'm sorry, Bampas.

196

The paint was slow to dry. . . ."

I was still connected when Cowboy got into the truck. I swiped the keys out of his hand just before he put them in the ignition. I gestured wildly at the phone in my hand and shushed him. When I hung up with Bampas, I turned on Cowboy. "What the hell? Did you want him to hear the engine? *Jesus!*"

He said nothing when I got out of his truck at his shop, nothing when I dragged my backpack onto my shoulders. Neither of us said goodbye. I hurried to meet my father. I was late by almost fifteen minutes. While Bampas berated me for making him wait, I thought about Cowboy. *I won't see him anymore*, I decided. But of course, it didn't go like that.

Twenty-nine

"Beta."

Better than *Bettina*, but boy, what an expressionless greeting. Perhaps I had startled him. I had called out at the door but the music was up louder than usual. He crossed toward me to turn it down. "Are you all right?" Cowboy asked. "I mean from that tumble?"

"Fine."

"Did you tell your parents?"

"No!" I said. "So don't worry, nobody will ever know that I know you." I sounded like a fifth grader, and I regretted it immediately.

"Come on. You know that isn't why I asked." Cowboy

shook his head. "But I was thinking . . . maybe you should stop coming around here." He turned away from me, and I tried to ignore the feeling that he'd just cut my legs out from under me. He made himself busy with something—new brakes for the Chevy, I think. "I'm buried in work. I've got calls to make and I'm waiting on parts that are going to have to be modified—"

"And none of that is new," I said. "Look, I didn't mean to mess everything up."

"There is no *everything*," he insisted. He still wouldn't look at me.

"Well, just the same . . ." The heat from the two coffees I held was coming through my thin gloves. I'd waited three long days to come back and, in that time, October had turned even colder. I had followed my breath to the shop. It was warmer inside. The aroma of the coffee was rising. I looked around me. Here were the shiny car parts, the tools along the wall strip, the neatly stacked tires. The cowboy. The shop was my haven. I had to be able to come here. I wondered if I could *ignore* my way back in—simply not hear what he was telling me.

"Listen, Beta." He spoke again. "It's not just you. I made a mistake too. I—I looked at you, felt you, underneath me like that and . . ." He closed his eyes for a second and chewed his lip. I remembered how he'd caught my hand between his chin and shoulder. "I guess I did the same thing you did. I got . . . confused, and—" He cut himself off with one deep breath.

"It *was* confusing," I said. "What I felt on that hill—it surprised me. And . . . I just wanted to be honest about it. You can blame me for that, for speaking. But I'll leave it there. I will. Don't kick me out." My eyes were full, near to spilling again, but I didn't care if he saw that. I held fast and kept my voice even. "I'll help you here. Or I'll just stay out of your way," I said. "Look, there's an awful lot that doesn't feel right out there." I pointed outside the shop, shook my head. "I—I need to be able to come here. Please."

Time stretched. Oh, damn him, how long could he stand there staring at the floor and not saying anything?

"I'm not confused anymore," I said, which was as true as a thing could be. I thrust a coffee forward. Slowly, he took it. I moved over to the bench and set my pack down. I pretended to get busy—pulled out my sketchbook and flipped it open.

I wasn't looking at him, but I heard him say it . . . finally.

"You can always come here."

Thirty

IN OUR KITCHEN, I LET THE SMELL OF THE COFFEE FILL MY head. Association was such a powerful thing. Coffee *was* Cowboy. Cowboy was good—good not to leave me taking all the blame for our "moment" on the mountain. That was crazy; we forgot what we are. That's what I told myself. Those several seconds of confusion belonged to both of us—

"Bettina."

I turned from the counter with my mug in my hand. Bampas motioned me over to the breakfast table where the newspaper lay open in front of him, just like most mornings. I thought he'd frown at my short skirt hem, or ask me to zip my sweater to my throat. Instead, he tapped a finger on a photo in the paper.

"Something you'll want to see," he said, smiling slightly.

"Oh? What's that?" I was hugely curious. Was there a new gallery? An art show opening? I leaned over Bampas's shoulder to have a look.

Newspaper photos never look like the person in them, at least not at first. A few seconds blinked by before I saw handsome Brady Cullen grinning up out of the ink.

Then I remembered. "Oh. Right. He said he would be giving an interview. . . ."

"A very nice interview," Bampas said.

"I didn't think it'd be in so soon. The first game is still weeks away."

"Priming the public for a big season," Bampas said. "Your young friend appears to be quite a standout. This is an honor that they interview him over a senior player. He expects a winning season."

"Hmm . . ." I scanned the article. "I hope he gets it," I said, and I meant it. I had been wishing good things for Brady. Some of that was guilt, I am sure. After all, I knew who I was: the girl with a recently sidetracked heart.

Ever since that serious talk with Brady Cullen, he'd been on good behavior. Some of it had made me uncomfortable; the little gifts he'd brought to my locker the first few mornings afterward had felt like Band-Aids, or worse, bribes. But there had been honest, wistful looks from him followed by appreciative hugs—the kind that gathered my bones together and felt truly *given*. Sometimes Brady could do that.

Bampas shifted, making the legs of his chair squeak on the kitchen floor. "And why wouldn't he have a winning season? Your tone is not very believing," he said.

"I didn't mean to sound that way," I said. I looked at Bampas, who appeared to be waiting for more. I so rarely had his attention this way. "I think he feels an awful lot of pressure," I said.

"Well then, you'll help him," Bampas said.

"I do, Bampas, I do help—"

"His challenge is your challenge. Now, if you are up to it, you will help him."

Help him. He'd said it twice. Bampas could not have known exactly what I meant; I'd kept secrets. Nonetheless, my father's words affixed themselves to me. He was right. I should help Brady, and I did. I bolstered and encouraged. I listened to him worry out loud. I helped him with his Spanish homework. I told him he'd be great. I tacked that newspaper clipping up on the inside of my locker door along with a mighty White Tigers emblem sticker I bought at the school store. I told myself we'd gotten past another bad patch.

Back on track, I went for broke. I helped the

Not-So-Cheerleaders. They needed a few dance moves that were easy and that would make us all look good. I had at least a dozen of those up my sleeve and we put them to work. I was remembering to bring my sneakers, and I made sure that I let it drop that all my body art was *temporary*. I'd be clean and shiny for them come time for "making states." From the sounds of things, that was still months away.

I helped. So when I wanted to cut a practice, I didn't feel so bad about it. The first few times I saw Cowboy after we'd struck our new deal, things were different. His greetings were abbreviated. He crawled into and under car carcasses and I took that as a message that he had work to do. Fine by me. I had my sketchbook. We melted our ice, and by the time November came, it was easy for me to walk through his door again.

One afternoon I told the cheerleaders that I was coming down with something—mid-November has a flu season, after all—and I cut out and went to SWS Classic Auto. I figured I'd try to drag Cowboy out, get him to take me for a truck ride. Maybe he'd let me drive. He'd been doing that, starting with an empty parking lot, and then the back roads. I guess that wasn't perfectly legal; he was not an instructor. But he was old enough, and I had a permit. Momma had taken me to the DMV right after my sixteenth birthday. But she had not had much nerve for letting me behind the wheel, and

Bampas—well, forget it. He would always find a reason why I did not need to have a license. He'd say something curt, like, "Well, and do you own a car to drive?"

But Cowboy said I was a natural. He'd sit in the passenger's seat, casually splitting his attention between what I was doing behind the wheel and the view out the window. He might say, "Hold your lane" or "Full stop, Beta." Mostly, he told me I was doing fine. I thought driving was kick-ass easy.

"Cowboy? I'm here. Are you?" I called.

"Yep."

Him and his single syllables; I could tell he needed to concentrate. I stood no chance of getting him out of the shop. Oh, well.

"Is this a tailpipe?" I tapped a finger on the broad tube of chrome at the bench. "And what does it want? A scrubbing with some steel wool and degreaser?"

"Yep."

"Want me to do it?"

"If you want to."

I wrapped my braid around my neck so it wouldn't swipe the garage floor and bent down to look at Cowboy underneath the Chevy. "Hello, by the way."

"Yep."

I laughed, stood myself back up, and spread a length of shop toweling onto the workbench surface. I squeezed into rubber gloves. I always used them, figuring I'd be questioned someday by Brady or my parents if I became noticeably grease stained.

Of all the odors inside SWS Classic Auto, degreaser was my favorite. I set to work on that tailpipe. A satisfying shine began to come through the grime. I suppose I was getting a little light-headed—just a nice sensation—but I realized suddenly that Cowboy was calling me.

"Beta! You still here? I could use some help."

"Yeah!" I called out.

"Can you bring me a towel?"

I grabbed a handful of clean toweling and hurried to him. Cowboy had crept out from under the Chevy. His eyes were shut tightly and he was blindly getting to his knees. "Here, here!" I pressed the toweling into his hands, still not sure what had happened. His face and head looked wet—and kind of citrus green. Slowly, he mopped the depressions near his eyes, then the rest of his face and head.

"Can you bring me the hose? Please."

I did, and Cowboy let the water fill his cupped hands. Over and over, he rinsed his face and head. Finally, he took a length of fresh toweling from me and dried his face. He opened his eyes slowly, blinking a bit.

"Hey, are you okay? I mean, your eyes?" *Your beautiful sea-green eyes.* "Should I be reading the contents off some container, Cowboy?" I was serious.

"No, I'm fine. Shit. That was stupid. I stuck my whole head right under the radiator. The thing took a leak all over me."

I had to laugh. "You're soaked," I said. The collar of his coverall was drenched and when he zipped out of that, the neck of his shirt showed a ring of wetness too. I watched him tie the empty arms of the coverall around his waist.

"You need a dry shirt," I said.

"Yep. I've got one out in the truck."

"I'll get it for you." I started for the door.

"No, no. You already did me one big favor. And thanks for that," he said.

Cowboy headed out. I started to follow him. I stopped near the door and watched him. He stood beside his truck and peeled off the damp shirt. At first, all I saw was a tight six-pack, his ribs and smooth chest. I'd only ever guessed at what his body looked like—*nice*—and probably I should not be looking. But a wave rolled through my center—the "want you" wave. He took a second to rub his wet hair with his shirt. I watched the long muscles in his arms, his skin riding over his ribs. This was no way to get rid of a wave. . . . Then he turned and reached into the truck.

It only took a second for me to see the white marks that scarred his back. Some were like dashes, some like teardrops.

My core clenched. I took one step backward toward the shop.

It was too late. He turned, our eyes caught. He knew I'd seen the dark history written on his back. Cowboy had secrets and I wanted to know them. I also knew not to ask—not then. I turned, and I pretended to be looking up at the sign above Unit 37.

"So, hey," I said. "You've never told me what SWS stands for."

He gave me a wary look as he put an arm into the fresh shirt. "You're right, I didn't."

"Come on," I said.

Come on, or I'll ask you about the scars on your back.

"My initials," he said as he buttoned.

"I figured that much. It isn't fair. You know my name, but I don't know yours."

Cowboy slid by me into the shop. He crawled right back underneath the Chevy. I sat on a short stack of tires next to the car and leaned into a backbend until I could see him.

"Jesus, you're flexible," he said, and he almost hit his head on the undercarriage. He started back to his work. "Silas Wolcott Shepherd." He let the words out the side of his mouth.

"SWS!" I said triumphantly. Then I flipped myself off the tires.

Coming back across the playing fields, I had Silas Wolcott

Shepherd on my mind, and so were his scars. I hadn't given it much thought before but I had noticed the scar across his brow back on the water property that day, and his bottom lip had a little white line through the middle of it. But Favian had that scar too, from falling forward out of a plastic kiddie car when he was four. The other scars, the ones on Cowboy's back, didn't look like they came from a single accident. But what the hell kind of *accident* could happen over and over again and make marks like that?

"Hey, P'teen-uh!" Brady startled the hell out of me. He came jogging up. "Hey, what gives? Coach let us out early and I went by the aux gym and the girls said you left sick or something." He looked me over, head to toe. There I was with my short, leather jacket open to a brisk November wind.

"Oh, yeah. I have a scratchy throat, is all. I didn't want to jump around and yell."

"You smell funny." He pinched the shoulder of my jacket and pulled me toward him. He took a whiff. "Where did you go?" He glanced off in the direction of the industrial park. Had he watched me come through there?

"That's the other reason I cut. I had to take a key to some-one over there." I pointed my thumb over my shoulder in the direction of the park.

"Oh, yeah? What? Something for your father?"

"Yes." I lied some more. Brady was already distracted—hands inside my jacket, indecent smile on his lips. What a ridiculous excuse. My father would never give me a key to anything! But all I needed was for Brady to buy it, and I guess he did.

Thirty-one

BRADY'S PRACTICES PICKED UP IN NOVEMBER AND SO DID mine. Our busyness was probably good for us both. We had avoided major incidents, mostly because I'd become so pre-emptive about not making him mad. We were also short on time to be alone. The basketball coach kept the team late on Friday nights now. They worked their tails off, and Brady would call me at 9:30 saying he'd just gotten out of the shower and was exhausted. I believed him. I could practically hear him falling asleep on his end of the line. Just as well, because Bampas said starting a date after 9:00 p.m. was out of the question.

Then one Friday night, Big Bonnie and some of the art

room kids were going to a silent movie mini-fest at the art cinema and she asked me to go. They were planning to go in costume just for fun.

"I'm wearing false eyelashes and a pillbox hat," she laughed. "So if you have anything vintage-y, wear that."

I dug out a pair of black lace gloves I'd found at the Goodwill store back in my days of running and shopping with Julia. But when I asked Bampas if he or Momma could take me downtown, he looked at me like I had three heads.

"No," he said. He pulled his chin in as if to say, *Why would I do that?* I pushed. I repeated the plan to him. He ignored me. Momma had an ear on the whole exchange.

"Why can't she go, Dinos?" she asked sweetly. "I can take her—"

"I told the girl no, Loreena," Bampas said firmly. Sometimes he had an ugly way with Momma. Was that new, or was I just noticing it lately? "Bettina, if your boyfriend is not available, you should stay home. It won't kill you. Think of him," he said. "This kind of thing hurts a boy's feelings if you go out when he cannot be with you." That was a little freaky even for Bampas—and it was as screwed up as it was true.

"But Bampas, it's just the art cinema—"

"Are you trying to order yourself up a grounding?" He put his attention back on his reader. *"Fili antio,"* he added.

"Or do you mean *siopi*?" I said. What was the difference? Kiss it goodbye or shut up.

"Take your pick," he said last-straw slowly, and he didn't even look at me.

Momma and I split a look. I went back to my bedroom and landed on my bed, face in my pillow. I let out a yell. Bampas was nuts, I thought. *Nuts!* I could hardly have had a more innocent plan than to visit the art cinema with Bonnie Swenson. But in my suck-it-up way, I backed off. I couldn't risk losing my afternoons at the school . . . or the industrial park.

The jock gatherings in the lobby by the White Tiger mosaic were still happening. I went to most of them with Brady, though I'd given up baking. One afternoon, as we made our way there, my hand tucked into his elbow, I heard music—great music.

"Oooh . . ." I looked up at Brady as we walked. "Do you hear that?"

"Yeah . . ." he said. He rattled an open snack bag full of potato chips in one hand. "Sounds like somebody invaded our space." He tilted his head up and sprinkled his mouth full of chips.

"Aw . . . but it sounds like a party!" I gave his hand a squeeze. He forced a smile with a full cheek as I pulled him along.

Turns out it was Tony Colletti on his saxophone along

with half a dozen other musicians. They were rocking that lobby. An open instrument case had a sign taped to it: HELP US GET TO STATES!

Man, *everybody* was trying to get to states.

Brady didn't blow at the sight of Tony. Maybe he just didn't see who it was. He had his face in that bag of chips, after all. He circled up with his friends, while I turned outward to watch the band.

They were good. I picked up the beat from the girl on the snare drum, started to click my fingers next to my thigh. That music found its way to my bones. I put some hip into it, still dancing in place. Across the way, I saw Emmy doing the same. She gave me a nod. I let go of Brady. Tony Colletti leaned forward into his sax. He opened his eyes wide to engage the crowd—so adorable! A cheer went up.

Emmy pointed at me with both hands as if to say, *You're on! Let's dance.* I sent her a body roll. She sent it back. Some cheerleaders joined in calling, "Oh yeah!" Soon, a dozen dancers were on the floor. Whistles squealed up from the crowd. People clapped to the music. A couple of teachers dance-bombed their way through the lobby to loud cheers. I'd never seen my school like that. I twirled, floated my hands over my head, and shimmied down. I was breaking a sweat, having a blast.

But before that number was done, Brady broke out of his

circle to collect me, and by that I mean he walked around the front of me, took hold of the edge of my jacket and turned me away from the band. He leaned into me. "Cut it out," he whispered through potato chip–breath. "That dancing shit is embarrassing. You make weird-ass faces." He made a long, slurring *S* sound at me.

"Oh. I guess everyone has a dance face," I said. Before we left the lobby, I put a few bucks into the instrument case and joined in the applause for the band as they tuned up for another number. Brady shook his head at me.

Thirty-two

THE WEEK BEFORE THE FIRST SCRIMMAGE, THE COACH gave the White Tigers the night off and, of all the crazy things, I felt my heart sink. Brady had the car and he took me up to one of the state college branch campuses about an hour from home. A former Tiger teammate of his was a student there—Spooner, the guy I'd met once or twice back when Brady and I were brand-new. He'd teased me about the way I dressed but I always thought he'd been warmer to me than anyone else. We met Spooner on campus, then drove out to an old farmhouse from there. It was just a few turns from campus, and it felt like the middle of nowhere.

All the people at the party were older, and not just

college-older either. They were adults, but not like the ones I knew. The property was full of motorcycles and farm animals. The few kids our age, well, they were probably crashers like us. But nobody cared, and nobody seemed worried about cops or any sort of trouble. They drank their beer and smoked their dope. A big guy with long hair and a bushy beard pumped a couple of beers out of a keg for us the second we walked onto the porch. I asked him for just half and he nodded and smiled when he handed it to me. The place was run-down, old, and beautiful. Inside, the walls were one big collage—a wallpaper-stripping project—that counted off the decades. A woodstove burned. Music played.

I sipped my beer and took it all in while Brady and Spooner shared odds on how their seasons would go. Eventually, Spooner drifted into another room. Brady nuzzled me and motioned for me to follow him up a sagging stairway. We found an empty bedroom where I lay underneath Brady, worrying just a little about fleas. We left most of our clothes on in case we had to get out in a hurry. But in that warm and drafty, music-filled house I relaxed swept up in a surreal feeling. I gripped Brady's solid body, pressed the bridge of my nose into his shoulder, and let out a throaty release.

"Jesus," he whispered in my ear, and we both laughed.

Afterward, we sat sipping our beers. I started to tell him about a poster design I'd been working on in art class. He

217

mocked me in a singsong: "Bettina's an art fairy."

"Fairies are awesome," I said. "Wouldn't you love a set of wings?"

"Only if they get me up to the hoop," he said. He rolled off the creaky bed and pulled his pants up without closing them. "I gotta take a piss."

Twenty minutes is one long pee. I straightened my clothes and the bedcovers and wandered out into the hall with the little bit of beer left in my cup. I passed the open bathroom door. No Brady. I started down the stairs. There he was, face-to-face with a girl. He gave her a lively grin. That was his "just-met-you" smile, I thought. Then damned if he didn't give that girl a "just-met-you" kiss. Well, holy shit! I didn't even know he had one of those. Then he saw me. He came quickly, met me at the bottom of the stairs, and hustled me into the next room.

"That chick, she was just being friendly," he told me. He leaned down and kissed me on my neck. A little stone dropped through my throat to my gut. *He does cheat*, I thought. Wow. How long? Maybe he doesn't do *everything* but he does what I just saw; he samples other girls. I thought about the girls in our school—there was that sophomore with big doe eyes—Courtney something. She had baked him brownies . . . and what about the Not-So-Cheerleaders? I wondered about all of it. But what amazed me most of all was that I wasn't

218

devastated, not mad. I actually felt sort of quiet inside.

Looking around that party, I wasn't sure what to want—except Cowboy. I could imagine him walking in—almost *expected* him to come around a corner. But that would *not* be good, not with Brady Cullen here. There was still great music playing and people were dancing. I liked the old farmhouse with its peeling paper walls.

"You want another beer?" Brady asked, giving me a one-armed hug. He was caught and he was nervous. I twisted the corner of my mouth at him. I showed him my cup. I still had a few swallows of beer left. We hung together for a while. He stood next to me, shifting his weight and craning his neck like he was late for an appointment. "I'm gonna go get you that refill," he insisted, and he left me alone again.

I dodged eye contact with a guy for a while. He had a head full of beautiful dreadlocks and a smile made of large, perfect teeth—not unlike mine, I thought. He crossed the room and greeted me. He seemed sober and he was polite.

"Dance?" he offered.

"Thanks," I said, "but I'm here with someone."

"I don't see *someone*." The guy looked all around us, and I had to smile.

"Really. Thanks anyway," I said.

"My loss." He nodded but he did not leave. He leaned against the same wall as me, his hand dangling very close to mine. I didn't own the wall. He could stand there if he felt like it. I drained my beer and closed my eyes. The music was good, the words and rhythm hot and slow. The singer crooned about love and hunger. Being the hungriest girl in the room, I was moved, and I began to move, just rocking, just a little. Music did that to me. Sometimes it was hard not to dance. My elbow brushed a loose curl of wallpaper. I felt the guy's fingertips, lightly under mine.

"It's just a dance," he said.

Yeah. It's just a dance.

I dropped my empty cup and let him lead me away from the wall.

I kept my eyes closed and stayed pretty much in one spot. I wasn't dancing *with* him—not really. In fact, he let go of my hands after he got me out to the floor. I suppose he was still near. I rolled with the music, danced myself in the swirls of humid, yeast-scented air. When the music faded away, I was sorry—same as when morning ends a good Saturday sleep.

I opened my eyes and saw Brady. And boy, was he pissed.

He strode over, wrapped a hand around my elbow, then closed tightly on it. In my ear, he said, "What are you doing? Huh?"

I felt dazed, slow. Beyond Brady, I could see the

dreadlocked guy watching me. He grinned and gave me a thumbs-up.

"You trying to get back at me? For that kiss? Huh, P'teen-uh?"

"No, no . . ." I almost blurted that I didn't care about that. Brady pulled me out of the room, back past the keg and into the yard where the scent of wood smoke hung in the cold, cloudy air.

"No more dancing, Goddamn it!" Brady punched his fist into his hand. "Why do you do that? You know I don't like it! Those guys in there wanted to jump you!"

"Oh, bull!" I said. I tried not to shout. This wasn't our peace to disturb. "It wasn't like that," I insisted.

"Everybody was watching you!" Brady spread his arms, palms up. "And *you* put on a show!"

"Brady! You make it sound like I was standing on a table, dropping my clothes. I wasn't the only one dancing. . . ."

"Listen," he said, putting his finger in my face, "you're smarter than me at school stuff, okay? But I'm smarter at this stuff."

I took a breath, trying to calm the both of us. "Hey, maybe you should go say goodbye to Spooner," I said. "We'll take this somewhere else, huh?"

"Are you hearing me? I'm telling you, *I know guys*."

"Brady. Take me home," I said. I turned toward the yard.

"P'teen-uh!" Brady reached for me. I jerked away. I stormed off toward the car, and Brady stormed after me, closing the gap with each step.

"I will, I will take you home and then I'll go out by myself and—"

My toe hit something with a thud. I fell forward. *Bam!* Pain shot through my cheek just below my eye. I was on the ground between two cars.

The dreadlocked dancing guy must have followed us because he was suddenly there, saying, "Oh, no! She went right over that landscape tie. I think she hit something on the way down." He was asking was I hurt and saying he'd get help. More people surrounded us. Brady was downplaying, telling everyone I was fine while he tried to yank me to my feet. Something warm and wet was running down my cheek.

"I think I hit the door handle," I mumbled. But I'm not sure anyone understood.

Spooner arrived and I think he was the one who walked Brady away from me. I heard him talking in a low voice. "Cullen, man. What is this fighting-with-your-girlfriend shit? This is *not* cool." Then he called, "Hey, is she really all right?"

My God, it was almost worth landing my face on that car just to hear someone take Brady to task—even just a little bit.

A woman wearing a flowy tunic brought ice. She

examined the cut under my eye, while someone else lit my face with a phone. I kept apologizing to them. My cheek started to numb out. "Hey, honey, I'm a nurse," she said. "I really think this needs a few stitches." Her voice was soft and sweet. I wilted from the inside out. I wished she would take me inside, sit me near that wood fire. Surely, she could knock me out with some herbs and sew me up herself.

Brady finally took me to the hospital; the people at the party insisted on it. They even helped me make a call to Bampas before we left. He arrived at the hospital shortly after I was triaged. He made sure that a plastic surgeon—the very best—was called. Then my father handed Brady Cullen a twenty and sent him home saying, "Thank you for taking care of my daughter."

Brady had lied smoothly—made up something about being at the branch campus for a pep rally. I didn't hear his version of how I had smacked my eye. We were lucky no one had Breathalyzed either of us, and lucky we smelled more like wood smoke than pot.

The plastic surgeon was a businesslike woman. I lay still while she stitched me. My father watched at first, but then settled into a corner of the room with his phone. I let a slow, steadying breath through my lips as I felt the tug of each suture. The surgeon said that I was a very good patient.

Thirty-three

At first, Cowboy seemed to be looking through me. Couldn't he see the bandaging, my hellacious black eye? He blinked, then strode over and took my chin in his hand. His touch took my breath. He tilted my face for a little more light. Then he shuddered—I felt it through his hand. He swore, and asked, "Did *he* do this?"

"No," I said, and I ducked out.

"Goddamn it, Beta!"

"No!" I repeated. "I fell. In the dark. I was mad. I was stomping. It was dumb."

"But he was there?"

"Yes."

"What's under the bandage?"

"A few stitches. But they did a real nice job. I'll just look real rugged until the color fades." I smiled a little.

Cowboy shook his head. "That's the trouble with you, Beta; you think you're tough." He turned and ducked under the hood of the Chevy like he was going to work on the engine.

Tough. That echoed. Regina Colletti had told me I was "tough" the last time I'd seen her. She had remembered me taking a digger in her garden when I was small. "A rambunctious dog took you out—topsy-turvy, you went off the steps," she had recalled. "Bloody legs, a knock on the chin—oh, my! But you didn't cry. I couldn't believe it," she'd said.

I looked at Cowboy now. He was not working on the engine. He was leaning on the car with his hands for support, his arms straight, his back rounded. It was a ruminating sort of pose, and I'd seen him do it before. "Cowboy," I said. "Tell me what happened to you."

I listened to him exhale.

"How did you get the scars?" I asked. "The ones on your back."

He let out an irritated huff. "I *know* the scars you're talking about."

I waited. He turned around, sat back against the car. He looked through me, like he was putting himself somewhere

where he could talk about it.

"My family," he spoke slowly, "was not very . . . *healthy.* Hmm. Actually, my dad is a sweetheart. My ma had problems."

"Problems?"

"Anger," he said.

"So *she* did that? She hurt you?"

"Yes."

"Oh, God. Cowboy!" I had not expected to hear that. I took a step toward him but the look in his eyes seemed to push me back. "And that's why the cops know you. . . ." I began to sort it out. "You said you took responsibility. But you didn't do wrong."

"There was an incident. Not the first one. She was already in trouble. I just protected her."

"But why? And you still live with her? I don't get it."

"My dad moved out, left her because of the things she did. We were all nearly grown by then. My brothers cut her off too. Ma had nobody."

"Well, yeah! For God's sake! Why don't you leave, too?"

He locked gray-green eyes on me. "Why don't *you*?" he said.

"Leave what? You mean Brady? That's completely different! Come on!" I threw my arms open. "It's your mother. You're a grown-up. You can leave."

"It's not that easy. There's something about being smacked around as a kid that makes it hard to move on."

"No. You're saying that because someone else said it. That's like . . . I don't know . . . it's what the pamphlet says."

He didn't even blink. The next silent seconds seemed to grind into both of us. My face felt hot. He looked like stone.

"Get out of here, Beta," he said.

I opened my mouth but he didn't let me speak.

"Get out," he said again.

I shouldered my pack and split.

I burned all the way back to school. I was mad at Cowboy. But by the time I reached the building, my heart ached for him. I felt like I'd said all the wrong things. I hid my face in my open locker and fought back tears. I touched my bruised cheek. *Don't get the bandage wet,* I remembered. I sucked it up. There was something awful and heavy settling over me— something hard to name, and it swam in my head for hours. Later, I knew, though I could barely acknowledge it; I felt a loss of respect for Cowboy. I was mad because someone had hurt him. And I was mad because he had stayed with the person who had done it.

Thirty-four

I'D FINISHED ICING MY FAT EYE. MY MOTHER INSISTED THAT I do it every night that week even though I told her it wouldn't help anymore. I was already dressed for bed and had said good night to Momma and Bampas when I heard a tap at my bedroom window. I thought it must be Brady, but he'd never done that before. I waited. Then I heard the voice. "Beta!" There was only one person in the world who called me that. I whipped the curtains aside.

Cowboy stepped back as I pushed the window open. "You scared me," I pretended to hiss, but I was glad at the sight of him. "What are you doing here?"

"Can you come out?" he whispered. "Let's talk."

"I'm in my nightgown," I said, but I guess both of us knew I'd go anyway—crazy and dangerous as it was. I could be caught. So could he. Still, I stepped into loose boots and grabbed the throw blanket off my bed. I gathered the skirt of my gown in one hand and stepped out through the window. The moonlight defined the way as I followed Cowboy back to the stand of pines where the rabbit cages were.

"How's this?" Cowboy tapped his own cheekbone to ask about mine.

"I'm taking care of it." I didn't want to talk about my black eye. "How did you know where to find me?"

"Your brothers told me. And so did you."

I opened my eyes wide. "What?"

"On ice-cream night, back in September. Remember? You were down by the river and you all pointed to the path."

"And you guessed at my room?"

"I figured it out." He shrugged. He glanced at the horse-shoe of rabbit hutches. "Nice gophers."

I smiled and pulled the blanket closer around me. Nobody else really knew about the rabbits, but it seemed right to be standing there with Cowboy.

"Not what I expected," he said, looking around him.

"The rabbits?"

"Not just that. Your house looks shut down from the front. From back here, it's almost . . . exposed. Well, once you come

229

through the garden. And yeah, sorry for creeping around." I gave him a smirk and a nod. He lifted his chin at me. "I won't make it a habit. I just felt like I had to find you. . . ."

"It's a weird house," I admitted. "The front is the back and the back is the front depending what road you're on."

"Right," he said. A second ticked by and he asked, "So, why rabbits?"

"Fertilizer." I shrugged.

"Guess that's working." Cowboy looked back toward the house where my father's plantings surrounded the pool and terrace. I was suddenly uncomfortable with the moon-lit beauty of the place. Nothing was blooming, but even in November the landscaping showed good bones. I cleared my throat.

"When I was little I wanted a dog. But I have rabbits because that's what my father said I could have—secondhand Easter bunnies. We find them in the paper. We call it our 'rabbit habit,'" I added.

"Well, you'd have to," Cowboy said. "You have a lot of the black-and-white ones," he noted.

"Yes, four of them," I said. "I did that."

"What do you mean?"

"We got two Dutches, one male, one female, when I was about twelve. My father had told me in no uncertain terms,

230

'Bettina, no visits between the two.'" I imitated Bampas. "So, knowing the possibilities . . ." Cowboy muffled a gulp. I hid a smile as best I could. "Yeah . . . I put them together first chance I got."

"Beta!"

"Twenty-eight days later, two Dutches turn into six Dutches. Little-bitty babies." I showed him with my fingers. "The parents are gone now and these guys are even getting a little old," I said. "But this big guy is our baby." I opened one cage and brought out the Giant Flemish buck and cradled him. His guard hairs glowed silvery white over his orange coat. "I love the shape of them," I said. "They're my favorite animals."

"What about horses?"

"Because all little girls love horses?" I shook my head no. "I'm afraid of horses."

"Not you. You're not afraid of anything." Cowboy set his fingers into the fur of the Flemish.

"Don't pat against the growth," I said. "He won't like that." I watched Cowboy correct. "So, you said that you wanted to talk."

"I'm sorry I kicked you out of the garage today. I don't talk about . . ." He didn't finish the sentence. "But you, you're different. I was an ass. I'm sorry."

"I shouldn't have pried."

He looked up at the night sky. "It's okay. You can pry," he said.

"Can I? Okay, then tell me something about your brothers," I said, and Cowboy let out a laugh.

"Well, one older, one younger. Michael and . . ."

"What's Michael's middle name?" I interrupted. "What goes with Silas Wolcott Shepherd?"

"Newlin. Michael Newlin. And the other one is Lincoln Hanley."

"Nice names," I said. "Huh, we both have two brothers."

"Yeah, I saw yours again tonight while I was skulking. Their curtains are open and they're looking at dirty pics on a tablet," he said.

"Way to go, boys!" I had to laugh. "I mean dirty pics are demoralizing. But the boys snuck that tablet away from my father. They are going to survive this household fine," I said. Cowboy smiled and we both fell silent for a moment. "So, I don't get it," I said. "How does someone make beautiful kids, give them beautiful names . . . and then one day start hurting them?"

"You've got a funny mind, Beta."

"No, I'm serious. I want to know." I eased the Flemish buck back into his hutch and gave him a few strokes before I latched the door. Cowboy held a cigarette between his lips and struck a match.

"Families," he mumbled. "Shit happens."

"That's not a reason to—"

"To beat your kids? It was for my ma."

I remembered Regina Colletti's story, what her father did to her. It was horrible, but different from what Cowboy's mother did to him. Cowboy shook out the match. His cigarette was still unlit and I watched him try again.

"Give it to me," I said.

"You're too young to smoke."

"Are you ever going to stop saying that to me? Anyone with lungs is old enough to smoke. Besides, I was just going to light it for you. I really only smoke when I *want* to feel bad," I said.

"Hmm . . . and I only smoke when I *do* feel bad. Like when I'm wrong—or when someone else is. This time," he said, giving me a nod, "I was wrong."

"Forgiven," I said. "Maybe we can both cut that out for good someday." I gestured at the cigarette, which now glowed at its tip. Then I asked him, "What set your mother off? What did you do?"

"Name it, I probably did it," he said coolly. "School stuff." He shook his head. "That was always tough. Late for supper, forgot to pick up the mail, mowed the friggin' lawn crooked. Everything pissed her off. *Everything.*" He knocked ashes

233

from the cigarette onto the ground at his feet. "Michael and Lincoln didn't catch as much of it. But I wasn't good at much except cars. I don't think she liked having a grease monkey for a son. She could go off like a gun, and grab a stick or a strap—" I let out a gasp and my hands went weak.

"What did you do?" I asked.

"When I was a kid, I protected my head until she was done," he said.

I could see him, a boy like Favian or Avel, ducking—it was unbearable. I brought my blanket up over my nose and wiped my eyes.

"Come on, Beta. No crying."

"No, no, I don't cry," I said. "But I just can't imagine it. Would you ever do that to your kids?"

"I'm not having kids."

"You don't know that."

"Yeah, I do," he said.

"That's giving up."

"I know whether or not I want kids."

"God! Why do you have to do that?" My tears were gone. "You tell me something important and then you cut me off as soon as I start to react. And I'm not even talking about *the stuff we never talk about*. I'm not—I'm not a stone, Cowboy."

He drew hard on the cigarette and nodded. "Good for you, Beta."

234

"Oh, screw off! That's condescending! I count on you *not* to do that to me."

"Not condescending. Serious," he said. "There is nothing better for me than seeing you stand up for you." He smiled at me. My heart turned to sauce.

"You make me really sad," I said, and I accidentally let out a little cry. "You don't know how much I wish we could both just . . . feel better." I gulped and ducked back into the blanket. I wanted to hold him, wanted him to hold me. "Are you seeing anyone? I mean do you have a girlfriend? Somebody you haven't told me about? Like, something physical—" I swallowed. He squinted at me—like I'd crossed a line.

"Physical? What? You want to know if I'm getting laid? God, there's a question I couldn't bear to ask you," he said.

I couldn't look at him. I glanced into the rabbit hutch where the Flemish had disappeared into his box for warmth. "I was talking about . . . I don't know . . . comfort, I guess."

"I've been there," he said. "It's not that comforting, Beta. You know that. Are you really happy with your dirtbag boyfriend? I mean, really?"

"*Happy* might not be the word," I conceded.

"But still, you choose him."

"I—I don't *have* choices," I said. My snappishness surprised me. "I let Brady in months ago. He was different then. Now, he's the boy my father lets me out of the house with.

I've tried. Truth is, I'm not very good to Brady—not any-more." I huffed a not-funny laugh. "I use him. I don't want to be home and alone all the time. So there. Now you know how horrible I am," I said, and I meant it.

"I don't think you're horrible." His singsong was unusual.

"He cares more than I do. . . ."

"Yeah, don't let that be your glue," Cowboy said.

"What I said about you seeing someone, I wasn't trying to be icky. I just meant that you have such a good heart—" My voice cracked, and I held on for a second. "And I—I want good things for you. That's all."

"You're sweet, Beta. But don't waste that on me. I'm fine," he said. "And you should go back in." He gestured toward the house. "I don't want to get you grounded."

"You go first," I said.

He did. I watched him disappearing down the swath until I couldn't see him anymore. I pictured his truck parked on River Road. I wanted to run down there in my blanket, catch up to Cowboy and just drive far, far away with him.

Thirty-five

THE MIGHTY WHITE TIGERS WERE GETTING READY FOR their first scrimmage. It was planned for just after Thanksgiving recess. The days before we went on that break felt like a lousy stretch when all I did was placate other people.

Brady was a wicked combo of pumped up and nervous. He'd been fretting over his grades; players had to have C's or better or they'd be benched. He'd been chewing his callused knuckles raw. I pleaded with him to leave them alone. He'd come to me for dabs of Momma's olive oil and rosemary.

Since he was so on edge all the time, I tried to be a sport about his latest trick: he kept dumping my books out of my arms in the middle of the hall. Then he'd bring out Mr.

Adorable to joke and apologize and pick them up for me, only to knock them away again. He did it more than once a day. It got so old that I just stood there and waited—looking like a bitch to everyone else, I am sure—while he handed me back my books.

One day he made me a public offer. "Here, baby, here. Take a shot. You dump mine." He offered me the armful.

"No," I said. "Because that's not nice."

"Ooo . . . temperamental . . ."

Ass hat. I left him and went to my class.

Meanwhile, Momma and Bampas were having a hard time getting their heads around my upcoming game schedule, which was sure to crash into our dinnertimes.

"We will reconsider this next year, Bettina. There'll be no signing up behind our backs again," Bampas told me. He looked up from reading the mail to wag a finger at me. "This has been most inconvenient."

Go ahead. Make me quit.

"Shall we all go to the game?" Momma asked.

I watched my father turn on his man-shoes so that both toes pointed at Momma. "And why?" he asked. "To add to our chaos, Loreena?"

"Well, the boys might like to see the game," Momma said. Her tone was wimpy, but boy, she had a plan. "And I would like to see Bettina cheer," she added.

Bampas peered over his glasses at her. "With the long days I put in, I want to be home at my quiet house come nighttime."

"It's not that much of a show, Momma," I said. "Not like dance recitals. And if you want, I will try to get a ride home—"

"No," Bampas said. It was his half-syllable no. Close to his *siopi*, but with less finality. "You will come home in my car. I will wait in the circle."

"Pickup is in the back lot on game nights. The visiting team's bus parks in the circle," I told him.

"More inconvenience . . ." he muttered.

Yeah, Bampas, but only for you.

Then there were the Not-So-Cheerleaders. They were all aflutter and had their eyes on my eye—my black eye—and perhaps it was their prayers that helped turn it from blue-purple to yellow-brown just in time for that first preseason game.

"I'm so glad that's getting better," one of the girls told me. "Does it hurt?"

"Not anymore," I said. I had wanted no conversation about it. No shudders, no glances.

"It must have been awful. What did you do? I heard you stepped off a log or something?"

"I just tripped," I said. I pretended to walk through a cheer, arms pumping.

239

"One of my cousins, man, she has the hardest time," one of the girls piped. "She's always getting hurt. We feel sorry for her. She's sort of a *klutz*!"

"Yeah, me too," I said. Then I excused myself to go into the bathroom and into a stall where I could ball my fists and silently scream at myself. *What are you saying? You are* not *a klutz! You have* never *been a klutz!*

Our barely there faculty advisor came to hand out crisp new cheerleading uniforms—white knit dresses with cap sleeves and "tiger-blue" trim, and matching compression trunks. I hated them. The look was so wholesome I felt like a walking milk carton. While the other girls discussed how best to bleach out future spots or stains, I imagined the dresses benefiting from a Jackson Pollock makeover—drizzles of blue and splatters of gray, our school colors.

Worst, worst, worst of all was the news that we had to wear them to school on game days. This was decided by a show of hands—eleven to one. Not surprising, I guess. I shrugged off the decision while Emmy gave me a silent, apologetic shrug.

Tiger spirit. I pulled myself into the dress the morning of the first scrimmage. I stood at my bathroom mirror and sighed. *Really? I have to walk around in this all day? How embarrassing.* I might have sooner gone to class in an old dance costume. Still, I scrubbed the final traces of a skull and bones tat off my thigh. I dotted cover stick on my healing eye and blended it.

It was not a coffee morning. No way was I going into SWS Auto wearing that getup. At school, I smiled genuinely when I saw Brady Cullen. He was buttoned up and wearing a tie as were his teammates. He was in good-behavior mode, required to act like a gentleman for game day, and I felt myself relaxing as we stood beside my locker.

"You girls look hot," he said with a grin. He reached down to my thigh and drew his finger just under the hem of one leg of my compression shorts.

"You're kidding, right?" I started to close my locker and he stopped me.

"You gotta lose the jean jacket."

"The uniform has short sleeves and I'm cold," I said. Partial truth. Brady shook his head at me. But he didn't dump my books.

All day long I wondered how the first game would go. I tried to picture myself out on the gym floor, doing the cheer thing. But I found I couldn't bear that image so I spent the rest of the day trying to put it out of my head.

"You look cute," Big Bonnie said. We were standing at the paper cutter together after last bell. Mr. Terrazzi needed a three-inch border for a display case. I was measuring; Bonnie was cutting.

"Eh," I replied. "White. It's all I can do to keep it clean, especially in here. And I can't think when I last wore sneakers for an entire day. I miss my boots. I think they hold me to the floor," I said.

Bonnie threw her head back, laughing. "Well, maybe it's not *your* look. But you're pulling it off anyway—"

"Hey! Hey, P'teenuh!" I looked up. Brady was leaning in at the door, jaw in the air. He swung one arm in a come-here motion. Not in the best mood, I could tell. "We're supposed to be down at the tiger," he said. His hard edge softened some when he saw that Bonnie was looking at him. Then he brought the back of his hand up to his mouth. He was biting his knuckles again.

"Be right back," I told Bonnie.

"I'll keep cutting," she said.

I shuffle-jogged toward Brady, my ridiculous cheer sneakers squeaking along the floors. "Hey, want some of that oil?" I asked. I opened my locker, uncapped my little bottle and tapped out a few drops of oil onto his cracked skin. He massaged it in with his own thumb, hissing and cussing about the sting.

He took a breath. "Okay, okay. Come on, let's go. We're friggin' late."

"I've got more paper strips to measure," I told him. I pointed my thumb toward the art room. "You go. And I'll be

242

right behind you." I reached into my locker to put the oil back on the shelf.

"Jesus, P'teen-uh! What the hell?" Brady swore. He slammed his palm on the locker next to mine. I jumped. "What the effin' hell!" He snarled.

His hand came up again. I flinched. He grabbed my braid and yanked it down—*hard*. He pushed me forward into my open locker. My fingers found the shelf to hold on to. Before I could get steady, my locker door bounced off me and crashed back. I stood clinging to that thin metal shelf.

In the quiet, I lowered my head and cupped one hand on the back of my neck. I tilted my head—carefully. Looking underneath my own elbow I saw the back of Brady striding away down the empty hallway. I let my head hang.

On the floor at my feet, a small, golden-green puddle of oil spread, all studded with shards of glass. It was the end of the day and the custodians would be coming around. I needed to clean that up. I felt shaky. My scalp burned and my neck felt strained—and something else hurt too. My hip, or was it sort of one side of my butt? And my shoulder? Or everything? I took a few seconds to breathe.

As soon as I felt like I could move, I scuffed into the art room for some paper towels. "I just broke a bottle in the hall," I told Bonnie, and she grabbed a can of cleanser. We blotted and scrubbed. I kept letting my head hang, trying to release tension and convince myself that my neck was okay.

Mid cleanup, Bonnie asked me, "Bettina, are you all right? You seem sort of . . . upset." It was clear she had not heard any commotion in the hall. For all I knew there had not been much to hear.

"I'm okay," I said. I stole a look at the locker next to mine. There was a new dent in the metal and when I opened my own locker door against it, the handle fit the mark. Brady had really whacked mine back off its hinges. "Come on, Bonnie," I said. "Let's go finish that job." I pushed my locker door to the closed position but it wouldn't go. Bonnie watched me pressure it into place with my whole body.

"Oh, wow." Bonnie cocked her head at my locker door. "You're warped."

"Yeah," I said. Then I lied, "It's been like that all year."

Thirty-six

I DIDN'T GET MUCH TIME WITH EVERYONE DOWN AT THE
White Tiger and I was fine with that. My parents were onto
the fact that, on game nights, there were no after-school practices, and therefore, no reason for me to be anywhere but
home. Momma picked me up after fetching Favian and Avel.
I moved stiffly as we rushed dinner onto the table, though
nobody noticed, and Bampas dropped me back to the school
before the game.

I could see evidence of electricity in the air. I truly wished
I could feel it. Even Big Bonnie was into it; she had covered a
giant hoop in crepe paper. When the announcer called for the
mighty White Tigers, the team burst through it. I watched

Brady circle out to the floor for warm-ups. I thought he might look for me, but he was all about the game. I watched the team do drills. I rolled my shoulders, I checked my neck.

As for the cheerleading, I jogged out to the center of the court when that first time-out came. I felt like a total ditz. Meanwhile, the space between my neck and my shoulder blades started cramping up. But that was secondary to the heat I felt in my face when I turned around in my position and saw the sea of Tiger fans filling out the bleachers. *People are going to* see *me do this cheerleading stuff,* I thought. *Why did I do this? Can't someone pull the fire alarm and get us all out of here?*

I began with the Not-So-Cheerleaders, my own lips barely moving. We sang out:

> *We are the Tigers,*
> *Mighty, mighty Tigers!*—

I felt a twinge in my neck when we tossed Emmy nine feet in the air. I felt it again just watching for her to come back down on my forearms. *Ugh.* I should not be catching a person—a person who was relying on me to be sturdy and accurate. I was aching. It was terrifying. But Emmy grinned as we leveraged her up to her own two feet. Success.

And we're outta here . . . thank God.

I got through the rest of the cheers, but barely. I wanted to get down on my back and pull my knees into my chest—fix my spine. Take some pressure off my neck. Sometime after the second half got underway, I saw Momma and my brothers standing against the wall of the gym. That was a surprise. Favian and Avel banged their hands together, point after point. The mighty White Tigers *trounced* their visitors, 68 to 41. Brady Cullen had a very good game.

It emerged that there was a postgame pizza-eating event, cheerleaders included. The booster club set that up in the cafeteria. All I wanted was three ibuprofens and a hot compress. I was pretty sure the boosters weren't catering to me. It was Momma who nodded at me to go join the others. If I didn't go, she'd wonder what was wrong and, of course, Brady was waiting for me. He was the high scorer. Twenty-eight points' worth of success drew his mouth up at both corners. He took a big hop toward me when I entered the cafeteria. He leaned down and put his arms around me. I stiffened.

"Was that crazy-great or what?" he asked me. "Did you see that? Twenty-eight points. That's my highest game ever."

"Congrats," I said.

"Hey, come here a minute." He took my hand and led me out to the quiet of the back corridor. Brady wiped his face with his hands. He sat back against the glass-block wall. "Phew," he said. "I'm so friggin' glad to have that game behind me. You have no idea. . . ."

"You did great," I said again.

"P'teenuh . . ." I looked at Brady Cullen. First, he tried to charm me with a smile and wide, playful eyes. But then he began tucking his chin. A second later, his eyes were all pinked up. "I'm sorry," he gulped. "Sorry about before."

"Yeah, I don't want to talk about that here," I told him.

A pair of custodians came into the hall. Now we really couldn't talk. Brady bit his knuckles. The workers collected their mops and rolling buckets and headed away.

"This game had me so stressed," he whispered.

"I know it did," I said. I tried to sound understanding. But it was a reply I might have given to a stranger. How could that be? All his familiar features were right there in front of me. But my sense of him was confused. So much of the boy I had been so taken with months ago was gone. I didn't want to talk to this Brady. I wanted to go home.

"Did you see me spell out your name on those three foul shots? The seven bounces? Did you tell your girlfriends I do that for you?"

I shrugged. "I don't tell them much of anything," I said, and I watched him wilt.

"Come on. Don't be mad. Don't be like that—"

"I have to go." I pointed a finger over my shoulder. "My mother is here to get me. My brothers are with her. You know how my father is. We need to go home."

248

"Wait—wait . . ." he stammered, then stopped. He looked helpless.

"Congrats again," I told him. "Really. The team looked awesome." I slid away to find Momma and the boys.

At home, Momma came into my room and perched on my bed. "Did you have a good time doing the cheers?" she asked.

I waited. "Did you think I looked like I had a good time?" I asked, no sarcasm.

"That's why I'm asking," she said softly.

The truth about Brady Cullen was right there like a welling bee sting on the tip of my tongue. But I couldn't bear to speak about it and it wasn't what Momma had asked.

"Bettina?"

"No," I whispered. "Momma, I hated cheering. I did fine, but it doesn't feel right. I'm horrible for saying so but it feels like a comedown from my dancing, Momma. I was embarrassed calling out those lame chants. And this dress feels like it belongs on anyone but me." I bit my lip. "And next week I have to do it again." A flood of tears got away from me. I scrambled to collect them before Momma could see. But I knew it was too late. "I know, I know," I said. "I can't be crying just because I am a cheerleader. . . ."

"I didn't say that," Momma said. She reached and covered my hand with hers. Why was she being so sweet about this?

I sniffed and I cleared my throat. "I'm okay," I said. I waved my hands to erase the air around me. "I am." I absently pulled up on the neck of the cheer dress and wiped my eyes on it. "Oh! Now I have mascara on it. What if this stains? Oh, hell! Oh, sorry, Momma." I did not usually swear even mildly in front of her.

"Bettina . . ." My mother leaned toward me. She set both hands on my shoulders. "It's only makeup. It comes off your eyes easily, it will come right out of the dress."

"Even a white dress?"

"Of course."

"Okay," I said. I sucked it up with all I had left in me. "I thought it was nice that you came to the game," I said. "That *awful* game," I added, and a laugh escaped through my quivering lips. Momma laughed too. She went into my bathroom and started a shower for me.

"Nice and warm." She shook water from her hand. "Come on," she said, switching places with me. "Hand me out the dress, and I'll put it to soak."

"Okay. Thank you. And Momma, don't say anything to Bampas. Please. I'm just PMS-ing or something. I don't even know why I'm so upset. I'll just finish the season. I'll be fine." I pushed off the dress and Momma took it at the door, gathering it into a neat roll.

"You'll feel better after a shower," she said.

Momma was exactly right. The shower helped. (Of course, I downed those ibuprofens too.) I let that hot water pour over my aches. I stood in my steamy bathroom afterward. I reached up to drop my nightgown over my head but stopped. I knew why my neck and shoulder muscles hurt, but why did I hurt along that one side? I wondered. I wiped down the mirror with a towel, held it to my chest and turned my bare back to the glass.

There wasn't much to see. But walking my fingers along my skin I could feel it—a new bruise rising. A set of bruises, actually. They were weirdly straight-line in shape and ran from the back of my shoulder down to my butt, skipping the hollows of my body. Cowboy would have referred to it as right, rear-quarter damage if I had been a car. What did this? Something long, and with an edge—

Oh. My locker door. That's what.

In the mirror where the steam was beginning to collect again, my reflection caught my eye and I looked at the girl through the haze—*really looked*. I let my towel slide down. I scanned the body in the glass, from head to breasts to hipbones and back up again to the staring gold eyes.

I asked that girl in a whisper, "How did you let him do that to you?" I thought of Cowboy and I started bawling into my bath towel.

Thirty-seven

IF THERE WAS ANYTHING GOOD ABOUT BASKETBALL SEA-
son, it was that those games ate up big chunks of time—the
time Brady and I usually spent alone together. We were both
too busy now. Funny thing, considering I'd taken up cheerleading in a move for solidarity. But I couldn't imagine that
now—not the solidarity, not the intimacy.

I couldn't deny it anymore; Brady Cullen was hurting me.
We were unfixable. But I knew that there was not a single
soul that I would ever tell that to. And I didn't know how I
was going to get myself away from him either. So many damn
things were tying us together.

I guess I would have been willing to flat out dump Brady

if all could be done with no fallout. *I'm out of here.* Right. Everyone would want to know the reason why. *Everyone.* His friends. The Not-So-Cheerleaders. My own parents.

If it wasn't enough that I felt ashamed and demeaned by the things that had happened, I was afraid too—afraid that nobody would understand. What does someone hear when the words are said? *He squeezed my fingers. He threw a ball at me. He pulled my hair. He slammed me in a locker.*

People adored Brady. They'd give him the benefit of the doubt. If I dumped him, the cheerleaders would despise me. I could not quit the squad. The season was about to begin— I'd made a commitment. Yet Brady was my only reason for being there.

But possibly the worst of all my thorn-covered thoughts was about Bampas. I believed that it would grieve him to learn that someone was hurting me—I did. But I feared he'd look upon this as *my* fail, nonetheless. He had said I was not mature enough for a relationship. What if he construed the facts as proof that he'd been right? I was afraid he'd criticize my judgment. I even feared he would think I hadn't done enough to support Brady Cullen. I didn't think I could bear that.

I was trapped. I hated everything I had going on as December rolled in. Brady and I went through the motions of being basketball star and cheer-girlfriend. He was affectionate toward me, as usual. He wanted me on his arm. He wanted us to cram into a booth at Minio's Pizzeria in the village with his friends after home games and wait for the ten o'clock news to light up the big screen over the bar with local sports coverage. I went sometimes—if Momma and Bampas gave me permission. But other times, I didn't even ask to go. I gave Brady excuses: They won't let me out tonight. I have to babysit. I have cramps.

I went home. Often, I thought about that kiss—the one he had planted on that college girl at the farm party. I actually hoped he'd go sampling some more. Maybe hook up with someone he could be nice to.

One night at Minio's, I sat watching him while he watched the television. Then we heard it: "The White Tigers are celebrating tonight—here's junior guard *Brady Cullen* turning in two of his *electrifying* twenty-six points—" There he was on the screen, looping a shot into the hoop. Our booth in the corner of Minio's roared. Brady pounded his fists on his chest then reached into the air with both arms. "Yes! Yes!" he hollered. He was glowing like he'd swallowed the moon. He didn't need to be alone with me; he'd found something better to get off on.

I didn't love those nights out—save the few times I ended up next to Emmy for a small conversation. But better to be out than on my back in Brady's basement. That hadn't happened in weeks. I sometimes wondered what he would have done if he'd seen that line of bruises skipping down my torso. He'd probably have ignored them. That seemed to be his way. But a couple of weeks went by and he didn't see me naked. The marks faded.

In spite of being dog-tired, Brady was always willing to go out of his way to take me home. "Gives me time to unwind," he said.

The Brady Cullen Dashboard Highlights Show, I thought. He looked wired, staring forward out the windshield, his eyes glossy and his smile crinkling his face every so often as he recapped his successes.

In the hallways at school, I held on to my braid—a new habit. I stood back from my locker door. I couldn't be sure but a couple of times, I had the feeling that Brady had rattled that sucker just to see me jerk. He'd look back at me, turn his palms up and shrug at me as if to say, *Why are you flinching?* I kept one eye on Brady.

At the end of the day we'd take a table in the library— a safe place to be—and I'd tutor him in Spanish while he bit his knuckles and filled in blanks on a practice sheet with his deliberate handwriting. Then we'd go off to our separate practices. One afternoon when we did gather at the White Tiger with his friends, one of the guys asked Brady, "Hey, Cullen, what happened with that Spanish grade this week?

Tell me you passed that test, man, 'cause we need you at guard on Friday night."

"B-friggin'-minus!" Brady answered. Then damned if he didn't drop his backpack so he could make a show of putting both his arms around me. "It's all P'teen-uh. She gets me through that shit."

For something so imperfect and doomed, Brady and I appeared orderly. What I wanted most, at least for the time being, was to have no drama. I insisted to myself that it was working. Soon two weeks were gone. Then another. And another. *Yes.*

Yes, because Brady was consumed and distracted by his sport. Yes, because I began to imagine that we'd come to a natural sort of end once basketball season wound down. I saw signs that he had the same thing in mind; he didn't seem to care that we weren't sleeping together. *He knows we are done,* I thought, *but he can't risk upsetting his season by stopping to face it.* Easier to keep everything in the box. I told myself to hold on and do the right thing. Stick by Brady. Stick by the Not-So-Cheerleaders. All of this will fade. But in the meantime, I prayed for a short season for the mighty White Tigers.

Visits to see Cowboy seemed far too few. But every time I saw him it was like putting a few necessary stitches in my soul. On a December afternoon, I cut practice and we took a ride in the truck, and when we reached the road out of town

256

I put down my window, stuck my head and torso out, and just let the cold, cloudy air wipe me clean. I suppose it was only a few seconds that I rode like that but when I plunked back into my seat and belted up again, Cowboy glanced over.

"Better now?" he asked.

"Yes," I said. I tucked back a few strands of hair and I mopped cold-wind tears out of the corners of my eyes. "It smells like snow out there," I said. Minutes later, flakes began to fall.

That was the day he brought me to a farm, and not just to the edge of some field with a ditch full of rotting apples either. (Although, I somehow felt we might be close to the place I had been caught during the rubber-band road prank.) He drove down a long driveway to a farmhouse with a covered porch, a barn, and rail fences. He parked the truck as if he had every right to be there. "Where are we?" I asked as I followed him out of the truck.

"This is Dad's place. But Dad's not here during the day and neither are the brothers," he said. "It's just us."

"And them," I said as three, then four, then six horses clomped into the back paddock. "Oh, you're going to make me be near those, aren't you?"

"I'm not going to make you do anything," he said. "Wait here." He jumped a fence and pulled open a gate to let just one horse into the front pen. Then he disappeared into the barn and came back with a bucket of oats. "Make a bowl, Beta," Cowboy said.

"Yeah, yeah, all right." I cupped my hands. He poured them full of oats. He made a kissy, clicking sound.

"Here comes Sweetie," Cowboy said, and up marched the chestnut.

I repeated a silent mantra: *Nice-Sweetie, Good-Sweetie, Nice-Sweetie, Good-Sweetie . . .*

I knew what I was supposed to do. I held my hands forward as she stepped toward me through the new-falling snow. Sweetie nosed into the oats while her jealous barn mates stood behind the second fence. I felt the breath and fleecy lips, brushing my palms. Her lip hairs tickled me. Her large eyes shone, and snowflakes from our first snow stopped like tiny stars on the horse's lashes.

"I might not be afraid of horses anymore," I whispered.

"Thought so," said Cowboy. He gave me a sideways hug, then he held me a little longer than I expected.

Thirty-eight

COME THE LAST DAY BEFORE WINTER RECESS, I TOLD
Cowboy I wouldn't see him for nearly two weeks. No way
was I going to be able to get to the auto shop during school
break. I dreaded those days off, which always grew too long at
home. Yet, I'd already chosen home over having to see Brady,
and I'd told him that my parents would keep me close during
the holidays. I would be released to cheer at several games
oh, joy.

As for missing Cowboy, I told myself it was best to avoid
a moment that might become sentimental—the way it sometimes goes with holidays. Still, I had little daydreams of him
finding his way to my father's garden again, to the rabbit

hutches, maybe on Christmas Eve just to say "Merry." But the night passed without his visit.

But then on New Year's Day, I woke to little *thunk-thunk-*ing sounds at my window. Plum-sized snowballs stuck and slid down the glass. Beyond them stood Cowboy. "Get dressed," he whispered. "I want to take you somewhere. Not far."

I was still soaked in my own sleepiness, but ignited by the fact that he had come. I hurried in the bathroom. I hopped around with my toothbrush in my mouth while I pulled on a skirt from the top of the hamper. I grabbed a few layers including a heavy wool sweater. I couldn't find leggings fast enough but I grabbed warm socks and stepped into my combat boots.

Cowboy offered me a hand as I climbed out the window. When he saw my bare knees, he said, "That's good—something practical. Jeez, Beta! It's January."

"Hey, these are my clothes," I told him. "Don't give me any sass."

A crusty snowfall had covered a day-old powdery one, and the weather had stayed mild after it. As we plodded down the swath, we broke through the surface, leaving craters for footprints.

"Oh, man, I need caffeine," I mumbled.

"Gotcha covered," he said.

Nothing felt better than climbing up into the warm truck.

I held the coffee cup in both my hands, and settled in for the drive. Cowboy had come *for me.* He kept his eyes on the road and was quiet, as usual.

"Did you celebrate Christmas?" I asked.

"Eh," he said. Then as if offering it to me, he added, "Christmas happened."

Outside, the new snow stuck to the trees and fences, roofs and mailboxes and, all along the roadsides, the plows had banked a clean path. I traced the hillsides and the tree line as we rode. Then I concentrated on the shadows on the snow. I promised myself I'd dig out my watercolors when I got home.

"You know what?" I said to Cowboy.

"What's that?"

"I think to paint snow you must have to paint everything *but* the snow."

"Hmm. To paint snow you throw a cherry slushie on it," he said.

I laughed, but then I pictured bright spills everywhere. "I could see that," I said. The truck slowed and I raised my chin to look. I recognized the turn to the water property.

"Uh . . . are you sure you want to bring me back here again?" I asked. That day seemed like long ago, and like yesterday all at the same time.

"Yup. There is another overlook, a shorter side to that hill. We'll take the truck to the top. Hike down instead of up.

Different view. Amazing view."

"Okay, I want to be surprised. I'm closing my eyes and you tell me when to open. Don't throw me out of the truck or anything."

"Okay, keep 'em closed," he said. I felt the truck turn and then lurch as he pulled up the brake. He killed the engine. "Hang on now," he said, and I heard him get out. He opened my door and helped me to the ground. "Keep 'em closed, keep 'em closed." He guided me forward, hands cupped over my elbows. "Okay," he said. I opened my eyes.

"Wow."

We stood above the bowl-shaped depression and looked over the tops of the trees. Snow clung to the branches, six inches deep in some places, and the sun shone on the glaze in morning pinks and yellows.

"Oh! The trees look like hills!" I said. "Like you could step out there and walk across them to the next county."

"Or drive it." He let out a long, fading whistle and let one hand glide over the other toward the treetops. I made a scared face at him and he let out one of those quiet laughs that I loved.

"Are we going down?" I asked.

"Yup. It's easier hiking than the trails we climbed in October. Not nearly as steep. I think those are closed under snow."

"Yeah, I'd close them under snow."

"Ready? I'll race ya," he said in a not-hurried voice. Then he jumped away and started down the crunchy white slope. I watched for a few seconds. He made big sideways hops as he went.

I called down to him, "I have better boots than you!"

All the way down, we played a sort of crazed game of hide-and-seek tag. The trees were weighted with snow—the saplings were bent into hoops, heads pinned to the ground. I'd slip behind a curtain of branches but then if he didn't come find me, I'd burst out and start looking for him. I'd hear him through the silence, breaking across the snow. Then I'd see him disappearing in and out of the tree trunks running toward me and I'd retreat again. It was never clear who was "it," and we both took amazing diggers through the crust of snow. We scrambled to get back on our feet—me, with the sting of the snow on my bare knees.

A snowball sailed past my shoulder and broke against a shaggy tree trunk. Our game changed. I thrust my hands into my own footprints, scooped the snow, and packed it into balls. We pelted each other over and over again—and hard too—so that we grunted when we were hit. We fought until we were both breathless. Finally, my own hands ached so much with the cold that all I could do was tuck them inside my sleeves and run away. When I couldn't run anymore, I stopped beneath a stand of pines and leaned helplessly against a tree.

Cowboy raced up to me and instead of showering me in snow, he offered, "Truce?" He could barely speak himself. We'd had a good match.

I fell onto my back in the crusty snow and he dropped down next to me. We lay looking up into the pines just catching our breath.

I was sweaty beneath my wool sweater, but snow cooled the backs of my legs. I breathed into my own hands, trying to warm them. A pair of cardinals moved into the trees above, their bodies the only colors against the gray-and-brown woods. I was sure Cowboy was watching them too. I whispered, "The males get all the attention, but I think the females are prettier." I watched the olive-colored bird with her pinkish beak switch branches above me. "Look at her," I whispered.

The female bird darted down from the trees and landed on the snow just twenty feet from were we lay. I propped myself on my elbows. The bird hopped nearer. "Isn't she the most beautiful thing you've ever seen?" I looked at Cowboy. He looked back at me with just the faintest smile. Then, he shifted his gaze to the bird.

Before long, I began to shiver. "Time to go," Cowboy said. He pulled me up out of broken snow saying, "Your hands are frozen!" He cupped them but his were not much warmer than mine, and that made us laugh. I was sorry when he let go of me. I loved his touch and I wondered, *When would there be a reason for him to reach for me like that again?* We happened to catch eyes exactly as I had the thought and I felt caught, as if I might have said it out loud. I was forever covering all the things I really wanted to say to him with a little sigh or a smile. I did that yet again. Then I pulled the cuffs of my damp sweater over my fingers and we began our march back up to the truck.

"Hey." I made sure I had his attention. "Thanks for coming to get me," I said. "I've never had a New Year's morning like this one. I am so glad I didn't miss this. How beautiful!" I looked over the snowscape, my arms open wide and thought where else, and with who else—

"Beta," Cowboy said, "you are the most beautiful thing I've ever seen."

Thirty-nine

Bampas was in a rage. "We had no idea where you were! And you did not answer your phone. I find only footprints from your bedroom window! Who is it that comes to your window in the morning, Bettina? How long has this been going on?"

My mother stood nearby, not speaking. But she was eyeing me in an unnerving way and listening to every word.

"Bampas, it was just Brady," I lied. "He just wanted to take a New Year's Day walk. I thought it was too early to wake you. I should have left a note, and I forgot the phone. I'm sorry."

"You were at a party last night with him, were you not?"

I had to think to remember the New Year's Eve party—it

266

had been dull. Brady had split to be with the guys most of the night while I'd sat on the outside of a cache of Not-So-Cheerleaders. "Yes," I said, looking Bampas in the eye.

"And he needs to see you again first thing this morning? Bettina, who told him he could park on River Road and walk my property this way?"

"Nobody, Bampas. He—he just figured it out."

"I cannot believe it! The same boy takes such good care of you the night you cut your eye, but he comes to a bedroom window to take you from our home?"

"Bampas, he didn't want to ring the doorbell. It was *my* mistake."

"I will want to see him and speak with him. Do you understand me?"

"I do," I said. He was mad but he was also losing interest already. Yet, my mother was standing just behind him, glaring at me. Something was up.

"He will use the front door from now on." My father was calmer now.

"Yes, that will be better," I said.

My father excused me and I went to get a hot shower. I was standing in my own bathroom, stark naked and water running, when my mother walked right in.

"Momma!" I yanked a towel from the bar and covered up. "You scared me!"

"Did I?" She pulled the door closed behind her and handed me a folded-over piece of paper.

"What's this?" I asked.

"There was a call for you on the house phone not fifteen minutes ago—someone who gave up trying to reach you on your phone," she replied.

I unfolded the paper. It was from Brady Cullen. I pulled my lips inside my teeth and bit down on my secret. She had me.

"Were you gone all night?" she asked me in her lowest whisper. "Or did someone spend the night in your room?"

"No! Neither," I said, and I wanted her to believe me. I was amazed she thought I'd be so bold. The bathroom was filling with steam. "Momma, we were just playing in the snow. Honest."

"*Honest.* There is a word you have no business using. Take your shower, Bettina. You're not seeing anyone else today. You'll go with us to the restaurant. There is plenty to clean up after all the celebrating last night. By the way," she said, turning at the door, "happy new year."

I got lucky. Bampas never confronted Brady because he never saw him. So my lie, which could have broken the universe open, stayed between Momma and me. The New Year's morning incident did win me another grounding. So went the final days of that school vacation.

Oddly, there was comfort in the confinement. I was not chomping at the bit to go back to school, to Brady and basketball games and my swinging locker door. At home, I listened to music and filled the last pages of a sketchbook with drawings of the god Janus for January with his two faces looking forward and back. Favian and Avel came in and out of my room to ask what I was listening to and I'd turn up an ethereal, Celtic tune that sounded like a walk through snow. I fantasized, at least six or seven times over, that someone was waiting just outside my window. The best reason to go back to school was morning coffee . . . and a new art class.

"I'm playing in clay again!" I couldn't stop myself grabbing the upper arms of Cowboy's coverall. I jumped up and down a few times while he stood there, straight-faced and cooperating the way a tree might. "I'm learning how to throw on the wheel! I'm really bad at it," I added without dropping my note of enthusiasm.

Cowboy did a rare thing then; he threw his head back and laughed out loud.

I let him go, and in a hyper sort of way switched to the Chevy. "Hey, it's really coming along! You've been putting in a lot of time." I walked around the car. "It has a great face," I said. "Check out that orthodontia smile—"

"*Orthodontia?* Aw, Beta. You're killing me."

"Oh, sorry!" All his hard work and now I had offended

269

him. "Sometimes I blurt," I said. "It's just—it looks like it wants to go full grin. But with all that metal in its mouth, it can't. It's a *good* look," I said. "You know it is. Is it ready for the road?"

"Nope. But I'm getting there," Cowboy said. "Little by little."

"Little by little. Maybe that's how I'll get through this clay class," I said. I drummed my fingers on my lip.

"You're all about art. You'll be fine."

"Working on the potter's wheel is different. You have to get that ball of clay centered." I showed him with my hands. "I think there's a knack to it," I said. "I'm not sure I have it."

"Well, you can develop a knack." He laughed at himself. "Nobody's born doing the thing they die doing."

As I watched Cowboy go back to work, I was filled with a bittersweet feeling. He had developed his knack, all right. He had waited a long time to be appreciated for his talents. I thought of his mother—her cruelty. How had he stood up under her lack of belief in him? Or had he used his passion for old cars to stay whole in spite of her? There were times I felt that way about art; I could always go to it. I just had never had it kick my ass the way the pottery wheel was these days.

Later the same day, I stood in the art room with my braid tucked down the back of my shirt. I wedged the air out of a ball of clay for the fifth time. I climbed onto the tractor seat of one of our potter's wheels. I threw the clay down as close to the center as I could. I hesitated. From where I sat I could see finished clay pots—however rudimentary—already turning leather-hard under loose plastic wrappings. My classmates were marching ahead. All my rotten realities rushed at me. It seemed like I wasn't getting anything right; boyfriend stuff was all a lie, cheerleading was awful—

"Hey, come on. Let's go." I blinked. Big Bonnie was in front of me. "You can do this."

"I can't get it centered. . . ." I whispered through gritted teeth. "It's like I don't have the power. This is my fifth try today."

"Let me watch you," Bonnie said. "Go on, kick it."

I started the wheel spinning and wet my hands. I seized the ball of clay, which immediately went to war with me—defying my grip. In a matter of seconds, I felt exhausted.

"Okay, okay. Don't be so frantic with it," Bonnie coached. She paused to think a second. "It's not about muscle. Hold your hands more loosely and lean into the clay—sort of with your core. But breathe, for heaven's sake. You're turning purple." Her voice turned meditative. "This is one of those 'be the clay' moments. Don't look at it. Feel it. Easy pressure . . ."

I did what she said. I even closed my eyes. I leaned up over the clay. A few tries and suddenly, it felt right. I stopped and looked at Bonnie.

"You *are* the clay!" she said. "That's centered." She pointed to the lump. "Now just play. Try bringing it up and see what you get."

The form I made that afternoon collapsed. But at least I knew where center was. Maybe that knack would follow.

Forty

THE SKY WAS OVERCAST BUT MOON-BRIGHT, AND I KNEW something must be up when I saw the '57 Chevy at the side of River Road that Saturday night.

He did it! He's got the Chevy up and running.

Anyone else might have missed it—just some old car pulling off on the shoulder. But I'd spent a lot of time with that car. I knew that shape, that chrome smile beneath the headlights. I knew the place where our swath met River Road. I had to get to Cowboy.

I was with Brady and he was about to drop me at home after one of those group pizza stops. We arrived at the front of my house. "Don't bother pulling in. Just let me out on the road, okay?"

"Whatever," he said. He leaned over to kiss me but I was on the move and he missed. We both ignored it. "See ya Monday," he said. He mumbled something else about me helping him with a Spanish essay. But his head was down and he was tapping something into his phone with his thumbs. I hustled to the front step and faked purse problems until Brady pulled away. As soon as he was out of sight, I went around the house to the backyard. I started running toward River Road.

"Don't-be-gone. Don't-be-gone." I breathed out a word for each step. We still had snow and it was softening in the February thaw. I picked my feet up higher. *"Don't-be-gone. Don't-be-gone."*

I realized that he could be heading down the swath toward me. I started to call for him. "Cowboy! Hey! Are you out there?" Finally, I reached the road and I saw the long, thin silhouette of him in his jean jacket. He was sitting against the front of the car. He held up one hand when he saw me.

"It's the Chevy!" I jogged to a stop and tried to catch my breath. "Wow. You did it!" I walked all the way around the car, admiring its completeness—even in the thin light of the night. "Oh, it's perfect. How's it running?"

"It's good," he said. "Just one purr short of a kitten. Maybe two."

"Did you come to get me? Take me for a ride?" I wiggled a little.

"Hmm . . . I think not quite yet," he said. "But we could sit in it a minute."

"Oh, yes!"

I'd been busy admiring the car and was only vaguely aware that Cowboy had been holding something in one hand. He wound his arm back and threw it—a snowball—toward the river. He pulled open the car door for me. I bounced onto the passenger's side of the long front seat. I drew my palm along the dashboard, which was shining like a glass Christmas tree ornament, while Cowboy slid in behind the steering wheel.

"You brought it back to life. It's beautiful." I looked at him and grinned. Then I saw the wide, swollen line across his right cheekbone. My heart struck my ribs. I looked closer. His face was damp, glistening with tiny, melting flecks of ice and snow. He kept looking down or out the front of the car, anywhere that wasn't at me.

"Cowboy? Were you in a fight—oh my God! Was it your mother? It happened again?" I pressed my hands on both sides of my face.

"Hmm." He nodded almost imperceptibly. "But it's okay."

"It is *not*!" I heard myself say. "It is *not* okay!"

"It will be okay. It's been a long time. I thought she was done," he said in a confounded sort of way. "But this is the last time. I'm going to stay in the shop tonight, then start looking for a place tomorrow. By the way, don't tell your father I'm sleeping at SWS. I could lose my lease."

"Cowboy, I'd *never* tell him." I reached toward his face. "Did you get this looked at? You can break those bones, you know. That surgeon who stitched my eye told me, they're like Ping-Pong balls and they dent until you reach a certain age and then—"

"Shh, shh! Never mind, Beta." He gently batted my hands away. "I'm glad this happened. I know that sounds screwed up. But it leaves no question." He lifted his hands off the steering wheel and dropped them back down on it again. "I didn't see this one coming. But you know what? There's always another one coming." He looked at me dead-on. "You have to get completely out of the way."

"Oh, man," I said. "We're not doing this again." I got out of the car. Cowboy was in front of me in an instant. I faced him. "I'm glad you're out of your mother's house," I said. "So glad. But I'm not the same as you—nobody swings boards at my face," I said.

"He hurts you, Beta." Cowboy spoke flatly.

I folded my arms, trying to hug away a sickish feeling that kept creeping in. We'd done so well not letting Brady Cullen seep into our time together. I hated this. I toed the dirty snow at the edge of the road.

"You don't have to look like ground meat for it to be wrong," he said. "What he does to you, it's wrong in a thousand ways."

"I know! All right? I have a cruddy boyfriend. It's complicated—I don't know exactly how to do it, but I am working my way away from him—"

"You are?"

"Yes."

"Oh! Thank God, thank God!" Cowboy made a triumphant fist. "Yes!"

He was cheering for me. In my chest I felt a knot undoing itself. Cowboy was firmly on my side—about all things. I guess I'd always felt that. Now it was so clear. I wanted to wrap my arms around him. Instead, I hugged myself, while I stared down and brushed at the ground with the sole of my boot.

I finally spoke again. "So . . . did you just come out here to harass me or what?"

"No. In fact, I didn't mean to bring him up at all," he said. "Forget that. I need to tell you something. Something crazy and important, Beta . . ." Cowboy was reaching for me. His arms were open—a strange sight. "I want to hold you," he said. "Please?"

"Hold me?" I stared back at him. "We don't . . . do this," I said. I waited, looking back into Cowboy's eyes, and

277

wondering if I was going to be sorry. But I did it. I stepped into the circle of his arms.

Slowly, he wrapped me, brought me close—*close*—against his long, straight body. His breath was warm on the top of my head. Something was different about Cowboy. "Ooo . . . you feel so good," he said, and held me tighter.

I could smell the faint odors of the garage on his clothes, and for the first time I was close enough for long enough to really smell his skin too. I took it in deeply. I lost my breath, then caught it again in a tiny sound I did not mean to make. "Cowboy . . ." I whispered while I clung to him.

He leaned down, brushed his fingers along my temple and behind my ear. His lips followed the same path. He kissed me—sweetly, slowly—little kisses that asked for permission, kisses that could melt snow. He kissed my lips, my mouth, and I tasted faraway mints, a tiny hint of tobacco, and Cowboy. Oh . . . he was easy to kiss. He brought me close over and over again. I stretched toward him for more. *But is he going to stop? Will he say this was a mistake?*

I pulled away—gulped on the night air. I looked right into his eyes.

"I love you," he whispered.

A strange yip of disbelief came from my throat. I squeezed the arm of Cowboy's jacket in my fingers. Thank God he spoke, because I could not.

278

"Long time now," he said. "I didn't mean to. I tried not to. But I do." He touched me under the chin. "And I don't know, but I think . . . you might love me too."

I took a step backward. "*Y-you* don't let me," I said, and Cowboy let out a small laugh. "You don't." I tried to be in control.

"I'm sorry," he said. "You're so young. I didn't ever see myself falling for—"

"A kid," I said, but I was not offended. "Y-you still think of me as a kid." Meanwhile, I gathered my bottom lip up in my fingertips and held it. I wanted another long, easy kiss.

"By laws and by birthdays. Yes." He shook his head. "I tried to make the facts change how I felt about you. I even told myself it was wrong, you know? Like, *creepy guy*," he said, and he tapped himself on the chest. "But none of that worked. Pushing you away . . . hmm . . . hardest thing ever, Beta." He opened his hand over his heart.

"I cannot believe you're saying all of this to me." My lip quivered. "You wouldn't joke. . . ." No. He was shaking his head no, and I knew better. He would never joke—not about this. My eyes filled.

"I'm letting go of old mind-sets tonight. I *see* us together. You could say it took somebody smacking me in the face—"

"Oh! That's not funny," I said. I wiped my eyes.

"It's sort of funny," he suggested. He caught my hand in

279

his and held it next to his lips. "I'm in, Beta. I want you. We're going to have to wait a while for . . . *some things*." He glanced skyward for a split second and came back to earth with a sigh. "That's not going to be easy."

I thought how it would be—making love with Cowboy— his fingers, his breath whispering along all my bare skin. We'd both be so ready. He'd be tender. I'd be feverish. Oh, I wanted him *now*.

"Not easy," I agreed with him. Then my mind leapt forward. "Oh . . . *my parents* . . ." I said, and I closed my teeth together. "How in hell . . ."

"We have to talk to them together." He gave a definitive nod.

"Oh, Cowboy. I don't know. . . ."

"I can't see you going into that alone. I wouldn't feel right about it. They'd think I was a dirtbag, and they'd be right."

I put my hands to my head. "Uh, God. I don't know, I don't know! I still can't believe we're even talking about this."

"Then, this is enough."

"Enough?"

"I've already searched my soul about this a hundred times over," he said. "But now I've sprung it on you. I need to leave you alone."

"Oh, no! Don't leave."

"Just to let you think," he said. "You know your parents better than I do."

"Yeah, and this might not go so well," I told him. I tried to run the conversation—huh! It would be no conversation. A shouting match, maybe. I put my hands to my ears. Cowboy brought them down for me and held them, swinging me gently.

"Beta," he whispered, "let's try to trust this." As the words left his lips and his fingers laced into mine, I had a moment of utter belief. Maybe the whole thing really was possible. Maybe Momma would help me. We could soften Bampas. Maybe . . .

"Don't go," I said again. I stood on my toes like a girl on a ladder and reached to kiss Cowboy while he held me in a beautiful embrace, his hands low on the small of my back. I drew the pads of my fingers along his collarbone. I slid my hand between his shirt buttons—just the littlest bit—and I found his warm, bare skin just below the hollow of his ribs. He made a low sound in his throat.

"Aw, Beta, if you knew what that did to me you wouldn't do it."

"Yes, I would," I said, and we split a gentle laugh. I put my ear to his chest and closed my eyes. His heart beat solidly, peacefully. I thought, *This heart loves me.* Cowboy's gentle hands traced the pearls of my spine. Then he twirled my braid gently in his fingers and brushed it across his lips.

He sighed. "I'm done feeling like this is wrong," he said. "I'm done feeling bad."

I looked up and smiled. I reached into the chest pocket of his jean jacket and took his cigarettes. "I remember what you said," I told him. "If you're done feeling bad, then you're done with these." I disappeared them into my own pocket. "They can kill you, and I won't have that."

"Thank you," Cowboy said. I circled my arms around him again. I nestled close, and couldn't help thinking that we fit well together.

"I could sleep here," I said. "Just like this."

"And I'd be a happy man," Cowboy said.

"Someday I will. But we'll dance together before we sleep."

"We'll dance," he said.

A fire of warmth burned between us. But Cowboy's jean jacket wasn't warm enough for the night. I felt him shiver. It was late, and I knew we had to separate. I could not let this come out to Momma and Bampas like a river of napalm.

Cowboy told me, "No matter what you decide about your parents—how to do this—I'm with you. But I'd like to be there." He traced my arms and shoulders with both his hands then let me go.

"I'm scared," I said. "I'm scared this won't be real in the light of day."

He shook his head no. "Check your pocket. You have my cigarettes. Proof that I was here." He grinned. "Don't get caught with those, now. Get rid of them." He was so light and easy, all I could do was smile back at him. "We're going to be good for each other, Beta."

"Yes, we will be."

Good has come, I told myself. I turned to go, took a few steps, then whirled back again. I saw him stoop to pick up another lump of snow. He held it to his bruising cheek.

"Promise me something," I called to him. I wanted to leave him laughing. "Promise you'll come back in that smiling Chevy." I cupped my hands together underneath my chin. "Take me for a ride on River Road."

Forty-one

NEEDLESS TO SAY, I GOT IN LATE. INSIDE THE KITCHEN, MY mother sat at the table with a wineglass and a crossword puzzle. She was dressed in her robe. She looked at me coldly.

"You are past curfew." She sounded almost bored. "And you are grounded."

"Okay," I said, glancing at the clock.

"I saw Brady's car pull away some time ago. I am assuming you have been with someone else since then."

"Yes."

She responded with nothing but her straight-line mouth. She pushed a small pharmacy bag toward me. "Bettina, I hope you've been careful, but you don't show good judgment, so . . ." She fluttered her hand at the bag as if to push it closer to me. I lifted one side of the bag open and saw a large, flat box of condoms inside.

"Momma," I said, and I sank into one of the chairs and hoped she couldn't hear the cellophane crackling on that pack of smokes inside my jacket. "Momma, I have something to . . ." Suddenly, I couldn't look at her. I stared at the bag on the table and tapped it with my finger. "You are right," I whispered. "But, Momma, not with *this* one, and I won't. We . . ."

"Don't try to conspire with me on this, Bettina. How old is he?"

"I think he's about twenty-five," I said softly.

She leaned forward. "*You think?* You're not sure of his age, but you're sure he's worth all this deception?"

"He has a business and he's—"

She cut me off again. "Oh, I'm sure that seems like so much to a high school girl. Don't be so sure you want to grow up this fast, Bettina."

I felt my eyes begin to pool. "It's *not* fast. He has been my friend—for a while. But now it's something more. I'm not rushing, Momma."

"He will *make* you rush. Men do not wait."

"He *has* waited!" I cried. "He will *still* wait. He talks to me, and he listens to me!"

"Keep your voice down!" Momma hissed. She glanced down the hall. Bampas must have been in bed already.

I wiped my eyes with the backs of my hands and whispered, "I know I always push, Momma. But it's because I don't get very far around here." Surely, she understood me. "I know all the things you're saying. But this is different. I have this calm feeling about him."

"Calm! How calm is sneaking out late at night?"

"I'm just trying to tell you—"

"And I'm telling you! You'll wake up and find emptiness one day."

"Why? Because *you* did?" I spat. "I've done the math. I know how young you were—how much older Bampas is. What happened, Momma? You weren't ready and he wouldn't wait? And now you're unhappy?"

Her fire turned to a vacant stare. I watched her eyes fill.

"Oh, God! I'm sorry!" I reached toward her, but then covered my mouth with my hands instead.

She blinked and took a heavy breath. "You don't know what is in my heart."

She pushed away from the table. She strode down the hall, her robe swishing behind her. I blotted my eyes on a paper napkin and blew my nose in it. Momma had left two inches of wine in her glass. I drank it. I stared at the crossword puzzle page and thought about my parents. I wished I could take back what I'd said to her. I'd had no right. I knew nothing—not for certain. A half-finished word on the puzzle grid caught my eye. I checked the clue: mutual interchange. I looked at my mother's faintly penciled letters in some of the blocks and filled in the rest with my own clean printing.

Reciprocity.

I folded the bag of condoms shut, took them to my room, and hid them in the back of my sweater drawer. I wasn't going to need condoms again for a long while.

Forty-two

I WOKE THAT NEXT MORNING, HUGGING MYSELF IN disbelief.

I'm going to be with Cowboy.

Oh, there were hundreds of thorns to pick out of my life. I went over them with myself: You took a cheap shot at Momma. You have to end things with Brady. You will have a Not-So-Cheerleading mess to clean up. Bampas's head will explode.

But there would be Cowboy, now—and in a different way than ever before. I was certain at the center of my being that things were coming right with my world. He *loved me*. The rest would work out.

I had twenty-four hours in the house, twenty-four hours basically to myself—the most bittersweet grounding of my life.

My parents and my brothers were home, but no one came into my room, and Brady didn't call. Neither did Cowboy— well, he'd never done that anyway. He didn't even have my number. I'd have to fix that. But he was also giving me time, and I thought he needed some too; he was probably out apartment hunting. I looked out my window, my escape route, and remembered the feel of him from the night before—the gentle pressure of his lips, the taste of him, the warmth of his skin. We had laughed—like lovers, I realized. I kept my jacket on all day long and checked for the pack of cigarettes over and over again.

Late in the afternoon, I ventured down the hall to my mother's room. I hesitated then brushed my knuckles against her door.

"Come in," she said. She was at her mirror combing her hair. "Oh, Bettina." She seemed surprised, and when I thought about it, I could not remember the last time I'd come to my parents' room.

"Hi," I said softly. I slipped in to sit on the edge of her bed. "I'm sorry about last night. I'm sorry for what I said to you."

She pressed her hand toward me. "Let's not," she said.

She collected her thick, dark hair in her hands. "So," she said rather suddenly, "you want something."

"Well." I cleared my throat. "I wanted to tell you about my . . . friend." My own choice of words surprised me at first, but then seemed right. I waited for Momma to interrupt me. She didn't. "His name is . . . Silas," I said, "but I call him Cowboy."

She made a little bit of a face. I ignored her.

I told her how I'd been taking him coffees, and cutting bits of school and cheerleading practice to see him. I told her that he owned a small classical-car restoration company and that he rented a unit at the complex that Bampas owned. Momma rolled her eyes. "Oh, Bettina. Your father will forbid this. You know that."

"But Cowboy really admires Bampas—"

"They *know* each other?" She raised her brow. "Dear God."

"They've met. To sign the lease. Business stuff."

My mother nodded. "So what else about him, Bettina?" she asked crisply. She wound her hair tightly at the back of her head and pinned it. "There was Brady Cullen, and I suspect, a few before him. What is it that makes you *have* to have this one—the older one?"

"Well, I'm not sure I can explain it, Momma." I began to try anyway. "He listens, and he likes the way I think. He believes in me as an artist and that makes me feel like I *am* someone. Momma, there is this exchange. . . ." I shifted my hands back and forth. "I've never had this before. But really, it's my heart. This is who my heart loves. I can't help that. The fact that he's older is . . . an obstacle. He and I both know that."

"I see," she said. "I'm surprised. I expected something more superficial."

"Nice, Momma."

"I don't mean to be unkind. It's just that—I know how it feels. You want to be swept away. You really do."

"So maybe there's no stopping that," I said. "He and I only just admitted this to each other, Momma. I haven't decided to marry him. I just want to be able to see him without lying. I want you to meet him. And someday I want him to come over and—oh, I don't know—wash cars in our driveway and have Sunday supper with us." I finished with a small, hopeful laugh. "Momma, will you meet him?"

"Possibly," she said. "I just don't know. I cannot imagine telling this to—"

My father strode into the room. "Loreena, I'm going to have a shower and—oh. Bettina." It was funny—he said my name just the way my mother had. He stood, looking back and forth between us, one hand poised on his top shirt button.

"I was just on my way out," I said. I gave my mother a

parting glance; she returned an unreadable one, but I realized, she had not said no.

On my way down the hall, I poked my head inside the boys' bedroom.

"Hey, nerds, wanna come out and shovel turds?"

"You rhymed!" Avel laughed. "You going to do the rabbits? Yeah, I'll come!" He jammed his feet into his sneakers.

"Wait, wait! Boots," I told him. "Snow's melting. It'll be muddy out there."

"I'm gonna come, too." Favian swung himself down from the upper bunk. "I haven't been out to see the rabbits in a while."

"Been checking out some *other* bunnies?" I poked him in the ribs. "You know. On Bampas's reader?" I raised my eyebrows.

"Avel, did you tell?" Favian reached to swat him and I caught his arm.

"He didn't tell," I said. "I just know *everything*."

"Are you gonna bust us?" Favian whispered. He shot a glance down the hallway toward Momma and Bampas's bedroom door.

"Not as long as you promise me that you'll always be nice to girls," I said. "And now, I *am* going to make you scoop *major* poop."

"Catch me first!" Favian hollered, and he took off down

the hall. I chased him to the kitchen and held him in a bear hug.

Avel came running. "Pig pile!" he hollered. He jumped on my back and knocked us all down on the kitchen floor. We lay there laughing until Avel—on top—said, "Uh-oh! I'm gonna pee my pants!" We were suddenly arms, legs, and torsos everywhere, as Favian and I scrambled to get out from under Avel.

I looked up and saw my mother in the hall. She wore a faint smile that broke open when she said, "What are you children doing?" I felt so much warmth from Momma at that moment. Once again, I believed that a good turn had come.

Forty-three

ALL I COULD THINK ABOUT ON MONDAY MORNING WAS getting over to the garage to see Cowboy. For the first time, I could go in there and hug him the way I'd always wanted to. What seemed right would be right. I could kiss him and know he'd kiss me back. That would get me through a long day at school.

I was excited, a little scared, and full to my brim. I didn't have our solution yet. I didn't know how to tell Bampas or how I was going to handle ending things with Brady. Big changes were coming. But all I could think of for the moment was that I was sure as heck going in there to tell Cowboy that

I loved him. I had never said the words on Friday night beside the river. I believed that he knew; he'd said it himself. But I was going to make sure—*this very morning*. I jingled some quarters, meant for our usual pair of coffees, in the hollows of my hands as I stepped into the kitchen.

"Twenty-six!" my father said loudly. He slapped his hand down on the morning paper, which lay open before him. The kitchen table shook. "I *know* this young man! This Silas Shepherd."

My breath stopped. I locked eyes with my mother.

Bampas knows? About Cowboy and me?

She stared back at me, seemingly frozen, frightened— and what else? What was that other look in her eyes? Helplessness? Yes, I thought so. I pressed my quarters hard between my hands. What was going on here?

"He ran SWS Auto at my Hamilton complex." My father went on. "Can you believe it, Loreena? *Dead*, at twenty-six."

Dead?

I looked at Momma. She covered her mouth with her hand and shook her head.

"No," I said. "No. That's not possible. . . ." I watched Momma's eyes begin to fill. Her face crumpled. The wall met my shoulder. "Bampas. No. You . . . you are wrong. . . ."

"What do you know of it?" Bampas said. His brow creased.

295

"It *is* so. It is written right *here*." He thumped a finger on the newspaper. "He is dead."

My quarters crashed to the floor. They bounced and spun with a horrible ringing. I slid lower and lower down the wall. I pushed words from my chest.

"Oh, no! No. Momma. *Please!*"

I watched the quarters rolling far away from me—away from my useless arms. Weightless hands.

Footsteps pounded. Bampas was there, kneeling next to me. He reached for me but did not touch me. "Loreena!" he called into the kitchen air. "What is the matter with her? Loreena, come to us!"

"Dinos," my mother said. She sniffled as she pushed into his place on the floor beside me. "It's about the boy in the newspaper." Her whispering filled the space all around me. She gathered me into her arms. My head fell heavily against her breastbone. She rocked me. "Bettina, take a breath," my mother begged. "Sweetheart, breathe!"

My lungs let in a painful rush of air. "Oh, Mom-ma, no! Tell Bampas he is *wrong*!" I cried. My body shook, my teeth chattered violently. I gripped the arm of her bathrobe in my fingers and wailed.

In the unearthly kitchen air, I heard Favian calling, "Bampas! Who? Who died? What's the matter with Bettina?" I saw his wide eyes, his open mouth. Then Avel's bewildered face mixed into the haze.

"Get a blanket for your sister, Favian." My mother spoke gently. "Dinos, go put the kettle on. Bettina needs to stay home today."

Forty-four

IT RAINED, OF COURSE, FOR THE GRAVESIDE SERVICE. AT first, I thought I would not go. I'd done nothing but stay home and ratchet my bedsheets into a knot since Monday morning when I'd dropped all the quarters in the kitchen. I still heard the ringing and the sound of them spinning—I still reached for them in replay.

Momma had tried to cook for me but I couldn't bear to feed the stone in my stomach. God knows why, she brought me the paper, showed me the report.

A twenty-six-year-old man had "perished" early Sunday morning. *Perished* struck me as such a gentle-sounding word. *Swished. Wished. Perished.* The Chevy had gone off the overlook at the water property and crashed in the branches of the trees. Not gentle. They put the time of the accident at 12:40 a.m.—about an hour after we'd parted.

Mechanical failure, road conditions, driver error—all were suspects. *What?* I thought. What could have happened? Did Cowboy really make a mistake—punch the gas? Was something wrong with the car? Was it those brakes I had watched him install? All the possibilities dug their jagged edges into me. I thought about what the report didn't say—didn't say because nobody knew: he had been with me minutes before.

I'd kept my phone off, while I'd balled myself into my sheets and salted my face with tears. When Sunday afternoon came, I was numbly conscious of needing to be at the service. I'd heard about "closure." But I didn't want to close this. I could not concede that Cowboy was gone. It was Momma who nudged me along.

She lent me her long, black skirt and her dress boots. She followed me out to the front step and dropped her gray tweed coat over my shoulders. She pressed the handle of her black umbrella into my palm. "Stay dry," she said.

She looked up into the weeping sky and I looked after her. Sometimes even grayness is too bright. I had to look away.

"Ready?" my father asked. He sounded like he was about to take me to the merry-go-round. Since the morning the news all came spilling out, I'd had the sense that Bampas was having as much trouble acknowledging the truth as I was. Momma had told him about Cowboy and me. He seemed dumbstruck, very unsure how to treat me.

As we neared the cemetery gate, I saw a dozen or so cars entering—some of them classics. My heart skipped. I'd seen the parts of those cars—the bolts, tailpipes, and radiator caps. I'd seen them before Cowboy had used them to make each car whole. I watched the cars park one behind the other in the long U-shaped drive. It dawned on me that none of them would be able to move until the first one did.

"Don't pull in," I told Bampas. "Drop me off here. I want to go alone."

"But Bettina . . ."

I had the car door open. I stepped out on the curb and let the umbrella pop up. "Just come back for me in an hour." I pressed one palm toward him.

"No, no. I will drive the way around and watch for you—"

"Go, Bampas. Please."

"We meet at this gate," he said.

The grass was spongy underfoot, still spotted with rain-weary snow. There was a tiny gathering, a circle of maybe thirty people. I stayed on the outside, my mother's umbrella open over my head.

There was the urn on a draped pedestal. It was simple—made of marble I guessed, ivory with gray veins. The base was narrow, and the shape rose to maybe fourteen inches. The top was full-shouldered. The rim narrowed to meet the flat lid cleanly.

It is not Cowboy. Cannot be Cowboy. I thought it over and over again.

The people stepped closer as the service started.

A solemn voice began, "The family would like to invite—"

I looked up. I saw them—the family. The four stood together beneath a portable awning that seemed to expose them more than it sheltered them. I saw the brothers with the beautiful names. And his mother—she was small—her hair in tight curls, her mouth a straight line. She held her own hands clasped at her chest. It seemed like my heart should go cold at the sight of her, knowing what I knew. But she looked like a mother, was all. I wondered what kind of sorrow she felt.

Behind her, a tall man stood with his hands on her shoulders. His sweet, sleepy eyes so much like Cowboy's. I stared at him. I watched his gaze move slowly around the circle of people, then to the outside until he was looking right at me. Then it hit me; I'd seen him before. He'd seen me too. I was the girl who had stared up at him from a ditch beside a back road while an apple rotted nearby. He was the man who'd let me go that night. "Shep"—that's what his friend had called him. Shep, like Shepherd. His eyes narrowed, he tilted his head at me—the tiniest of movements—as if to ask, *Why are you here?* I think he smiled at me. Then he bowed his head.

A flicker of color caught the corner of my eye. A little girl in a bright blue coat and tights was stepping up and down over the footstones well outside the circle. She held a yellow umbrella almost over her head. She tipped and bobbed like a toy against the gray-flannel backdrop. Mud began to dot her tights. But she didn't seem to notice. I glanced back into the circle where Cowboy's father stood pressing his thumb and finger into his eyes. The woman in front of him stood unblinking. Two brothers stared at the ground. I turned my gaze back to the little girl and watched her while all the words rasped the air.

"Hello." Large, cool hands closed briefly over mine as I held the handle of Momma's umbrella. Startled, I stared up at the moon-faced man. "I'm Kenneth Shepherd," he said. I managed to give him my name. He waited, then asked, "You a friend of Silas's?"

"Mmm." I nodded.

"Well, that's nice for Silas," he said, but not in an indecent way. He sounded equally sincere and surprised. "Thank you for coming." He faltered a little. "There's a small reception at my farm. Would you like directions? Or can we take you with us?"

The small crowd was breaking away in pieces all around us.

"N-no. Thank you," I said.

"Another time then," he said. He smiled such a sad smile.

"I'm sorry," I said, and I meant for his loss—the way people say. He was a father with a dead son. My throat was in a horrible cramp. I couldn't form another word. I nodded at Mr. Shepherd one last time. Then I turned and walked away as if I had somewhere to go.

It'd taken only thirty minutes for them to say goodbye to him—their brother, their son. Bampas might not be back for a while, so I walked. The ground made sucking noises under my mother's boots. I reached the opposite end of the cemetery and turned to start back again. But then I got off course. I could not find the shoveled path, nor my own footprints. No matter where I looked I saw no one. Even the awning was gone. *So quickly? That's how this works? You just fold up? How is that enough?* The tallest monuments in the yard made a dizzying pattern, like pieces on a giant disorderly chessboard.

Where is the place I was just standing? Where is the urn? Why does the whole world keep warping?

Finally, the trampled and melted snow gave it away. The awning was on the ground, rolled and packed to go. But the urn was still on its little temporary stage. Not a soul stood near it now. I stepped up and held Momma's umbrella over the urn and over me. If that was really Cowboy, what could I say to him? What words could I whisper—

"Bettina?"

303

I gripped the umbrella handle and turned. Bonnie Swenson blinked back at me.

"Whu—?"

"My dad threw out his back so I'm helping today," she said quickly. She gestured. I looked and saw a lone van slowly making a turn near the cemetery gate. Its taillights glowed and a funnel of exhaust rose from its tailpipe.

"Oh. He's waiting for you," I said.

"He'll pull around," Bonnie said. Then speaking in a very gentle way, she added, "We have to take the urn."

I looked slowly from Bonnie to the urn, and back again. Maybe I looked like I was guarding it. I took a step back.

"I-it's really sad," Bonnie said. "He was so young."

I nodded.

She hesitated then asked, "How did you know him?"

"He was . . . my friend," I said. I swallowed hard. "Like . . . the best . . ."

"I'm so sorry," Bonnie whispered. She touched my arm and let her hand slide gently down to mine. She held my fingers for a second. She stepped toward the vessel.

"Wh-where do you take it now? The urn?" I asked.

"Storage," she answered. I hated that. "The remains won't be interred until later. Some families make that request."

"Really?" I said. *Why?* I wondered. What was the point of a graveside service then? I did not ask that question, but

304

Bonnie was on a roll, talking shop.

"Sometimes unmarried children are buried alongside their parents. . . ."

Suddenly, I felt like I would puke in the mud. I stepped back from my own feet and leaned forward. Bonnie hushed. A few seconds throbbed by, and the feeling passed.

"I'm sorry, Bettina," she said again.

I nodded and took a deep breath. "I better go. My father is meeting me at the gate." I started away.

"Bettina?"

I turned back to see her holding the urn in her capable, chapped hands.

"Are you going to come back to clay class soon? I've missed you."

Beyond Bonnie I could see Bampas pulling the car to the side of the street and motioning with one hand for me to come. "I—I don't know," I said, shaking my head. "I don't know."

Forty-five

FOR THE REST OF THAT DAY I DIDN'T KNOW WHAT I should be doing. Closure did not show up to put its armor around me. All I felt was dread for each new minute. My phone was off but I heard the house phone several times. Momma did not make me take the calls. But she told me, "Brady again. It is the third time. I know you are hurting but, Bettina, we don't know what to tell him." She did seem helpless. "And now the cheerleaders have called too."

"I—I can't talk to anyone," I said, putting my hands up like a shield. "Not yet. I'll—I'll do something. Soon. I will."

I slipped away to my bedroom and stared out the window at the place where Cowboy had stood the couple of times he had come for me—the place I would never see him again. *All* places were like that now. He would not be anywhere . . . unless I could dream him. I watched the world beginning to refreeze in a changing wind. *All that early drizzle had been a waste of a good snow*, I thought.

Later, I went into the kitchen and I carried a shopping bag in my hand. Neither of my parents saw me in the doorway.

"Loreena, *this* you should have told me!" My father towered close to my mother as if he would step on her feet.

"Two days, Dinos! Two days I knew about it! Then he is dead!" She brought her hands to her head. "I didn't have time to tell you. I was still trying to think."

"To think?" My father stepped back and brought his fist down onto the counter with a thud. "That is the problem then!"

"Dinos, you are being unfair," my mother insisted. Her eyes were filling.

"He was twenty-six, Loreena! The girl is fifteen. . . ."

"Sixteen," I interrupted hoarsely. "I'm sixteen. Seventeen soon."

They both looked at me.

"Bettina!" My mother reached for me, trying to apologize for my father's mistake. I wanted to say that it didn't matter. Instead, I held the bag out to her.

"Momma, I need you to turn this in," I said. "It's my

307

cheerleading dress. You have to tell them I am not coming back."

"No, no," Bampas started up. "Bettina, quitting is not the answer—"

"Bampas . . ." I cut him off with a whisper. "Do I look like I can jump up and down and make noise? Do you think I can care about *ridiculous* basketball after everything that has ha—" I choked. It took a huge effort but I pulled myself together. "Don't you understand why I won't take Brady Cullen's phone calls? Because *I can't!*" He stared back at me. I actually had his attention. "And Bampas, I hope you never blame Momma for any of this again," I said. "I sprung it on her—the whole thing. She did her best." I turned to face my mother. I held out the bag. "Take it to the school for me, Momma, please. The cheerleaders will need to make other plans. There is a Jenna Somebody. She can step in. I won't hold them up any longer."

"I'll do it," Momma said, and she took the bag.

Forty-six

MY BED BECAME MY NEST; MY NIGHTGOWN WAS MY cocoon. I wanted to sleep. I wanted to find Cowboy in a dream.

My parents left me to it. They brought cups of tea and small dishes of food. The boys knocked softly on my door in the afternoons, as if they were wearing mittens. For all those days they whispered my name, whispered offers of card games and cocoas and videos. I couldn't do any of it. They looked at me with big, round eyes every time they closed my door.

There was no single thing that dragged me from that bed. But three or four days after the funeral, I got up. I stepped

309

straight into my clothes, slid my window open, and walked out into the snow. I walked the swath to River Road. When I saw the place I had last seen Cowboy—the place where we'd held each other—I reached into my jacket to check for his cigarettes. I turned left and kept on going for an hour, or maybe it was more, until I reached the water property.

In the ruined and refrozen snow, there was evidence of something having been pulled up and out. There were muddy gashes in the hillside from heavy equipment. These scars in the earth were right where Cowboy and I had stood together on New Year's Day. I wondered, did he think about telling me he loved me that day? And if he had, how would that have made this day different? I looked into the bowl below and saw the split treetops, the sickening hole in the snow—the place where the Chevy had to have lain with Cowboy in it. I twisted my arms together and held them to my chest.

I asked myself again, *What could have gone so wrong that night after he left me?* But no answer could ever unbreak my heart.

The little mental movie played—us running along the snowy ground—clouds of Cowboy's breath—gray bark on winter trees—the pair of cardinals.

And cold hands holding cold hands.

It seemed like a time to cry or scream. But I was perfectly silent.

When the cop car pulled up behind me I realized my mistake; I'd left home without telling anyone. The cop ushered me onto the seat of the patrol car. I heard him radio in to the station. "Have someone phone Dinos," he said. "I'll have her home in fifteen minutes." He gave me a glance, shook his head, sighed through his nose.

At home, my frantic parents slipped into their roles: Bampas playing "good host" to the officer, pouring him coffee, and making light of everything, and Momma following me to my bedroom. "I'll start your shower," she said. "After, I'll help you with your hair."

I went along with that. My mother came in and out of my bathroom several times, the shower curtain billowing to announce her each time. She left fresh towels, then came back and handed me her bottle of rosemary and olive oil— Old World hair conditioner. "Suppresses the tresses," we'd always said. I poured a small puddle of the oil into one hand then spread it between both palms. I drew my hands through my hair, then rinsed and watched the water falling toward the drain. My arms and shoulders were tired; my wet hair was heavy. Even my fingers felt weak. I rinsed one last time and shut the shower off. I wrapped my head in one towel and my body in another. My mother tapped on the door.

"I'm leaving a clean nightgown on the hook."

"I want the one I've been wearing," I said.

"It's stale. I'm washing it," my mother answered. I don't know why but I wilted over that loss. When I came out, she was tossing a crisp, clean top sheet over a fresh fitted one on my bed. The windows were open to the cold day. She was airing me. I shivered.

"Put it on." My mother gestured at the clean gown. "Your robe too. You can have tea if you want it. I'll close the windows after a few minutes."

It was late afternoon, the winter sun dropping and fading, when my mother gently braided my damp hair for me and told me how fine I was going to be. When she left, I tried to find my way to sleep, and to a dream where I might glimpse Cowboy. But sleep didn't come. I twisted in my fresh bed. My hair caught underneath me. For years I had never cared that my braid made my nightgown damp, that it was heavy and so constantly *with me*. Now, I remembered the day Brady Cullen had jerked my head back so hard.

I sat up in bed. The scissors were there on the nightstand. The next thing I knew, I was halfway through that rope of hair. It was quite a *thing*—that braid—hanging from the grip of my finger and thumb. I don't know what gave me the thought that it had to be kept together but I twisted an elastic band onto the chopped end. I dropped the braid and folded myself back between my sheets.

There was the awful moment when my lamp came on.

My mother screamed. She was frantic, searching the back of my head and finding only a short cob of hair left there. She was still breathless when my father's form filled the doorway. "Does this do it, Dinos?" Her voice was hoarse. She swept the braid off the floor and shook it at him. "Can you see that beneath this roof there is a heart that must be mended? And will you help me? Because if you will not . . . I will ask you to leave so I can do it alone."

That about blew me out of my bed.

Leave? What had I done to them? "Oh, Momma! No!" I cried and begged her to understand. "It's j-just hair!" I stammered. "It felt wet—it was twisting around me—and I was tired of it, is all. Momma, it doesn't matter."

Her face ran with tears and her lip quivered uncontrollably. I looked at Bampas, who stood still as granite and looked empty as a cardboard box. I turned back to my mother. "Please, Momma," I said. "I'm sorry."

I suppose I did sleep that night once they left the room. But I kept opening my eyes wide in the darkness. I could not dream.

When I came into the kitchen the next morning, both my little brothers looked at me with big eyes and mouths wide open. I caught my bowed reflection in the cupboard glass. My hair had sprung into wild spirals and uneven lengths. I should've said something to Favian and Avel. But Bampas

313

excused them before their cereal bowls were empty.

I put the kettle on, flicked the burner to high, and watched the flame. I stared at the fire below the kettle and twisted the knob. Flame up. Flame down.

My mother glanced at me, at my hair. She turned away to face the kitchen sink.

"Bettina . . ." My father cleared his throat. "Tomorrow you need to get up and go back to school. This has been enough," he said. He endorsed his own words with a nod.

"Enough?" I said. My lips felt numb. "No. I can't go back. Really, I can't."

"Your mother will take you to have something done about your hair, which you have ruined—"

"Dinos!" My mother turned from the sink so fast, one of her bones cracked. "Please don't say that Bettina's hair is *ruined*—"

"I don't care," I said. I paused to touch the springs of hair. How quickly it had untamed itself. I couldn't stand it if Bampas got on Momma's case, any more than I couldn't bear the mention of anyone leaving. "I don't want the hair fixed," I said. "But okay, I will go to school. I will try."

Forty-seven

BRADY CULLEN WAS WAITING AT MY LOCKER. I ARRIVED
in front of him on hollow legs.

"What the hell . . . ?" He stared at my hair and walked
around me until our places were switched and I was against
my locker door. "You look like barf. What is this?" He reached
toward me, flicked a few wiggly strands. He stood there, mouth
like a trout, and let out little gasps and swears. "What gives?
I've sent you a shit-ton of messages, I've been calling you. . . ."

I knew that this was true.

"How come you don't answer me? Huh? I wanna know."
He put his finger in my face. "'Cause what I hear . . . is that
you cheated on me?"

He knows. How does he know?

"Like, for a while." He went on. "Some way older dude? A guy that's *dead* now?"

I stood with my back pasted to my locker. I tried for loud and clear but all that came out was a whisper. "I can't be with you anymore. I should have broken it off—"

Bam! Brady slammed his fist into the locker close to the side of my head. My heart lurched inside my chest. He swore at me. He flicked at my hair. He put his face right up to mine. He pounded his fist into the metal for every word: "You. Look. Like. A. *Freak!*" He went away down the corridor, bashing more lockers on his way.

The space around me grew quiet, though there were people everywhere. I glanced up. A sea of faces loomed, so many eyes on me.

Tony Colletti must have come around the corner right after Brady's storm. "Hey, Bettina." He grinned, same as he always did. I looked up, watched him striding by. "Hey, where ya been?" he asked. He turned, took a few backward steps, and panned the nearly silent crowd around us. "Missed you the past couple of weeks," he said. Now he looked bewildered.

I went in and out of classes, picking up packets of missed work. By noon, I felt like I'd collected a stack of paving stones. I dumped the work in my dented-up locker and walked out to

316

the far end of the parking lot for my lunch period. I stared out at the industrial park—couldn't help it. I lit one of Cowboy's cigarettes and took long, hard drags on it. The smoke was horrible and perfect going into my lungs. I shivered in the open cold. If I could get caught, maybe I could get suspended. No such luck. I finally put the butt out under the toe of my boot and went back inside.

All through the day, I felt people staring, heard them whispering. At first, I thought it was because of what I'd done to my hair. Surely, I looked bizarre. But soon, I understood that word had gotten around that I'd done Brady Cullen wrong. I had cheated on him. He'd said it himself. I pushed past all the whisperers in the hall and went to clay class.

One glance to the back of the room and I saw them, a neat row of mugs and teapots—teapots with spouts and lids—all ready for the kiln. I pressed the heels of my hands into my eye sockets. I sucked at this before, and now I was two weeks behind. The art room seemed like a foreign country to me—in fact, my whole life did.

Big Bonnie stopped beside my desk. She leaned down and slipped some pages of notes between my elbows. I darted a look at her. She seemed a dispirited version of herself. Slack-faced. "I copied these for you," she whispered. "It's not much since the class is mostly about throwing clay." I think she might have felt bad after she said it; after all, I was the girl who had thrown *no* clay—not successfully. "When you're ready, I'll help you at the wheel," she added.

I couldn't speak, but I weighted the pages with my elbows. I was grateful to Bonnie Swenson; she was good to her core. But I knew that something bigger was driving her this time, and that something was *guilt*. Bonnie had to be the person who'd told Brady Cullen about Cowboy and me.

Forty-eight

"SLUT."

Not again.

One of the basketball players spoke loudly behind me as I stood in the bus circle. I did not turn. The White Tigers were having a perfect season, and now, a handful of Brady's best buds were having open season on me. I had done their homeboy dirty.

"I hear you could *do me* right off a cliff!" the same one called out again.

My stomach turned. I closed my eyes and swallowed hard. If only the buses would move. Mine wouldn't make it to me until the second wave. I couldn't even see it yet. Still, I inched closer to the curb.

Everybody knew about Silas Shepherd now—or thought they did. What they really knew were just a few things about me. I had been seen at his funeral; I was absent from school for forever; when I came back I was weird and my hair was all chopped off. I hated that they were talking about Cowboy, guessing, and making things up. None of them knew him. They had no right. I was ashamed of feeling too weak to defend him.

"How do you like your ho-down?" A mock conversation began maybe ten feet behind my back. Bastards. They weren't even taking buses. Why couldn't they just go back to their gym?

"Like my ho-down—on her back!"

I clenched my jaw until it ached.

"Hey, I'll bet there's a tramp stamp over that ass—"

Somebody touched me from behind. I jumped the bus line. I crossed straight through the circle. A driver shouted down at me from his window. "Hey, what kinda stunt is that? My kindergartner knows you don't walk between the buses! Use the crosswalk or I'll write you up next time. Hear me?"

I stumbled onto the sidewalk and went on blindly, and with no idea where I was headed. I wiped my face in the bend of my elbow a few times. I sniffed hard and walked on until I reached the shelter of the business buildings in the next block.

Tony Colletti appeared out of nowhere—perhaps from the drugstore. "Hey, Bettina. What's the matter? You doing okay?" he asked. He pressed a clean cloth handkerchief into my hand and I pressed it into my eyes. He leaned against the building beside me and just waited. I started to hand him back his handkerchief but changed my mind. I'd soaked it wet.

"Let's walk," Tony said. He took my pack without asking. We started off again. Suddenly, I turned and pushed my face into poor Tony Colletti's chest. I kept pushing. Tony managed to walk me around to the side drive of one of the town houses. We sank down into a little stone stairwell for shelter. He put his arm around me while I cried my head off.

Every so often he gave me a squeeze. When I wasn't sobbing, I could hear him humming softly.

I cried until I was done. Tony never asked me why, and it was amazing, I thought, to let go like that—no one to tell me to kiss my feelings goodbye.

When I finally collected myself, I blew my nose and I said the only thing I could think to say. "Thank you, Tony. Thank you. I'll wash this," I added, holding up the balled handkerchief in one hand.

"Or keep it," he said. I laughed just a little. I thought it was sweet that he carried a handkerchief when most guys were more likely to be packing a condom. "Hey, it's Tuesday," Tony said, "and Tuesday is your day to visit my nonna."

"Oh. Y-yes. I meant to keep going. . . ." I actually missed Regina. It had been weeks, and it wasn't right I'd been sloppy about my promise. "I still want to help you fix her fountain."

"Oh, that," he said. "If I live a hundred years . . ." He made us both laugh.

"Anyway, I'm sorry. I've been so . . ." All I could do was shake my head.

"It's okay, it's okay," he said. "I know things haven't been easy."

"Yeah?" I sniffed again. "Are you hearing a bunch of weird shit about me at school?" I asked.

"Eh. I hear, but I don't listen so much." He jostled me just a little. "You should come see my nonna. Just something to do. Might take your mind off other things."

"Tony, I want to see her but I don't know if I'm any match for Regina today."

"She is spicy," he said. "Look, walk with me. If you don't want to go in, I'll take you home in my ma's car. Come on. What else are you doing?" He didn't give me time to say no. "You got your phone? Call your mom so she won't worry," he said.

I heard myself say okay.

Forty-nine

"OH, MY GIRL, MY GIRL!" CONCERN SEEMED WRITTEN all over Regina Colletti's face. I wondered what she was reading on mine. Once again, she got rid of Tony as quickly as she could, though he okayed that with me twice before he left. I took my spot on the edge of her bed. "Are you all right?" Regina sat forward and whispered as if we shared a secret. "You look exhausted." She invited me onto a bigger patch of her bed with a pat of her hand. I obliged.

Regina reached up and pushed her fingers into my wild hair. I pretended not to care that she was looking it over. Working her way down, she brushed my jaw with her fingertips. Then she squeezed my upper arms in her hands—kneaded me like I was dough. "Poor girl, poor girl," Regina said. "Tony told me something terrible happened. He heard you lost someone," she said. Her voice was breaking. "Someone special," she went on. "Tell me about it. Who was that? Was he the first one you loved?"

I felt like she'd thrown a lit match at me but her head was bowed in a sympathetic way. Being with Regina was like that, I realized. You got both sides of everything from her. I closed my eyes, dipped my chin. She had my wrists now and I stretched my rigid arms long but she would not let go.

"Stop," I said. "Y-you don't know. . . ."

"Then tell me," she said. All I wanted to tell Regina was that she had to stop hanging on to me like she was. She let go and grabbed one of her snow globes from her bedside table and pushed it into my hands. It was the one with the little Chinese boy inside who flew his kite in a whirl of stars—it was the one that, if you took it away from all the others, was actually beautiful. "Tell me all of it," she said.

"If I tell you, you cannot tell anyone else—"

"If I do, you can feed me cat shit when I am not looking. I would expect you to," Regina said. She squeezed me.

"I—I'm not sure how to tell it. . . ."

Regina waited.

"I called him Cowboy," I said. "I never would have met him if I hadn't run from my so-called boyfriend one day."

"How long ago?" Regina whispered.

"September."

Regina settled back to listen, her eyes intently on me—too much. I could tell her, I thought, but not while she was looking at me. I tipped myself onto the gold velvet pillows with my back to her. I pulled my knees up and held her snow globe to my chest.

I told everything. The good. The best. The rotten. While I talked, I did not so much cry, as leak from the corners of my eyes. My cheeks grew wet and tears seeped onto the velvet pillow shams. Regina listened the whole time. She was so silent I thought she'd fallen asleep. But then she spoke.

"You are always going to love him," she said. "You're stuck with that."

Fifty

AT HOME, I FOUND MY MOTHER AT THE KITCHEN TABLE.
She was near tears.

Must be a crying day all over.

"Momma? What's the matter?"

"Oh, just all these things," she muttered. She waved her
fingers in the air. "You know, so much hurting in this house."
At that, she began to weep.

I could not remember seeing her like this. When I thought
about it, it seemed to me that my mother had always been
smiling sweetly—and maybe preemptively. But in the last
few months, I'd seen her cry several times, and I remembered
her words, so shot-through with pain, when she'd suggested

that Bampas should leave.

I pulled a chair out and sat down. "Did you and Bampas fight again? It's not about me, is it?"

"No, no, no," my mother said. "Well, it *is* about you, but no fight with your bampas. It's just that . . . I felt like I should tell you . . . I have thought of *him* often since we read the bad news that morning. I know that will sound strange to you, Bettina." She rubbed the back of her hand against her nose.

I handed her a napkin. "Him? Momma, are you talking about Cowboy?"

She nodded.

"Well . . . what do you mean? What have you thought?"

"That morning you told me about him, and then I saw you playing with your little brothers in the kitchen. The three of you went outdoors and I watched you. I thought about the possibility, you know?" She twisted the napkin into a fat worm, wrapped it around her knuckle, and pressed it to her nose.

"Momma, I don't think I understand."

"I mean I saw him in my mind's eye. Your friend. I imagined it, Bettina. I imagined that he was out back with you and the boys. And I thought, what's so bad? We could welcome him—somehow—we could reach an understanding. I would have tried for you. I would have helped you tell your bampas." My mother reached for me and I let her take my hands.

"I am so sorry we never got that chance." She ended on a high and piping note.

I closed my eyes and imagined Cowboy at our supper table, Cowboy with Avel swinging from his strong arms, and Cowboy pouring a glass of wine in our kitchen. That was what I'd really wanted—to let him into my family and do some very ordinary things together.

"Thank you, Momma," I said, and I kissed her on the cheek. She clung hard to me and kissed me back.

Fifty-one

"BETTINA."

I opened my eyes. It was Bampas saying my name so sharply. I'd been snoozing at the kitchen table, my head on my outstretched arm. The heartbreaking smell of coffee reminded me that it was morning. My days had been drag-ass at best. Some were worse than others. This day was one of the deadly ones; it had stabbed me awake just before dawn. Now here I was, having to come around to it for the second time. I tried not to blame Bampas; it was not his fault that the sun had come up again.

"Your mother will be down the hall with the boys shortly," he warned. "And I will expect to leave on time."

Great. I was still in my nightgown. Slowly, I pushed away from the table. If he saw me moving maybe he'd leave me alone. I stood at the counter and poured myself a cup of coffee. Bampas gave a small, satisfied nod.

"*Fili antio*," he said.

Kiss it goodbye.

The words looped through the air like a fireball. I drew a breath.

"*Don't* say that to me." My voice crackled. I looked directly at Bampas. "*Don't you dare.* I am *not* a little girl with scraped knees."

My father raised his brow and looked away from me.

"No, no! You have to listen," I said. "I cannot just shut this down. I have lost my love! *Really* lost him!" I chugged a breath into my lungs. "*He is dead!*" I shook my head. "Th-this has never happened to you. Do you want to know how it is?"

Bampas was not looking at me but he had to be hearing.

"I hate waking," I said. "I'm waiting for the morning that it will feel okay to put my feet out of my bed again. I am pushing and shoving my way through every minute of every day." I waited in the hush of our kitchen. From my aching throat, I pressed the words again. "He is dead. I'll *never* get over it. This is not a thing I can just kiss goodbye, Bampas. I won't get off that easy. I have to feel the whole thing. So *don't* say that to me."

My father stood looking down the long road of his own cheekbones into his china cup. He stirred his coffee. The spoon clinked shakily against the porcelain.

Avel trotted in. Momma and Favian followed just behind him. I marveled at them walking through fire like that. They were in a conversation—something about lunch money.

"I need quarters," Avel strained. "The lunch ladies get crabby about giving change."

My mother's open purse dangled from her arm while she fished its depths. Her hair was caught up loosely in a clip with strands falling all around her face.

Meanwhile, Favian overshot his cereal bowl and little sugar-coated balls rolled across the countertop.

"Momma, did you find the quarters?" Avel was focused.

Momma shook her head no. "Dinos, do you have any?" she asked.

Bampas set his cup down with a clank and shoved his hands into his pockets. Happy for a reason not to look at me, I could not help thinking. I watched him pat himself down, his good gray pants staying knife sharp at the front crease. I followed the line down. The toes of his shoes happened to be pointing right at the dark slot beneath the refrigerator.

I went to the pantry and I took out the broom. "Excuse me, Bampas," I said, and he moved out of my way.

I wound the hem of my nightgown up in one wrist. I

crouched down in front of the fridge and slid the head of the broom underneath it. *Swat-bang, swat-bang.* One, then two, and then two more quarters slid out. Avel scrambled for them as if they'd fallen from a piñata.

I stood still. My family stared. When I tried to move, I accidentally let go of the broom and the handle hit the floor with a loud crack that made all of us jump. Favian and Avel both clapped hands over their ears.

It took me a second to find my voice. "I am walking to school today," I said.

"Walking? Oh, but it's so far—there is isn't time." Poor Momma was confused.

"I'm walking," I repeated. "I'll call you when I get there." My father stepped forward but before he could say a word I told him, "Don't follow me." I held both my palms toward him. *"Don't."*

Fifty-two

THE SCHOOL SECRETARY WAS CHIRPING AT ME. ALL I HAD said was "I'm late." Stating the obvious. My walk had been the right choice—possibly the only way to make the blood move inside of me this morning. Nonetheless, it was an hour past homeroom.

"Okay, so how about I give you this . . ." She drew a yellow pass out of her drawer. In a fluid motion, she checked the clock and scribbled the time on the proper line. Though I was holding my cell in my hand, she said, "And how about I call home for you . . ." She picked up the office phone. "I'll let them know you are here. . . ." *Chirp.*

It was known, I guess, by school administration that I'd

been through *something*. Nobody harassed me about the classes I was now failing. Maybe it was understood that for now, Bettina Vasilis was just making it through each day.

In clay class, everyone but me had managed to bring up a required vessel—fourteen inches or more. They talked about "tall forms" and every time I heard the words, I dissolved a little more. It was my fault. I wouldn't get up there on the wheel. I lay on my arm and drew in a sketchbook. I was hung up on little female figures. I had a half dozen pages of them. They looked like wingless fairies or naked witches; I couldn't decide. But it didn't matter because they were not *for* anything.

Mr. Terrazzi was friendly without bothering me. Bonnie said nothing, but I think she was afraid and guilty still. I didn't mean to keep her on the hook—I didn't even blame her. I missed her and I wanted to talk to her. But I couldn't reach out.

I'd asked to be picked up by my parents every day. Imagine that. Either Momma or Bampas had been fetching me on their way to pick up Favian and Avel. I stayed in the art room after last bell most afternoons, avoiding the basketball jocks until my ride came. It wasn't that those guys looked for me every day—I am sure I wasn't worth that much to them. But staying away from the bus circle seemed like an easy move in favor of myself.

One afternoon, Bonnie was loading the kiln in the back while I sat at a desk close to the art room door. I sketched more of my strange womenfolk until I saw the last bus wind its way out of the circle. I packed up. In the hallway, I forced my crooked locker door shut and shouldered my jacket. When I turned around, several of Brady's teammates were running up at me. One hollered my name. I turned in time to see him holding his crotch and lunging toward me. He grunted, then gasped, and sent a plug of spit into my locker door. A second wad hit my jacket.

"Oh, oh—*oh*—my G-G-God!" he said as if in great relief. "I just had to get rid of that. Sperm pressure's a killer, man!" He and the others ran down the hall, laughing.

The milky wad clung to the steel door right about eye level, then began to slide down. I felt myself dry heave. I turned toward the girls' room but caught sight of Big Bonnie standing in the doorway of the art room, a look of pain in her eyes.

"Slobs," she muttered. She looked down the hall where Brady's minions had paused to congratulate themselves on being disgusting. "Come back in here," she said. She glanced at the spit wad on my jacket. "Maybe we could sponge that."

I followed her inside the art room and over to the big sink. Bonnie started with a paper towel, then wet the sponge. "Hmm . . . think this is okay for leather?" I shrugged. She began to dab. I felt bad. That hocker was nasty. "Are you all right, Bettina? You look like you're about to fall over." Bonnie reached like she was going to put a hand on my shoulder but she hesitated.

"Actually . . . I don't feel so good," I said. I hadn't eaten all day—stupid—and now I was grossed out. I let myself down onto a stool, and Bonnie slid my jacket off my shoulder. She went after that gob spot with her sponge, brave soul.

In the art room, there are several old mirrors, all rough and spattered with clay and paint. Drawing classes used them for the obligatory self-portraits. I sometimes held my sketches up to the glass to see them reversed and anew. But that day, I was looking at myself. The afternoon light came in through the windows and illuminated me. I was startled. No makeup, which almost knocked me off my perch. Had I not looked into my mirror at home lately? I didn't look so bad, just different. But my hair—oh, man. I tilted my head trying to see the sides.

Bonnie had come over to stand behind me and together we regarded the girl in the mirror. "Why did you cut it?" she asked softly.

I shrugged.

She began to walk around me. I looked up at her and remembered the day I heard one of the Not-So-Cheerleaders say that I'd be nothing without my boyfriend or my braid. "I think I just wanted it off," I told Bonnie.

She reached for a strand. "Do you mind?" she asked.

I sat still. Bonnie drew my hair out through her finger-tips. She lifted a corkscrew here, set another one down there like she was rearranging them. "Will you let me trim it?" she asked. "Just to even out the lengths?"

She reached for a pair of art room scissors and gave them a critical inspection. "What do you think?"

"Yeah." I nodded.

I watched in the mirror while Bonnie worked. She gently pulled the strands up and out, matching the ends. Then she closed the scissor blades across them. Her chapped knuckles brushed my cheek as she came around to the front. "Should I do the bangs a little bit shorter maybe?"

"Sure."

"You've got the best hair," she said. Gently, she snipped little ends of all the coils. I saw her reflection in the mirror. She was smiling.

"Do you mean I *used* to have the best hair?"

"No. I mean now." Bonnie set the scissors down and scooted a chair around in front of me. "Bettina," she said. Her head was low. "Can I tell you how sorry I am? Those guys—the way they're treating you—it's my fault." She began to tear up.

"No. Bonnie, stop." I could hardly stand it.

"*I* told Brady you were at that funeral," Bonnie confessed. "It was *me*." She shook her head.

"I know. It's okay," I said.

"I—I felt sorry for him. He waited at your locker every morning. He looked lost. And nobody knew where you were—even the freakin' rumor mill wasn't coughing anything out—not at first." I nodded at that. "So, I finally told him I had seen you at a service. He asked which one. That's *all* I told him, I swear. I didn't make anything up."

"No . . . I'm sure that played out in imaginations. And text messages."

"I guess." Bonnie sighed. "Bettina, I admit it, I *liked* having a reason to speak to Brady Cullen. I know it was lame."

"It's okay. He would have found out anyway."

"But there was probably a better way for that to happen."

"I can't think of a better way." I shrugged. I looked Bonnie right in her teary eyes and told her, "I mean that. So don't think about it again."

Poor Bonnie. Such a look of alarm crossed her face when Bampas and the high school principal came rushing into the art room.

"Bettina!" Bampas looked like he was about to lose it. "Oh! You are here!" He breathed a huge sigh. "We are running late to get the boys," he said. He glanced at the principal and added, "My two young sons at the elementary."

The principal muttered something tranquilizing.

"Yes, yes." Bampas was beginning to calm down now. He looked at me. "It's just . . . I was waiting for you in the circle," he said. He wasn't usually like this—putting salve on a tense moment instead of thumping it flat with his fist. We'd had a bad morning; maybe he was afraid I'd start yelling at him here in the art room. The principal excused himself, and Bampas relaxed just a hitch more.

"This was really my fault," Bonnie piped up. "I held Bettina up. I'm sor —"

"No, no," I said. "There was something stuck to my jacket—something sickening. This is my friend Bonnie, and she helped me clean it up." I tucked my fingers up to my hair but decided not to mention the new trim. "She helped me," I said.

Bampas nodded slightly. "Well, do you have your things? We should go now." He started toward the doorway. I looked down at all my little hair twists on the floor.

"Go, go," Bonnie said. "I'll sweep up."

"Thank you," I said.

I hooked my jacket on my shoulder and hurried to catch up to Bampas.

Fifty-three

"I'M GOING UP TO THE GARDEN," I CALLED INTO THE hallway from my bedroom door. Nobody answered. "I'm *not* missing," I added a little louder. Well, at least I had tried.

Beside our semi-frozen swimming pool, I lit Cowboy's last cigarette. I wasn't bothering to hide them, and neither Momma nor Bampas had said anything to me.

I sat on the iron bench and pulled my knees up to my chest. From there I could look across the pool and down toward the house. Favian and Avel were having a ferocious, forbidden pillow fight in the lit-up living room below me. I was glad to see it.

Poor Avel had not spent his quarters. He'd brought them to me before supper time, opening his hand and whispering, "These are yours."

"What? Oh, no! Avel, you didn't eat lunch?" His eyes had filled with tears and his small face had crumpled. My heart had melted. I'd crushed him in a hug. With all his little bones squeezed up in my arms, he had felt like a big baby bird with finger-tipped wings clutching my back. I had rocked him, trying to keep back all the sobs that wanted out of me so that I wouldn't freak him out. But in the end we'd both cried. When Avel and I had finally both blown our noses and laughed about our snots, I had called Favian into my room too. I'd told them about Cowboy—the guy in the pickup who'd let us cross River Road with our parfait dishes. They had remembered him. They'd been stunned and sorry.

Now in the garden, I thought back on it and I felt grateful that the boys had, just that once, laid eyes on Cowboy. There were so few stories to tell. I wiped my face with my sleeve and took a hard drag on the cigarette.

Then I saw Bampas. He was squeezing out of my bedroom window, awkwardly lifting his knee to his chest so his foot would clear the sill. What in the world? He looked like a bear in a charcoal-gray man-suit. He took a hop to draw that second foot through the opening. Never had I seen my father *hop*. *Here comes the anti-Bampas*, I thought. I snorted a laugh.

"I'm here. I'm fine," I called from my spot on the bench. I hoped that might turn him back. Instead, he crossed the terrace. *Damn*. I wanted to have my smoke and watch the boys through the glass by myself.

"You left your bedroom window open," he said.

I fed him the next line before he could say it: "'I do not need to heat the out of doors, Bettina.'"

"Well, it's true, you know," he said. "At least you are not smoking inside."

"You could say I'm *always* smoking inside, Bampas." I gave my chest a thump.

He sat down next to me and asked me if I was cold. I shrugged, then hid a shiver. "Almost March," he said, and he looked up at the night sky. "Hard to believe it, my bulbs will come up soon."

I nodded.

He sighed heavily and let the breath go out his nose slowly. Men do that, I have noticed. You don't usually hear women nose-sighing but men do it all the time.

"You know, your momma, she tells me to notice you better," he said.

"That must be hard," I said. I blew a smoke ring and watched it disappear.

"She says I should hug you and not to be the first to let go," my father said.

"Hmm. We could have a contest."

Bampas laughed softly. Together, we watched Favian and Avel run through the lighted living room. "Wild boys," my father mumbled. "How many times do you suppose we have told them not to roughhouse in the living room?"

"How many times have you told me not to heat the out of doors?"

My father waited. Both of us stayed fixed on the living room windows. The boys went on boxing with the sofa pillows—close to the lamps with their back swings, accurate on each other with their uppercuts. Bampas pulled a few breaths now and then as he watched. "I suppose they do what they want anytime that I am not looking, hey?"

"Well, they put a lot of heart into it," I said.

Bampas kept watching the boys. I realized something; he didn't really care that they were being disobedient, breaking rules. I felt captivated by this. What about all the rules he set for me? Did he actually expect that I'd break them?

"Bettina . . . you were close to this Silas Shepherd?" my father asked. My train of thought snapped in two.

I closed my eyes tightly and opened them again. "Yes," I said. "Very much so."

"What does that mean, Bettina? Did you . . . Did he ever . . ."

Then I knew what he really wanted to know, and I burned with insult. But this was a chance—my chance—to stand up for Cowboy. I flicked the ashes off the tip of my cigarette and scrubbed at them with the toe of my boot. "He was faultless with me, Bampas. No agenda but to love me, and that only came at the end. He had been a good friend before that. We kissed. Only once." I stared across the garden and blinked off a bit of moisture. "I wish it had been more times," I said.

I felt my father breathe out. He leaned back and put his arm around me. I nestled the least-offended side of me into him. "I'm sorry," he whispered. "You are right, what you said to me—you are much too young to suffer this loss."

Loss. Well, there. He had said it.

"I want you to be strong. . . ."

"I know that. I'm trying. But you know what I learned this year? I learned that if you don't acknowledge pain, you're not really safe." I collected the next thought. "Pain is . . . a message. True for heart, body, and soul." I let the words go in a veil of white smoke. We sat closely and quietly for a moment.

"One of us will have to be the first to let go," I said, "or we'll freeze our butts to this bench."

Bampas laughed out loud. I passed the cigarette to him—down to half now. I meant for him to snuff it out. Instead he held the butt in front of him, regarded it a moment, and then put it to his lips. He took a drag then blew the smoke away. "Terrible," he mumbled, and he handed it back to me.

"Awful," I agreed. "This is the last one."

Bampas and I polished off that cigarette together while we watched Favian and Avel slug on.

Fifty-four

SOMETIME AROUND THE BEGINNING OF APRIL, TONY Colletti's schedule became filled with music. Concert season was coming and the band was all doubled up on practices. It was Tuesday and I was set to head to Regina's on my own. But first, I crouched at my locker in the silent hallway and tried to concentrate. If I could remember to pack up all the things I needed, then school might start to go better.

"Bettina?"

I looked up and saw Emmy.

"Hi," she said. She gave a sigh followed by a gentle smile.

"Hey," I said. I had not spoken to any of the Not-So-Cheerleaders. Who could guess what they believed about me? I had no energy for it. I turned my attention back to the inside of my locker to buy time.

"I've missed you," Emmy said. "On the squad. I mean it."

"That's really nice," I said. I stood up and looked her in the eye. Emmy shifted her feet where she stood.

"Hey . . ." She hesitated. "Brady Cullen asked me out." She gave me an apologetic shrug.

"Did he?"

"Yeah . . . and I know a lot has happened with that . . . but I consider you a friend, Bettina. So I just wondered . . . would you be hurt if I went?"

Quickly, I shook my head no. I fussed with the books and papers in my arms. Then I stopped. I looked at Emmy again. Little-bitty, *happy* Emmy. "I wouldn't be hurt," I said. "But you might be."

"*I* might be?" She put her finger to her breastbone. Her mouth hung open for a few seconds. "But what do you mean?" Slowly, her eyes opened up wide. "Are you talking about . . . like . . . that time you had the black eye—"

"Emmy . . ." I drew my mouth into a line and shook my head as if to say, *Don't do it.* I backed myself against my battered locker door. I pushed once, then again, harder, to get it to close. "Look, I have to go. I have to be somewhere," I said. I started away.

347

"Okay. Hey, Bettina, I'm not going to cheer next year," Emmy said.

That stopped me. "Oh, no?"

"What I really want to do is dance. The school charter says anyone can start any kind of club they want. But the thing is, I haven't done that much dancing. Like, none. But if you—"

"Eh . . . I don't know, Emmy." I was about to tell her that I was pretty sure I'd be poison for any club. But then I remembered back to the day Tony and his bandmates had set up in the lobby, how much fun that one-number dance party had been. "Actually, Emmy . . . this could be brilliant," I said. "If I had time I'd talk it out with you right now. I really do have to go. But, yes. I'm in. As long as we don't have to 'make states' I'm in."

"Oh, good! Put your number in my phone. Please!" Emmy said. "I'll call you."

I did that. Then I hustled on down the hall, crossed over the White Tiger mosaic in the lobby, and headed out the door.

I must have been walking fast because before I knew it, I was in the same block as Alcott Elementary. Tony and I had passed the school on plenty of Tuesday afternoons and I never stopped noticing how beautiful it was. Funny how in a town where there is more than one place to attend the early grades, you never really lose that sense of mystery about the school you *didn't* go to. In junior high when everyone is tossed together, you hear little bits about the *other* principal, the building, and the teachers you never had. I had gone to Whitman, the new school outside of the village. It was built from block that could only be described as dust-pink. Alcott was generations older, made with real red bricks and layers of yellow paint on the window trim. Much better. Add that to the ancient maple trees in the play yard and the fact that it had been named for a woman and, well, I'd always wished I'd gone there.

I looked up at the maple buds all about to burst. I was thinking about Emmy's idea and wondering what it would take to wake my body up and get it to dance again. I was glad I'd had the guts to warn Emmy about Brady, and just as that thought came and was about to go, I heard the hollow sound of a basketball thumping on the pavement.

Speak of the devil.

Brady Cullen was all by himself on the blacktop at Alcott Elementary. He bounced the ball a few times—not seven, I noticed. He was about to take a shot when he caught sight of me. He froze. I too stopped in my tracks.

"Hey," he said.

"Hey," I answered.

So how great is this—six feet of chain-link fence standing strong between you and me. I would have loved to say it. But what I felt wasn't fear.

Brady bounced the ball and pumped it toward the hoop. The ball hit the rim with a reverberating *chink-a-ching* sound. I hated that noise. A few dirty gray strings were all that remained of the net and they quivered after the shot.

"What are you doing here?" Brady wanted to know.

"Passing by," I said. "But I'm sort of glad I ran into you. I . . . I've actually wanted to tell you something. I know it has been weeks, even months . . . but I was wrong."

He turned away from me and shot the ball at the hoop again.

"Is this about that guy you were seeing behind my back?"

I thought for a second. "Not so much," I said. "I was wrong not to break things off with you. Not because of him. Because everything was wrong with us."

"How can you say that?" Brady's volume rose. His voice was rough and his face was turning red. "You know, P'teen-uh . . . you really *hurt* me!"

"You hurt me too," I said. "Bruises, in fact."

"Bruises? Bullshit on that," he said.

"Short memory," I said.

He kept his eyes on the ball while he pounded it into the ground a few times. "I—I might have done some things," he mumbled. "But I was always just joking around with you. Just playing."

"It wasn't fun," I said.

350

"You know what I can't believe about all this?" Brady stood with his hands up, the basketball balanced in one of them. "I just always thought I had you. We were good. With all the other bad stuff—you were the one thing I thought I didn't have to worry about." His eyes began to rim up red. "Ya know, P'teen-uh, I never loved anything like I loved you."

"Yeah? Well, don't ever love any *thing* like that again."

I turned to go. Brady must have heaved that ball at the hoop because it hit the backboard like a hundred slamming doors. The noise made me turn around again.

"So that guy, he really did die, huh?"

I wondered if he'd meant to sting me so. "Yes," I said. I took a few slow, backward steps.

"That must have sucked." He jumped and shot the basketball again.

"Still does," I said. I don't think he heard me over the rattling of the hoop.

"So, P'teen-uh," Brady said, and he didn't look at me, he bounced the ball through his legs and turned to grab it up again. "Listen, about that stuff with the guys from the team—I didn't know they were bugging you. It won't happen anymore. If it does, I'll rip somebody's face off."

"Right." I sighed toward the sky.

I walked away from Alcott Elementary School. I walked away from Brady Cullen.

September

I WOKE BEFORE DAWN THIS MORNING, AND NOW, I AM
standing across the street from the high school. I'm getting it
together for the first day of senior year. I've got my skirt. I've
got my boots. I've got one cup of coffee. There's a breeze and
it's rolling the corkscrew curls on my head this way and that
way. There is a key in my hip pocket. I keep checking for
it—not going to lose that.

It is September. But I keep running snippets from June.
I'm thinking about the ways people cheer. Oh, I know, that
isn't supposed to be my thing. But all through the longest
June of my life, it happened all around me. It was the season; things culminated and they all wanted to be clapped for.

Like when Tony Colletti absolutely killed a saxophone solo at the stage band concert, you can bet I cheered for him—a little payback for a guy who has always rooted for me. The cheerleaders made states and, guess what, people cheered for them.

It can be loud. But sometimes cheering makes no sound at all.

Momma cheers with a breath and a smile, from across the room. I saw that the day Bampas gave me this key. And Bampas, well, he packaged a cheer for his daughter in a business transaction. But that was okay by me. I wanted a job and when he said the words "Money for art school," well, that sounded like a cheer too.

My teachers cheered; they gave me Incompletes instead of F's, and summer school wasn't really so bad. I did most of the work at home.

When I kicked the potter's wheel for a final pass up the ugliest cylinder of clay ever, Bonnie stood by. She clutched her ruler and we both hoped for a tall form that would be tall enough. When my pot swallowed up those inches, she hollered, *"Yes! That's tall!"* I spent the next class breaking open all the too-thin places on the walls of that form. I was flirting with disaster; it was supposed to be a vessel—something to hold water. But it seemed more like a place to me, a place crying out for dwellers. I sculpted tiny clay women and nestled them into all the waiting spaces, while poor Bonnie fretted for my grade. But Mr. Terrazzi saw what I was up to.

"Aha! That's right!" he cheered. "It's not about the assignment now. It's about the art."

In June, Regina Colletti's little-boy fountain became a beautiful, pissing thing again, thanks to Tony and me—and Bonnie. Bonnie snuck a winky's worth of porcelain, crafted by yours truly, into the kiln for the final firing of the year. When the little boy started to shoot his stream again, Regina leaned from her open upstairs window. Arms spread wide, she cheered, *Gloria! Gloria! In tutta la sua gloria pipì!* Her neighbors came to their windows and cats arrived to drink. The next week, I cheered for Regina when she said the word "Remission," and she cheered for me when I passed my driver's test.

This key in my pocket is not for a car. It is for the door to a potbelly building at 66 Green Street. Anastasia, an excellent employee at Loreena's Downtown, well, she needed a new position where she could be closer to her children's school in the afternoons. Bampas paid me for the design work. Bonnie and I painted a kick-ass mural of a Steampunk world on the inside wall this summer. I'll take over for Anastasia behind the counter this afternoon in time for her to meet the school bus. Tony will be my Italian ice man—or as he says, the *Italian,* Italian ice man—and help me pull the boxes off the truck and shoulder them to the freezer. Bampas was right. We cannot sell fine Greek pastries to high school students, but gelatos, soy lattes, and bagels, yes. Can't lose this key; I'm responsible for locking up the busy Steam & Bean at 66 Green.

It is September and I'm sighing back at the breeze. Not a day has gone by that I have not ached for my Cowboy.

He finally showed up. Last night. Beside my bed. It slowly dawned on me that he was there. I heard his voice— either spoken or otherwise conveyed—"Beta . . . I love your curls." He was a warm outline of light that disintegrated ever so slowly—like tiny stars blinking away. I lay in my bed, eyes open. A sense of calm settled over me. In the dark I smiled and whispered, "Did you have to wait so long?"

Before the sun rose, I went and whispered Momma awake. I asked for the keys to her car and promised I'd be back before breakfast. I drove myself and my old, lopped-off braid up to the overlook at the water property. I flung that thing off into the treetops below. I watched it go, chasing end after end until I couldn't see it anymore. I found sweet, soft morning music on the car radio and I slow danced myself around in the gravel until the sun rested on the earth.

It is September and the season is returning—the time of year that I loved Cowboy. There will come another October sky all washed in yellow light, a snowy day with cardinals in the treetops. When my heart cracks—and I know that it will—I'm going to try to think of it as *open*. Open to the spaces and places that are keeping Cowboy for me. Open to the good that has come from loving him. Open.

Acknowledgments

WITH MY HEART BRIMMING, I OFFER MY THANKS:

To my writing friends who listened endlessly and responded with their helpful hearts: Sandi Shelton, Nancy Hall, Doe Boyle, Leslie Bulion, Mary-Kelly Busch, Lorraine Jay, Kay Kudlinski, Judy Theise, and Nancy Elizabeth Wallace.

To Katherine Tegen (who is *unsinkable*, just by the way) for her steadfast trust in me.

To everyone at HarperCollins for the good care all my work receives at every stage. Special nods to Katie Bignell for escorting me to the finish; the art department for being so receptive; Brenna Franzitta and the copy editors for putting on the polish; and especially to Susan Jeffers Casel for leaving that uplifting note for me at the very end. (I never really know what the copy editor is thinking!)

To Jennie Dunham for good navigation.

To my Jonathan for all that you do for all of us.

To Sam, Marley, and Ian for the many text messages regarding the modern lexicon.

To my parents, my siblings, and the many branches of my family tree for always asking, "Hey, what's next?"

Finally, to my own high school art teacher Phil Spaziani, who became my dear friend, and who blew on the spark for so many of us . . . I wonder if anyone has ever tried to count us all.